———————— ★ ————————

Ginny hit the dirt as another shot rang out. Blood pounded in her ears, drowning out everything else.

After a moment, she cautiously raised her head and peered around. Her heart slowed as the seconds went by. One by one, Coffee Creek's normal late-night sounds filtered back into her awareness.

She started to feel silly. She hadn't imagined the shots, but she did seem to be the only person who had taken notice of them. Certainly the only one lying in the dirt.

Then she heard a moan.

———————— ★ ————————

"Readers will come away from this smartly told story with a better understanding of the heated issue of clear-cutting."

—*Publishers Weekly*

"[Wallingford] offers an original plot with a nice balance of humor, romance, and action..."

—*Booklist*

Also available from Worldwide Mystery by
LEE WALLINGFORD

COLD TRACKS

CLEAR-CUT MURDER

LEE WALLINGFORD

WORLDWIDE.

TORONTO • NEW YORK • LONDON
AMSTERDAM • PARIS • SYDNEY • HAMBURG
STOCKHOLM • ATHENS • TOKYO • MILAN
MADRID • WARSAW • BUDAPEST • AUCKLAND

CLEAR-CUT MURDER

A Worldwide Mystery/April 1995

This edition is reprinted by arrangement with
Walker and Company.

ISBN 0-373-26165-9

For Ed, who can see both sides

ONE

COFFEE CREEK Ranger District was three hours from Galina, four if you took the trouble to go to Longmont first. That was what Ginny Trask did, stopping at the supervisor's office to see Frank Carver. The highway wound over the south flank of Mouse Mountain where sunbeams, piercing the stands of fir, set the dust motes dancing and gave the woods an open, airy feel. The trees gave way at regular intervals to clear-cuts—stumps and seedlings dotted across acres of cutover land. The most recent were still black from last summer's slash burns. In the older units taller established trees thrust their leaders above the brush. Clear-cuts were part of the reason Ginny was going to Coffee Creek.

Clear-cuts and a threatening letter.

She pulled over at the top of the pass to stretch her legs. The loggers had been up here, too, leveling a thirty-acre tract. That had been five years ago. She remembered the traffic delays while they maneuvered the yarding tower into place. At one point logs had been cold-decked for a few weeks in the eastbound lane. This was private land, on the south side of Mouse Mountain. Forest Service employees driving between Longmont and the Galina Range Station watched the show with interest, commenting on practices no longer permitted on public land. Now early summer flowers—foxglove, fireweed, Indian paintbrush—grew thick among the young trees. Wild iris, white and violet-blue, dotted the edges of the road.

Was it ugly? Ginny couldn't tell anymore. The first clear-cut she'd seen had left her feeling sick—a battlefield littered with root wads, limbs, and discarded chunks of log. She had walked through a couple hundred of them since then, developing a professional interest. Slowly, and with help from her husband, Dale, before he died, she had come to see them in a new light. Here on the west side, so different from the desert country where she had grown up, nature veiled human activity with amazing speed. This clear-cut, for instance, planted four years earlier, was now prime wildlife habitat. Tourists on their way to the coast stopped to watch elk feeding on the lower benches. A walk through the brush would scare up rabbits, quail, half-a-dozen species of ground-nesting birds. Deer and coyotes still followed their ancient trails, the terrain apparently engraved in their genes. Clear-cuts could be heaven to the kind of wildlife that made people stop and get out of their cars.

She picked a handful of iris, clipping the stems with her pocketknife. Frank would like them. Frank Carver, special agent in charge of law enforcement for the Neskanie National Forest, had during the past few weeks developed the complaint of the deskbound worker—he didn't get out into the field enough. Everyone in the SO—the supervisor's office—complained about the paperwork, but she was surprised that Frank expected anything different. After all, he'd spent twenty years with the Seattle police.

A few flowers weren't going to make up for being inside on a day like this, but she liked to bring him something. Back in the car, she caught a brief glimpse of the Willamette Valley, veiled in a light summer haze. Far to the east the tall peaks of the Cascades, still capped with snow, glinted in the sun. Then the road dropped and plunged again into the shadowy, sun-speckled woods.

The Neskanie SO was a handsome new building set in Longmont's technological park. Long, narrow windows gleamed among the wood-sheathed walls, giving the people inside glimpses of Mouse Mountain and Prairie off to the south. Ginny drove past the visitors' slots in the front and headed for the staff parking lot. Most of the SO's green fleet was back there. On a district compound, those rigs would have been gone for the day. Frank Carver was not the only person in the SO who didn't get out into the field enough.

The receptionist, pinned to the telephone, flashed Ginny a smile and waved her down the hall. She stopped at the rest room, a luxurious affair by federal standards, with flowered wallpaper and a dish of potpourri beside the sink. She glanced at the mirror. A month ago, in May, just before her thirty-second birthday, she had noticed a definite thickening around the waist. The agency's severely tailored uniform really did make her look thinner. At the district, working in Dispatch or out in the woods, she wore jeans and flannel shirts. She had reservations about the uniform—any minute now she expected to be mistaken for a Girl Scout cookie chairman—but she had to admit it gave her the tremendously competent look.

She was going to need all the competence she could lay her hands on for this assignment.

Frank's office was on the third floor. She ignored the elevator and took the stairs, going for the exercise. She knew, too, that Frank's ears were tuned to the sound of the elevator doors. She wanted to surprise him.

She sneaked down the hall, the carpet muffling her steps. That carpet must drive Frank nuts. She stopped just beyond the line of sight from the open door and slowly craned her neck around. He was at his desk, shoulders hunched over some kind of paperwork. His grizzled hair thinned at the top of his head to reveal a small, vulnerable-looking patch of scalp. The air conditioner hummed softly, almost muffling the faint scratch of his pencil.

She ducked back as Frank lifted his head. He scanned the hall outside his door. Had someone hurried past? He still wasn't used to having his own office, to the isolation of four walls and a carpet. For years in Seattle he had worked in a big linoleum-floored room echoing with footsteps, voices, typewriters, radio chatter, all the hustle of a big police station. You could spot a visitor from the other side of the room in a place like that, and even after it was divided up into cubicles you still knew whenever something happened. Now he had to listen for the gentle swoosh of the elevator doors. He checked the hall one more time.

"Okay, Trask, you'd better come in."

Ginny peered around the door. "How did you know?"

He lifted his eyebrows and glanced over his desk at the hall floor.

She looked down. A lavender petal lay on the carpet. "Damn."

"Besides, I could hear you breathing."

"Now, that I don't believe." She came in and sat down. The desk was covered with a litter of papers that almost hid the telephone and a hand-held radio. A government-issue computer terminal sat mutely on a small stand near the window.

"Why not? You sound like a winded horse after climbing all those stairs."

"That's the sound of lungs, Frank. Good, healthy lungs." She gave the ashtray on his desk a meaningful glance.

"One thing at a time," Frank said. He should never have told her he planned to quit. Eat salad, walk four times a week, and quit smoking. At least he was managing the first two.

Christ, but she looked good—broken arm as good as new. He hardly recognized the skinny, rain-drenched kid he'd met only six months before. She sure didn't look like a kid now. That's because you're a horny old man, he told himself, and looked again. Wrong. Even the uniform couldn't hide the fact that she had breasts, and nice ones, too.

"How's that kid of yours?" he asked, forcing his thoughts somewhere else. Anywhere else. "Still playing hearts?"

"Whenever she can talk someone into it. Susie and I both know better."

He finally smiled. They hadn't seen much of each other lately. He hadn't felt it was right, with the formal interview for the Galina law enforcement position coming up. At least, that was what he told himself. There were five applicants, and Ginny had barely made it into the top three. This detail at Coffee Creek should give her a chance to show how well she could perform. Instincts based on twenty years of office politics told him to hold back. He could give her chances, but he couldn't give her the job.

That was one reason. The other he had already noted.

"Susie's still staying with you?"

"Yeah. Now that the baby's here, though, she's talking about getting her own place. I want her to stay. It's been a lifesaver, having her around. Almost as good as two parents."

Frank nodded. Ginny's status as the single parent of a ten-year-old had already been discussed. Could she handle a job that called for travel and irregular hours? Before meeting her, Frank would have had doubts, but not now. Ginny was resourceful, and she had a lot of friends in Galina.

"You've got to come out and see the baby, Frank. She's the cutest thing."

He smiled uncomfortably. He could have found an excuse any time in the past few weeks to visit the house on Tenmile Road. "What's her name again?"

"Angelica. I'm afraid Susie's an incurable romantic."

Often, at night, he closed his eyes and thought about the few days he had spent there in December. He thought about Ginny's hair, her warm, slightly musky scent as her shoulder brushed his arm. Sometimes he thought about other things, too. As long as they kept to business, he could handle it. Today, they had a lot of business.

He glanced up at the clock. "You have room for lunch, Deputy?" He'd given her the nickname last winter, and he still liked it. Reminded him of old cowboy movies.

"You bet. I always have room for lunch."

They drove downtown, the new technology park as yet bare of eating establishments. Longmont was a university town, with a good selection of ethnic and health-food restaurants. Ginny wanted to try a vegetarian place a few blocks from campus. Tofu-burgers with alfalfa sprouts. Frank groaned inwardly and ordered the heftiest item on the menu, a giant burrito. They went through the salad bar and settled down at a table under an enormous spider plant that looked as though it lived on leftovers.

Frank was, as usual, sifting his way through mounds of paperwork—it was June, the marijuana-eradication program was starting up again, logging was in full swing, tourists were making their pilgrimages to the forest's recreation areas, and then, wham in the middle of it all, the latest spotted owl report had blown up in their faces. If clear-cuts and a threatening letter were two reasons Ginny was going off-district, the spotted owl was another. The last was Ward Tomasovic.

"He grew up in Coffee Creek," Frank explained over lunch. "Left as soon as he got out of high school. That was twenty-two years ago. He hasn't been back since."

"So now he's going to tell the loggers they can live with the spotted owl?" Ginny had a pretty good idea of how Tomasovic's former neighbors would take that suggestion.

"Hell, I don't know what he's going to tell them. He's making a big deal about how he grew up in a logging town, how he sees both sides of the issue. His line seems to be that environmentalists aren't the enemy, the mill towns can survive the spotted owl, the wilderness areas, the timber cutbacks."

Ginny shook her head. "I would not call that a popular position, out in the Coast Range. Not with yellow ribbons draped through half the countryside." It had started ten years earlier, during the Iran hostage crisis, this display of yellow ribbons—actually the indispensable plastic flagging used in the woods. You couldn't drive from one town to another without seeing them everywhere. She turned her thoughts back to Ward Tomasovic. "Isn't he a biologist?"

"Fisheries."

A wildlifer. Not many jobs in fisheries. "Government?"

"Academic."

"Wasn't he in D.C. for a while, with the National Environmental League?"

Frank nodded. "Just over a year."

"That's not very long. Why'd he leave?"

"Ask him. He showed up in Oregon about six months ago. He's been speaking here and up around Washington since he got back."

"And now he's coming home."

"I guess so. Kind of funny, isn't it, growing up in a logging town and coming back an environmentalist?"

Now it was Ginny's turn to shrug. Tomasovic hadn't been much more than a kid when he left Coffee Creek. He might have gone in any direction. "Is someone sponsoring him, or is this his own idea?"

"There's a group in Coffee Creek making the arrangements. I've talked to one of them on the phone—Gayle Wallace. Nice lady. Here in Longmont she'd be considered middle-of-the-road on environmental issues, but in Coffee Creek I expect she and her friends are flaming radicals. So Tomasovic does have some local support."

"He's going to need it," Ginny said dryly.

"Here's that letter." Frank opened a large manila envelope and slipped out a piece of paper. "A copy. The original's in my office."

The words had been cut from newspaper headlines: GET TOMASOVIC OUT. Below the words was a photograph, torn into pieces, each shred carefully set in its proper place. Below that another line of type, the letters cut out individually: OR WE'LL DO IT FOR YOU.

The copier had blurred the photo, but Ginny recognized it. Ward Tomasovic.

She looked up. "This must have come from that big supplement the Portland paper ran a few weeks ago."

Frank nodded. "There was an article on Tomasovic. That's how they got his name in one piece."

"The photo was in one piece too, as I recall."

"Yes, I'd say this is meant to be a threat."

"It came to the SO?"

"Three days ago. We've had two phone calls since then, too."

"Oh?" She had only heard about the letter.

"A man's voice. The gal at the front desk took the first one. Shook her up a bit. He has a pretty foul mouth. She put the next call through to me."

"And?"

"Ever hear a chain saw over the telephone?"

Ginny winced. "Loggers aren't very subtle."

Frank slipped the paper back into the envelope. "They got the Coffee Creek station, too."

"Same thing?"

He nodded. "Phone calls are easy to make. So are threats. Bowers is on his toes, but we don't expect any serious trouble."

Ginny was quiet for a moment. She didn't like the image called up by the shredded photo and the chain saw.

"What's Bowers like?" she asked. Bruce Bowers was the Coffee Creek law enforcement officer—LEO, in the alphabet soup used by the Forest Service. If she got the new Galina LEO position, they would be counterparts.

"Seems like a nice enough guy. Competent, came to us with good recommendations."

"He was with ATF?"

"Yeah, Alcohol, Tobacco, and Firearms. Heavy on the firearms—he's supposed to be a crack shot."

"Why did he change agencies?"

"Said he didn't see much future in working with things that blow up. Those guys get all the explosives, you know." He chuckled. "Real organized. When he requested extra bodies for the weekend, he had three options laid out already. Plan A, Plan B, Plan C."

"Which plan was I?"

"D. You were Plan D."

"Your idea, then. He doesn't mind?"

Frank shrugged. "He didn't object."

Frank had called her three days ago to ask if she would be available over the weekend for a security assignment in Coffee Creek. She had guessed right away that it involved Burnt Meadows. Everyone in the Neskanie knew that

EarthAction had gone to court in an effort to stop the sale. Two days ago the Ninth Circuit Court judge had handed down his decision—the sale was legal, and logging could proceed. No one had any doubt that there would be an appeal. Meanwhile, the Forest Service was trying to prevent a showdown between EarthAction and Zellers Wood Products, the top bidder on the sale. The appearance of a nationally known environmentalist in Coffee Creek, where Zellers had its headquarters and biggest mill, was a setup for major trouble.

To make things even more exciting, EarthAction planned a gathering at the Burnt Meadows campground tomorrow, the day after Tomasovic's talk. The Neskanie forest supervisor felt strongly that the gathering should be permitted. His concerns were with public relations; Frank's were with security, and the Burnt Meadows campground was a security nightmare. He needed twenty bodies to do the job right. He had three. EarthAction expected about fifty people in the campground Friday night, with another hundred or so arriving for workshops and lunch. They said they planned to go home after that, but no one knew what might happen once they got revved up.

"Does Bowers have any background on these people?" Ginny asked.

"I sent a copy of our file over. Mostly newspaper clippings. You can look at it when you get there."

She sat quietly for a moment. As a general thing, she agreed with the environmentalists. There *had* been too much cutting, too little concern for the future. On the other hand, she made her living in the woods, as did most of her neighbors. What would happen to the little towns like Galina and Coffee Creek if logging was shut down for good?

"Once Tomasovic starts spouting off, those loggers will throw tomatoes at him till he looks like a spaghetti dinner. Not to mention chain saws."

Frank chuckled, which was a mistake. A tomato wedge caught in his throat. He choked politely for a moment, then set his fork down and glared at a stray piece of lettuce. No wonder he hated salad. Ginny watched with interest as he stabbed the piece of lettuce and returned it to his plate. Who said tomatoes weren't deadly?

"Our job," he said, "is to make sure it's nothing worse."

TWO

ALAN BRECKENRIDGE PULLED the battered VW van to a stop and shut the engine off. The silence was sudden, startling. He sat still, letting the sounds of the woods seep into his awareness. Insects whirred and hummed in the hot June sun. Somewhere in the distance a thrush called out with a single high note. A squirrel, noting the invader, chattered from the trunk of a big fir.

Alan dropped his hands into his lap and closed his eyes, letting the sounds flow over him like a benediction. His shoulders, tensed for the last ten miles, slowly relaxed. The knots in his stomach loosened, and he felt a sudden, overpowering urge to take a dump. Damn! He grabbed the roll of toilet paper from the glove compartment, jerked the door open, and plunged into the brush.

The squirrel's chatter erupted again, then slowly died away. A dragonfly skimmed past Alan's head, wings shimmering in the sun. The warm, resinous breeze caressed his face. He stood up, zipped his jeans, found a stick, and began to methodically bury the signs of his presence. You'd think, after all these years, he'd have gotten over the uptight anticipation, the sudden need to empty his bowels. But no, it was just as bad now as it had been that first time, in Arizona, when they'd dismantled a bulldozer at a dam site.

Now, that had been an event. They'd driven out together late at night, drinking beer and making up raunchy songs about dams and men who needed big machines. Three of them, Alan, Bob somebody, and Rachel Davis. As they neared the dam site, Bob shut off the headlights and they drove by the light of the stars, through the wide, eerie majesty of the open desert. They had all met for the first time just a few days earlier, brought together through their mutual contacts with EarthAction.

Rachel had been tight, intense, charged with recklessness and sex, her dark hair twisting like a living creature in the breeze. Both men were stunned—it was a reaction Alan was to see again and again through the next few years. Bob was the local contact, the one who knew the area and had planned the action. Rachel knew about bulldozers. A few months later, in a house in New Mexico, Alan had seen a poorly printed manual giving step-by-step instructions for destroying heavy equipment. Rachel's nom de guerre, Red Tail, was on the cover.

Alan went back to the van and slid the side door open. Now he mostly operated on his own. It was easier, and tended to reduce the risk. He'd asked Rachel to come along, though. For old times' sake. She had turned him down. She was too well known; a criminal charge against her would destroy the credibility of the Eugene Environmental Coalition. It was true, as far as it went, but the real reason, Alan knew, was that she was still hung up on Ward Tomasovic. Two years ago she had been passionately in love with Ward; now she hated him with equal vehemence. What did it matter? Alan thought morosely. She was still hung up on Tomasovic, maybe would be for the rest of her life. Or his.

He got his map out. It was an official Forest Service map of the Burnt Meadows sale, obtained openly and aboveboard as part of the packet sent out to anyone interested in bidding on the timber. He had been careful, though, not to mark it in any way. Leave no trace—it was a good wilderness motto, and even better in this line of work. He spread the map, located his position, then traced a route to the closest unit in the sale. The trick was to come up to it from the back. He had driven along the highway, turned off just past town, turned again at Fish Hatchery Road, and again onto Forest Service Road 1006. That was the route shown on the map, the route the log trucks would take. But then he had stopped, because that was undoubtedly the route the Freddies had wired.

They might have wired a few other places, too. It was a mistake to underestimate the Freddies, especially the cops. They went through the same training as the FBI, and they had access to the same antiterrorist technology. A few days ago an anonymous caller had filled Alan in on the security precautions surrounding the Burnt Meadows sale. Based on the information, Alan guessed he worked for the Forest Service, or was in touch with someone who did.

The van was parked near a trailhead, in full view of the road. Anyone driving by would assume it belonged to hikers. The first unit of the Burnt Meadows sale was over a mile away cross-country, more by road. Alan hauled his dusty backpack out of the van, hefted it up on his shoulders, and set off into the woods.

A few yards down the trail he veered into the brush, heading downhill. With each step the fifty pounds of nails in his pack clanked softly. He crossed a draw, climbed steadily uphill, then paused at the top of the ridge to take a long drink from his canteen. From the edge of a clear-cut he caught a glimpse of Road 1006 winding along the opposite slope. Last week a couple of Freddies had been sitting there, keeping an eye on the Burnt Meadows area. With Ward scheduled to speak in Coffee Creek tonight, though, they'd pulled everyone off for a few days, leaving only the radio sensors. The anonymous caller had known about the sensors, but he had not known enough.

Alan shifted the heavy pack and started down the hill. Across the draw, just where the slope broke, he spotted the line of yellow flags marking the unit boundary. Now came the sticky part. Most of the sensors were located across the top of the unit, but a few had been placed inside. They could pick up a deer, the caller had said, definitely a bear, but the people monitoring them back at the station would disregard such signals. They were interested in vehicles and steady, regular vibration. The kind of vibration set up by a hammer driving a six-inch spike into a tree.

Last year some of the EarthActioners had made a big deal about giving up spiking. They weren't going to do anything that might injure people. Hell, he didn't want anybody to get hurt, either. He'd make a few changes in technique, but he wasn't about to give up one of his best tactics.

He paused, walked a few steps, paused again. He crossed through the line of yellow flags dangling in the brush, doing his best to move like a deer. Would the Freddies go all the way into the unit? Most of them kept to the cleared boundary lines; they didn't like beating brush. How good were those sensors? Could they pick up vibrations from a hundred yards? Two hundred? A quarter-mile?

Alan started to sweat. He had done a couple of actions in wired areas before, and they made him extremely nervous. He couldn't reason away the paralyzing fear of getting caught. Damn it, so what if they caught him? It would be great publicity, and at worst he'd get a few months in jail. His stomach knotted at the thought. He paused, took a few steps, paused again. He must be a third of the way across the unit by now. It was as good a place as any.

High above his head branches swayed in the breeze. Sunlight poured down, picking out patches of lime-green moss on the forest floor. Alan looked at the big fir in front of him, took a deep breath, and nodded. Rachel would have said some kind of prayer, asking the tree's spirit for forgiveness. He wondered if she said the same prayer before lighting into a human being.

He took the first nail from his pack. With four strong, practiced blows, he drove it knee-high into the trunk. Twenty more nails followed, laced around the tree in a helix pattern. He straightened up, took a can of paint from his pack, and sprayed a big white *S* on the trunk. Spiked. The fallers wouldn't touch it. Not knowing if he had spiked all the trees or not, they wouldn't touch any of them. He moved on to the next big fir.

WARD TOMASOVIC SHIFTED down into second as he took the turn off Coffee Creek Road. The Toyota van responded instantly, gripping the pavement and then skidding slightly as the road turned to gravel. Dust plumed out behind the tires. Ward pushed a button and the driver's window slid halfway up. He slowed as the fish hatchery came into view.

Twenty-two years. He had been gone for twenty-two years. He could vaguely remember a field trip to the fish hatchery. Fifth grade? Must have been sixth? The place had grown. He could see at least twenty ponds. The van slowed to a crawl. Amazing that he had almost forgotten that field trip. There had to be a connection between the fisheries biologist he was today and the gawky twelve-year-old who had once peered in fascination at the swarming mass of young salmon.

The hatchery had always been a popular destination for families out for a drive. Kids could buy packages of fish food from an ancient vending machine and toss them into the ponds, creating a minor feeding frenzy. Today a young couple stood on the little bridge over the chute where water gushed into the ponds. Three kids ran down the concrete walkways. Ward smiled as he caught a glimpse of a No

Running sign. Most of the kids in that sixth-grade class had run, too.

Above the hatchery the road curved and you got your first good look at the creek. Pasture bordered the far side, fields of grass dotted with black-and-white cows. They looked like the same damn cows he remembered from twenty-two years ago. He pulled over and stopped just below the point where Coffee Creek widened, spilling from a deep pool into a series of riffles. He'd spent a lot of time at that pool, especially after Billy Ney drowned.

He'd been a fool even to take the drift boat out. He knew it wasn't safe, hadn't been properly caulked and sealed since the year before, but the Ney kid had begged him until he promised, and then nagged him until he'd made good on the promise. The boat capsized and he watched the kid drown, had almost drowned himself. After that he stopped fishing the Neskanie.

Hell, after that he'd met Debbie, and fishing took a back seat, along with everything else in his life. He started the van again. Was there still a wild salmon run? Or did all the Coffee Creek fish come from the hatchery now?

Too damn much cutting. Too many goddamn roads. Rip the trees off the slopes and for years afterward mud poured into the creek, silting up the gravel in the spawning beds. Cut the trees in the riparian zone, let the sun beat down on the creek, and the water got too warm for fingerlings. Oregon had once had one of the world's greatest anadromous fisheries. Now it was all gone, canneries rotting on their piles in the tidewater rivers, the fishing fleets bare tokens of their former selves. Oh, the creeks still had fish—hatchery fish. You could still buy a license, climb into a drift boat, and catch a few. But the giant runs, the fish unbelievable in their numbers, were history now, all their beauty and wildness destroyed.

Destroyed by men like Ward's father, Nick Tomasovic, a gyppo logger scratching to support his family. By men like the Zellerses, with their fallers, their buckers and choker setters, their yarding towers, log trucks, and mills. Coffee Creek was, for all intents and purposes, a company town, and the company was Zellers Wood Products.

Ward frowned and gripped the steering wheel tighter as the road began to climb. Was it a mistake, coming back? Would anybody listen to him? They probably hated him, Ward Tomasovic, big-time Washington environmentalist, out to take their jobs away and condemn their town to a slow death. He was ready to do everything he could to reach them tonight, really reach into their hearts and convince them that saving the last of the salmon and the old-growth trees didn't have to mean the end of their way of life.

His former colleagues in the National Environmental League thought he was a fool for even trying. It was Ward's opinion that environmentalists at the national level had simply written off the people who stood to lose the most from protective timber legislation: the mill workers, the loggers, and the thousands of small business people who depended on timber dollars.

Two years ago, when he had first gone to Washington, he had been starry-eyed at the chance to work with people who could really make a difference. Surely the representatives, the senators, the lobbyists, the committee members could draft legislation that would halt the massive overcutting of the Pacific Northwest forests. His job was to provide scientific support for proposed legislation. He had a doctorate in fisheries and plenty of experience in the movement. What he didn't have, he soon found, was any notion of how things were done in the nation's capital.

It had been, as they said, a learning experience. The money had been good—the money had been excellent, more than he'd ever made. He'd sent double child support to his ex-wife, trying to make up for the lean years when the kids were babies. And he'd bought this van. The first brand-new vehicle he had ever owned. Hell, no one in his family had ever bought something straight off the showroom floor. He smiled, remembering the admiration in his mother's eyes when she had seen it for the first time last week. Old Harold Jacobson, her second husband, would never own a rig like this.

So far the road didn't seem to have changed much; there should be a campground right around the next bend. Ward swung the van to the left, then hit the brakes with a jolt that almost sent him through the windshield. Gone were the trees that had once lined the side of the road. Spread across the slope overlooking Coffee Creek was one of the most godawful clear-cuts he had ever seen.

He pulled the van over and got out. The scar running down the side of Prairie had to be a hundred acres, maybe more. He walked along the edge of the road, peering over the side at the raw, red earth, the charred stumps, the first tendrils of green creeping out from thickets blackened by fire. Twelve-inch fir seedlings marched down the gutted hillside in straight, regular lines, each one a regulation ten feet from the next. Ward walked out to the point of a nearby landing, kicking at sticks and slabs of bark left by the loggers. Far below, sunlight glinted off moving water—Coffee Creek, exposed to the mud, the silt, and the heat. They hadn't even bothered to leave a buffer of trees. Take every last stick, that was the Zellerses motto.

It had to be them. They wouldn't let timber this close to home go to anyone else. The land itself might be private, or it might be Forest Service—the Jackson River area was a patchwork of private and public ownership. But the logging had been done by Zellers crews, and the timber had ended up in the Zellers mills. Zellers, Zellers, Zellers. Damn every single one of them.

Ward slowly unclenched his fists. He had left Coffee Creek twenty-two years ago because of the Zellerses. Because of Charlie Zellers, specifically, the head of the clan and Debbie's father. Charlie Zellers must be over seventy by now. Ward knew from his mother that the old man was still alive, and just as domineering and contentious as ever. Ward had been eighteen when Charlie Zellers drove him out of town rather than see him marry Debbie. Ward was forty now, and Debbie was a woman with grown children of her own. Charlie couldn't stand between them this time.

He would see her tonight.

He turned away from the devastated landscape, his heart rising at the thought. Somewhere below a vehicle geared down to take a turn, the transmission growling as the tires hit gravel. After the reception, the speech, the refreshments, Debbie would be waiting for him at the end of the old road where they had first made love when they were still kids. He had seen her twice since coming back to Oregon. They had both known instantly that the magic was still there, the almost magnetic attraction for each other. The first time, meeting by arrangement at a freeway restaurant, they had ended up in a motel bed within an hour. The second time had been just a week before, out at the coast. And now, tonight, he would see her again.

In a couple of hours he would head back to Coffee Creek to meet with Friends of Burnt Meadows, the group sponsoring his talk. He had come out early so that he could do just this, drive around and remember. He climbed back into the van and started up the road. Fifteen minutes later, rounding a curve, he spotted a van parked at the Prairie Mountain trailhead.

Ward had not seen Alan Breckenridge in two years, but he would have known that van anywhere, a battered red Volkswagen with air scoops improvised from a plastic dishpan. He parked alongside. A decoration made from feathers hung from the rearview mirror. One from a bald eagle, two from red-tailed hawks, and one from a great horned owl. He had given the owl feather to Alan himself.

The van door was locked. He peered inside, but could make out nothing in the dim light. He walked around the van, thinking. It was, of course, possible that Alan was hiking the Prairie Mountain trail. A lot of people did, especially during the last six months, when the controversy over the nearby Burnt Meadows sale had hit the newspapers and television.

Ward took his daypack from the back of his van, checked to see that the canteen was full, and pulled out a map of the Neskanie National Forest. He studied it for a moment, then set off up the trail. A hundred yards in he spotted what he was looking for—a flattened patch of grass and a dislodged stone. He nodded with satisfaction. After all those years in graduate school, postdoc work, and teaching, with another year in Washington, he could still find his way around the woods.

He left the trail, pushing the brush aside. Once, before meeting Rachel, he and Alan had been the closest of friends. Now they were enemies. He still knew Alan's mind, though, and he knew his tactics. It didn't matter that EarthAction had renounced tactics that might endanger people. Alan Breckenridge was somewhere in the Burnt Meadows sale right this moment, and he was spiking trees.

A FEW MINUTES LATER a third vehicle, a green pickup with the Forest Service emblem on the doors, pulled over and parked at the Prairie Mountain trailhead. Bruce Bowers, the

Coffee Creek law enforcement officer, got out and stood for a moment, studying the two vans. The Toyota he knew already, having followed it from the ranger station, where Tomasovic had stopped to pick up a map. They had an appointment to meet at four that afternoon, but he couldn't pass up the chance to tail the environmentalist and see what he was up to. Now he took out a small notebook and jotted down the plate number of the beat-up Volks. Probably more hikers from Eugene—who else would drive such a leftover from the psychedelic era? He tucked the notebook into his uniform pocket and walked around the vans, peering through the windows. All the doors on both vehicles were locked.

Bowers stood still and listened. A breeze sighed through the firs, carrying the faint growl of a log truck from the highway a thousand feet below. A squirrel chattered. Insects hummed in the warm sunshine. The radio inside his truck sputtered as a dispatcher called in to the SO.

He got back in, started the truck, and pulled out onto the road. A few hundred yards below the trailhead he turned onto an old logging track that would have been impassable in wet weather. His truck jounced through the ruts, crushing the young alders that had struggled up through the compacted soil. He parked a little way in, out of sight of the road, and hiked back to the trail.

He saw the flattened patch of grass, the dislodged stone. He stopped to study them, then turned to consider the trail that wound its way up Prairie Mountain. Bruce Bowers nodded, unconsciously touched the gun holstered under his arm, and stepped off the trail into the brush.

THREE

GINNY GLANCED at her watch, then flicked her gaze up to the clock on the wall. They both said she had been waiting for almost an hour. Coffee Creek's assistant dispatcher, a high-school student on her first summer job, had already offered her coffee, shown her around the station, and made an unsuccessful attempt to raise Bowers on the radio. Then Ginny spent a few minutes looking over the radio that received signals from the remote sensors in the Burnt Meadows sale. Now Tiffany—that was the dispatcher's name—had disappeared on business of her own. Ginny settled down behind Bowers's desk with a copy of *Magnetic Point Sensors: Deployment Considerations*. Irritation prickled across her shoulders like a heat rash. Where was the guy?

She and Bowers had an appointment to meet Tomasovic at four, and it was a quarter till. She wasn't surprised that Tiffany couldn't call him. Her own district's location was just as bad, tucked among the hills and deep, folded valleys of the Coast Range. Bowers was probably down in a hole somewhere, out of radio contact, but he should have let them know he'd be late.

She wandered back down to Dispatch. Tiffany was calling the afternoon weather readings in to the SO. When she finished, Ginny's own assistant, Sue Frank, came on the air with Galina's report. Ginny listened for a moment, then asked Tiffany to try Bowers again.

She switched the radio to the district frequency. "Bowers, Coffee Creek."

The receiver crackled. "Bowers."

Ginny leaned over to speak into the mike. "Trask here. What's your ETA?"

"Ten minutes."

She glanced at the clock. Five till four. "Where are we meeting Tomasovic?"

"At the high school. My screwup. Let's go to Plan B—I'll meet you there, by the main entrance."

His voice was light, almost boyish. Ginny's irritation started to fade. "Ten-four. Trask clear." She paused, racking her brain for the station number she needed to recite as per FCC regulations. Then she had it. "AUB528."

She turned to Tiffany. "How old is Bowers, anyway?"

"Oh, jeez, he's old. At least thirty."

Ginny strode across the compound parking lot, shaking her head. God knew what Tiffany would call Frank—elderly, perhaps? Ancient? She reached the chain-link fence that separated the Forest Service compound from the school playing field and slipped through an open gate near a towering scoreboard. The field smelled of freshly mowed grass. Her feet sank into the turf as though into a carpet, while overhead sunlight poured out of the perfect blue dome of the sky.

Years ago, before Dale had died, she would have spent an afternoon like this on the back porch with a pad of drawing paper and a pen, adding to the portfolio she regularly shipped to New York. But here she was instead, earning a living. She rarely thought about it anymore, except on near-perfect days like this, when she itched for a pencil and the smooth, cool feel of paper beneath her hand. Tomasovic's speech was scheduled for the high-school gym at seven that evening. They had arranged to meet at the school to look things over. Bill Larkin, Coffee Creek's deputy sheriff, was in charge of security at the talk itself. Ginny and Bowers were handling arrangements for EarthAction's gathering at the Forest Service campground the next day. Some of Tomasovic's audience was expected to spend the night at the campground, as well. That had been enough to generate a request from the county sheriff, perennially short of staff, for help.

Halfway across the field, Ginny spotted Larkin's pickup and a Toyota van parked in front of the high school. Three people, one in uniform, sat on a sunny patch of grass near the front steps. She kept walking, uncomfortably aware that they had fallen silent and were watching her with open curiosity.

The tall, thin man wearing a brown uniform unfolded himself and stood up, holding out his hand. "Bill Larkin, deputy sheriff. You must be Mrs. Trask."

His hand was warm, dry, and oddly comforting. She nodded. "Officer Bowers will be a few minutes late."

Larkin smiled. He had a nice smile, slow and a little toothy. "I suppose we can wait for him. Let me introduce these folks."

Ginny had already recognized Ward Tomasovic, but his newspaper pictures had not prepared her for the crackling intensity of the man himself. Even sitting down, his legs sprawled across the grass, he radiated energy. He was about forty, thin like Larkin but, when he stood up to take her hand, a few inches shorter. His dark, curly hair wasn't as long as she had expected, and his neatly trimmed beard was touched with gray.

He took her hand with a quick, almost eager clasp. "Glad to meet you, Officer. I appreciate the trouble all of you are going to." His eyes gazed directly into hers, claiming her attention, demanding a response.

She mumbled something and pulled back, emotional alarms clanging. Women probably tripped over each other trying to get to this man. It wasn't sexual, though sex had something to do with it. It was his enthusiasm, his focus, the way his gaze jolted through her like an electric shock.

She turned with relief to Gayle Wallace, a comfortable, plump woman in her mid-fifties, who greeted her with a warm smile, asking if she knew Nora Henderson, a fourth-grade teacher in Galina.

"My daughter was in her class last year," Ginny said. Ward Tomasovic was still looking at her. She kept talking to Gayle. "Do you teach?"

"I took early retirement just last month, so I really don't, anymore, but I still feel like I do." Gayle's short hair was permed into a gray frizz, she wore no makeup, and a pair of gold hoops dangled from her ears. Ginny made a show of admiring her dress, made from some ethnic fabric—Guatemalan, she guessed, full of bright strips.

"I got it for the party tonight. Ward's homecoming party." She gave Ward a smile, including him in the conversation. "A lot of people were pretty surprised that you wanted to come back."

Something flashed in Tomasovic's eyes, then vanished, replaced by a bland friendliness. "Yes, well, I've wanted to visit ever since I got back from D.C."

"Having you here has made us get organized." She turned to Ginny with an apologetic grin. "The biggest problem we've had is finding a name."

"Your group isn't part of EarthAction?"

Gayle shook her head. "None of us would dare join anything so radical."

"I'm glad of it, myself," said Ward. "The whole issue has gotten so polarized that the extremists on both sides have stopped trying to find a workable solution." After his eyes, his voice had to be his second big asset. Ginny could imagine him in a classroom, every student transfixed. It was a politician's voice, a preacher's voice without the proselytizing. She waited, hoping he would speak again, but that appeared to be all he had to say.

She turned to Gayle. "What *do* you call yourselves?"

"Friends of Burnt Meadows," said Gayle happily. "We just came up with it last night."

A moment later a Forest Service pickup pulled into the parking lot, kicking up gravel as it made the turn. Bruce Bowers slowed and came to a stop beside Ward's van. Now Ginny was part of the watching group and she was, perhaps, the most curious.

Coffee Creek's new LEO walked toward them with a relaxed, unhurried gait, as though unaware that he was ten minutes late. He was blond, clean-shaven, with a face that matched his boyish voice. He nodded to Bill Larkin and then to Ginny, giving her a friendly grin of recognition. *We're a team,* he seemed to say, *let's not let them know we haven't met.* She returned his smile before she knew it.

Once again Larkin made the introductions. Gayle unlocked the door and led them in. Ginny started up the steps, then paused to wait for Ward, who was studying the inscription over the doorway: "Coffee Creek School, 1905." He turned and squinted at the surrounding hills. The lowering sun picked out creases in his face that she had not noticed before.

"When I lived here," he said quietly, as much to himself as to her, "those hills were one unbroken blanket of green. The easy timber was almost gone, but the hills were untouched. Look at them now."

She looked, and what she saw she could have seen in Galina or any of a dozen other Coast Range towns. The hills no longer wore a blanket of green—now it was a patchwork quilt: squares of brown earth, some black from recent slash burns, squares of verdant new growth, with only a few patches of the original deep, dark green. The silhouettes of the ridges no longer flowed smoothly from height to valley floor, but dropped in jagged lines from mature timber to bare clear-cuts. Ginny's eye, trained in color and form, saw it the way Ward saw it and her hand, trained to draw, longed for a pen and brush.

"I could paint that," she said softly. "Paint it the way it used to be, and the way it is now."

"Could you?" He turned to her and smiled. "That's a picture I'd like to see."

THE HIGH-SCHOOL GYM was packed. Over five hundred people, Ginny estimated, pretty impressive for a town with an official population of seven hundred and twenty-three. Not everyone, of course, was from Coffee Creek. She had already spotted a few of her own neighbors from Galina. A good half of the crowd was probably from out of town.

It was quite a mix. Some of the men were still in work clothes, boots exchanged for sneakers in deference to the gym's wooden floors. Ginny counted at least eight sets of suspenders from where she was standing, near the big double doors of the back of the gym. Loggers tended to feel more comfortable in work shirts and jeans—she knew the feeling herself. The women wore slacks and flowered shirts or housedresses. The teenagers looked like teenagers anywhere. Ginny was surprised to see so many of them, with school out for the summer. Perhaps there wasn't much else to do in town on this particular Friday night.

So far everything was running smoothly, due, she suspected, to Bruce Bowers as much as Gayle Wallace. She and Bruce had grabbed hamburgers at the café a little earlier, and while they ate he had filled her in on the preparations. Frank was right—Bowers was a planner. He had a minute-by-minute schedule for the evening, seating charts (they were keeping the loggers and the environmentalists separate), a list of people he wanted to keep an eye on, and alternative plans in case anything went wrong. He seemed a bit abstracted, as though he had something else on his mind, but Ginny could tell he was enjoying himself.

Friends of Burnt Meadows had set up a table in the hall just outside the gym, with a hand-lettered sign advertising their new name. A couple with a young child sat there now, earnestly offering leaflets with titles like *Save the Ancient Forests* and *Trees Are Life*. Among them were copies of Tomasovic's scientific articles on salmon. Ginny had thumbed through one of these earlier, and found most of it unintelligible. Frank Carver, who fished with almost religious devotion, would probably have known what the paper was about. She hoped Ward planned to use more down-to-earth language with his audience tonight.

The steady flow of people into the building had begun to thin when a new commotion reached Ginny's ears. She turned around to see a tall woman wearing a long green robe pause in the doorway. More people crowded in behind her, just inside the hallway. The first woman held what looked like a bush. As she lifted it Ginny saw that it was a wreath of leaves. The woman settled it on her head, squared her shoulders, and walked down the hall, eyes straight ahead, and into the gym.

The rest came right behind her, about thirty adults and a dozen children. They wore T-shirts with slogans, pictures of trees, and satellite photos of the planet, with the phrase "Earth: Love It or Leave It" scrawled in a circle. All the kids, and many of the adults, had their faces painted with flowers, rainbows, and peace symbols. As they went by, Ginny counted five posters and eleven more wreaths.

The crowd inside the gym started to murmur. She keyed her radio and called Bowers in a low, urgent voice. "Looks like EarthAction is here."

"Well, we expected that. I'm tied up on the stage. Get out on the floor and keep an eye on them until I get there."

"Ten-four."

"Larkin, do you copy?"

"Copy," the deputy sheriff responded. He was somewhere in the west bleachers, near the area set aside for Zellers Wood Products. Quite a few Zellers employees had brought their own signs, and a lot of the noise inside the gym at that moment was coming from their area.

The chairs right in front of the stage had, as usual, been left almost empty. The EarthAction group headed straight for them. The noise level inside the gym rose appreciably.

Two women from the group started unrolling a banner. People in the bleachers shifted and stood, craning their necks to see better. Ginny eased her way through a clump of kids wearing face paint. One of the agreements with Gayle Wallace's group was no demonstrations inside the gymnasium. She reached the front of the gym just as the two women got the banner stretched out enough to read: EARTH FIRST! PROFITS LAST!

"I'm afraid that will have to come down," Ginny said, addressing the older of the two, the one whose long gray hair was braided with strips of bright ribbon.

The entire group turned to listen. Ginny saw a few more banners, not yet unfurled, tucked under their chairs.

"Are you a cop?" the woman asked.

"Forest Service," Ginny replied. "Security."

"What are the Freddies doing here?" demanded the woman holding the other end of the banner. She was younger, with unruly black hair flying loose around her face. "This isn't federal property."

The earphone tucked uncomfortably in Ginny's ear squawked her name. She punched the send button on her radio. "Trask here."

It was Bill Larkin, his voice almost unintelligible in the hubbub. It took her a moment to figure out that he was asking if she needed help. She scanned the gym and found the deputy sheriff near the bleachers, his height and brown uniform setting him apart. He looked as though he had his hands full with the Zellers crowd. Bowers was nowhere in sight, which worried her. She caught Larkin's eye and lifted her hand. "Under control so far. Trask out."

The EarthAction people were watching her, and the banner was still up. The murmur from the section of bleachers that could see the words was getting louder. She turned back to the task at hand. Her one-hour session on crowd control, taken two years ago, had not prepared her to confront a woman old enough to be her mother.

"We have an agreement with the sponsoring group that there will be no demonstrations in the gym." Thank God her voice was steady. "Please take the banner down."

Sympathy flickered in the older woman's eyes, but she held her ground. "No one told us about an agreement."

She simply was not going to budge until she got a concession. Ginny recognized the tactic from dealings with her ten-year-old daughter. Her choice now was to back down, call in reinforcements, or shift the discussion to something they could agree on.

"We went over all this with Gayle Wallace this afternoon. Have you talked to her?"

The woman nodded. "Last week, when we first heard that Ward would be here."

"We've made arrangements since then. Gayle's up on stage. Why don't you check with her?"

A smile crossed the woman's lips, then vanished. "All right, we'll do that."

It occurred to Ginny that she was facing an adversary with considerably more experience than herself. The woman looked as though she had spent a lifetime facing down authority figures.

"The banner," Ginny said.

The group was still watching her, silent.

"It still has to come down."

The woman sighed and lowered the pole holding her end. She began rolling the banner up. "John," she said, without glancing up, "go and find Gayle Wallace. We'd better get an update on the rules."

One of the men left the group and headed for the stage. The noise from the crowd in the bleachers had begun to subside as soon as the banner came down. Now it was time for Ginny to make a concession.

"No one else has banners or signs, either."

"They don't need them," the younger woman snapped. "Not with all those yellow ribbons."

It was true. That afternoon someone had decorated every possible object in the gym with yellow flagging. Two women were handing out yellow ribbons at the door—over half the crowd wore them on their arms.

"We just want to make sure no one gets hurt," Ginny said.

"A laudable objective, and one we share," said the older woman. The banner was completely rolled up. She tied a piece of string around the two poles, pulling the knots tight. "We just extend it to other species, as well."

There was no answer to that. Ginny thanked them and headed back to her position by the doors. The gym was completely full. Tomasovic's talk was scheduled to start in three minutes.

WARD TOMASOVIC LEANED forward on the lectern and waited, giving the audience a break before he swung into the "There Are Solutions" part of his talk. Things were going great so far. He had the audience, he could feel it. There had been skepticism at first, distrust, hostility, but now he had them. Every logger and mill worker out there was convinced that he, Ward Tomasovic, understood their problems.

Six months ago no one had believed he could do it. He was an academic, for chrissakes, a college professor. So he'd helped found an environmental organization. Big deal. Talking to the true believers. That didn't mean he could talk to anyone else.

They had underestimated him, his colleagues in Washington. They hadn't realized what kind of college professor he had been. He hadn't been one to hide out in a lab, or spend most of his time alone in the field. He cared passionately about fish, and therefore about water and the land. Not one student walked away from his courses without realizing that he cared. He took his classes out into the woods for days at a time, building gabions and clearing logjams, trying to undo some of the damage humans had caused in the last two hundred years. Most of his students left with a new awareness of their relation to the natural world, a new feeling that they could make a difference, a new sense of mission.

What he had proved, in the last six months, was that he could bring about that change in other people, too, not just college students. This audience, right here in Coffee Creek, was the toughest he had ever faced. But he had done it. He could feel it, the high, heady sense of connection, of empathy, of power. The loggers, the mill workers, the salesclerks and waitresses, the farmers, the teachers, the backpackers and birdwatchers—everyone in the audience was waiting for him, Ward Tomasovic, to tell them the answers.

Now came the hardest part of all, the part his fellow environmentalists could not forgive. They were here tonight, in their theatrical getups, just as they had been at every talk he'd given since returning to Oregon. He even thought he'd seen Rachel out there. Dedicated, visionary, unyielding in the purity of their purpose. Not one more tree, not one more fish (well, he had to agree about the fish). We are guilty, we will pay the price. Except that middle-class environmentalists didn't pay the price. That was done by working people in towns like Coffee Creek.

He reached into his pocket and touched the folded scrap of paper with the message from Debbie. She would meet him at eleven, under the scoreboard. A change of plans. He scanned the audience one more time, looking for her face. She must be out there, somewhere. Her father was there, old Charlie Zellers, dead center in the second row, flanked by his two sons. Debbie was probably somewhere in back, with her husband and kids. Ward remembered Ed Kurtz as an okay guy, not too bright, pulling green chain when he'd last known him. Now he had some middle-management job at Zellers Wood Products, thanks no doubt to his marriage to the boss's daughter. Ward didn't hold it against him. Ed Kurtz, in fact, was exactly the kind of person he wanted to reach. He pitched his voice low and started to speak, aiming his remarks at Ed Kurtz and all the others like him.

"There are answers," he began. The last few heads lifted, turned in his direction. "Answers that might cost you your job, but not your home, or your chance to earn a living. Answers that will bring big changes to Coffee Creek, but that won't leave the town to die. We can live on this land without destroying it."

He paused. There was silence now, no restlessness, no fidgeting. A baby whimpered from the bleachers.

"There are answers, but I don't have them." He waited, sensing the crowd's letdown, the beginning of disappointment. "You do. You have the answers."

Now he was off again, building their hope, giving them a sense of their own power. He glanced at the clock. Ten after nine, right on schedule. Plenty of time to stay and talk with the dozens of people who would want to shake his hand, argue, criticize, find a way to help. Gayle Wallace had a big party planned at her place afterward, but he would still have time to meet Debbie, under the scoreboard, where they had met so many times before, twenty-two years ago.

APPLAUSE THUNDERED through the gymnasium as the first few families came through the double doors, herding small children down the hall and directly to the parking lot. They were so intent on getting home that at first Ginny thought no one else had been so strongly, powerfully moved by Tomasovic's talk. He was a fine speaker, would have made a good preacher. Perhaps he was a preacher who had found his true calling.

She left her station in the hall to peer through the open doors into the gym. People were leaving their seats, crowding toward the doors. There seemed to be some commotion up near the stage. She thumbed her radio, calling Bruce Bowers.

"What's going on up front?"

"Just a lot of people wanting to talk to this guy."

She was about to ask if he needed help when the EarthAction group spilled into the hall. The rest of the crowd pulled away, giving them room, so that they passed like the Israelites through a parted sea of hostile faces. Did they support Tomasovic? Oppose him? Or did they just have their own agenda? In any case, they had a powerful unifying effect on the rest of the crowd.

More people came through the doors, eddying past the literature table on their way out. A few stopped to take pamphlets. Ginny made her way out to the parking lot, where she directed traffic for another fifteen minutes.

Finally, the gym was almost empty. Bowers and Larkin joined her outside.

"Well, that's over," the deputy sheriff said.

"It went real well," Bowers said. "No major problems." He turned to Ginny. "Larkin told me how you handled those EarthActioners. Good job."

She shrugged, but the praise felt good. It had been a busy night, with more to come. She glanced around the parking lot. A few vehicles remained, among them Tomasovic's van.

"Didn't he take off with the rest of them?" she asked, nodding toward the van.

"Maybe he plans to pick it up after the party," Bruce said.

"That party," moaned Bill Larkin. "Between that and the tavern, I'm going to have my hands full tonight."

Bruce chuckled. "Better you than us, brother."

"Yeah, you federales aren't any too popular around here, with either side."

"Go chase drunks, Larkin. I'll be up on the hill, making sure no one hassles the save-the-trees crowd."

"Watching them dance naked around the campfire, more likely. All those big tits."

Ginny's smile vanished. She stared across the playing field, suddenly intent on the scoreboard at the far end. She liked men, she reminded herself. Bill Larkin seemed like a nice guy. His wife had been in the audience that evening, along with their two children. Bruce Bowers seemed like a nice guy, too. So why was it that when two nice guys got together they started sounding like a couple of jerks?

Bruce evidently noticed her reaction. "I guess we'd better get going. See you later, Bill."

They took a final swing past the gymnasium, where the janitor was locking up. The Friends of Burnt Meadows and their table of literature were gone. The place had the empty, eerie feel of a school building at night.

Bruce shoved his hands into his pocket. "That was a pretty dumb comment. I'm sorry."

"You don't have to apologize for Bill Larkin."

"Well, maybe I do. I don't want you to think all men are like that."

"I know they aren't," she said shortly. How naive did he think she was? She was quiet for a moment, and then she realized he was watching her, concerned. He didn't look so much like a kid anymore. She took a breath and sighed. "I'm sorry. Guess I've just heard too many of those dumb comments."

He smiled. "You did a real good job tonight, you know. Frank says you're up for the Galina LEO job?"

She nodded.

"Good luck. I hope you get it."

They went back outside. There was an awkward silence.

"You want a lift?" he asked.

She looked up at the sky, thick with stars. Frogs chirped in the grass like nocturnal birds. "Thanks, but I think I'll walk. Meet you at road 1006?"

"Three a.m." He swung into the cab of his pickup, all business again. The engine started up, the lights came on. He pulled out onto the highway. Ginny sighed and started walking.

She would sleep while Bruce took the first shift on vehicle patrol. The plan was for Frank Carver to relieve them in the morning. If EarthAction stayed at the campground until Sunday, which was possible, they would have another night of patrol after this.

The ranger station was locked, with a single light burning in the reception area and a couple of others on in back. Ginny let herself in through a side door. She glanced at her watch—too late to call home. Rebecca, Susie, and the baby would all be asleep. She would call in the morning, after breakfast.

Tiffany was in Dispatch, reading a magazine. She got up when Ginny came in. "Pretty quiet in here."

"Well, that's good, isn't it?" Tiffany was putting in extra hours, too, monitoring the remote sensors in the Burnt Meadows sale.

"Yeah, I guess so." She stifled a yawn. They talked for a minute and then Tiffany left for home. She would be back in the morning to cover Dispatch. Ginny spread her foam pad and sleeping bag out on the floor, opened her pack, and took out her toilet kit and nightgown. She took her jacket off but, instead of undressing, went to the window. She pulled the curtain aside to peer out, moved to the door, then back to the window. She was restless, still keyed up by Ward's speech. She glanced at the clock. Eleven p.m. Gayle Wallace's party should be well off the ground by now. She wished for a moment that she were there, celebrating Tomasovic's homecoming.

She cranked the window open a notch and let the breeze in. The cool air still smelled of mown grass. She shrugged her jacket back on, checked to make sure she had her keys, and headed for the door.

A thin summer haze had gathered, dimming the stars. She stopped in the shadows just outside the door, suddenly alert. Someone was talking, not too far away. The voice murmured, rose and fell. Another voice joined in, both talked together for a moment, then the first voice again. She turned her head slowly, trying to determine the source. The voices seemed to come from the school playing field, just beyond the chain-link fence separating it from the ranger station. The scoreboard loomed above the fence, silhouetted against the sodium-vapor lights of the distant school building.

Something moved in the shadows below the scoreboard. Ginny tensed, straining her eyes and ears. Teenagers? It looked like a place where kids would meet, late at night. She held perfectly still, listening, but the voices had stopped. No sounds interrupted the steady chorus of frogs.

She stepped away from the door just as a gunshot crashed through the still night air.

FOUR

GINNY HIT THE DIRT as another shot rang out. She flattened herself into the shadows along the building's foundation, fingers scrabbling in the bark mulch underneath the shrubs. Blood pounded in her ears, drowning out everything else.

After a moment she cautiously raised her head and peered around. A floodlamp hidden in the bushes cast a pool of yellow light, blinding her to anything beyond. Her heart slowed as the seconds went by. One by one Coffee Creek's normal late-night sounds filtered back into her awareness. A vehicle roared off somewhere down the highway. A dog barked. Another dog answered, and another, until the canine chorus was cut short by an irate yell. A steady, low hum blanketed the town, broken by occasional loud thumps. The night shift was starting up at the Zellers mill.

Ginny wiggled a bit as a twig poked her under the arm. She looked at her watch—eleven-fifteen. She was starting to feel silly. She hadn't imagined the shots, but she did seem to be the only person who had taken notice of them. Certainly the only one lying in the dirt.

She got up and brushed bark mulch off her jacket. A gunshot, after all, was not so unusual. It could have been someone whooping it up in the tavern parking lot, shooting into the air. Or someone scaring coyotes away from a chicken coop. In some places—places like Pendleton, for instance, around rodeo time—shooting guns off was considered a recreational activity.

Then she heard a moan.

She turned slowly toward the school playing field, her heart catching in her chest. She swallowed. Something stirred in the shadows on the other side of the fence. She flicked her flashlight on. The beam played through the chain-link, coursed over the grass, reached the area beneath the scoreboard, and stopped. One of the shadows did not move.

She ran, feet slapping on the pavement, the radio thumping against her hip. Through the opening in the fence, into the school grounds, still running, a voice pounding inside her head. Please God, please, please. Please don't let it be.

He was sprawled awkwardly across the grass, one leg bent beneath the other, caught there when he fell. She flicked the light over his face. Ward Tomasovic. His eyes were open, gazing at her with wide, childish wonder. She knelt beside him.

"It's going to be okay," she murmured. She reached out to brush the hair back from his forehead. His skin was cold. Shock. He blinked. She flicked the flashlight down. His chest moved as he gasped for breath. At first she thought he wasn't badly hurt, but then she saw the blood, seeping into the grass beneath the body. A lot of blood.

She slipped her hand along his neck, searching for the carotid pulse. There it was, a faint throb. She lost it. She pressed again, but it was gone. Blood bubbled up from his mouth. His chest stopped moving.

She pulled his head around. His skin felt chill and lifeless. His eyes, still open, were already filmed. All the things she was trained to do—CPR, mouth-to-mouth, pressure points—all were useless.

She tugged her radio out of the belt holder, pressed the send button, and tried to raise Bruce Bowers. No response. He must be out of range, and the small hand-held was good for only the Forest Service frequency. She was going to have to leave to get help. Frank had told her how important it was to stay at the scene. Now she wondered about the reasons behind that procedure. As the more chilling possibilities occurred, she glanced apprehensively into the darkness. The shots had to have come from somewhere nearby.

Her feelings seemed to have shut down completely. She hurried into the station, grabbed the telephone, and called 911. The Coffee Creek fire siren started to blow before she even hung up. She turned to the radio and called Bowers.

He responded at once. "Hey, Ginny, what are you doing awake?"

She told him what had happened.

His tone turned abrupt, professional. She should get hold of Carver, then go back to the scene. He would be there ASAP.

"What about Larkin?"

"He'll respond to the 911 call. And, Ginny?" His voice softened. "You don't have a gun, do you?"

"Negative."

"Look, there's a little Smith and Wesson in the lower right-hand drawer of my desk, behind the files. The key to the drawer is under the pepperomia."

"Under the what?"

"The pepperomia plant, on the table in the corner."

Now she remembered that Bowers had half-a-dozen house plants scattered around his office. She had wondered at the time if they were really his. They must be, if he knew them by name.

"Okay, I'll find it."

"Good. I'm on my way. Bowers clear."

She picked up the telephone again and punched in Frank Carver's number. He answered after the second ring, his voice groggy with sleep.

"Carver here."

"Frank, it's Ginny. You'd better come down to Coffee Creek right away. Someone's shot Ward Tomasovic."

IT WAS ALMOST 3:00 a.m. when Frank Carver spotted the glow from the Zellers mill. Even with only the haze for reflection, Coffee Creek's sole industry managed to light up the night sky. He stubbed out his cigarette, swung the truck around the last corner, and drove past the mill complex. Sodium lamps, set on tall poles, shed their harsh orange light on the area. Roads snaked off among the buildings, past an enormous log dump that stretched for a quarter of a mile along the highway. In a long, open shed men in T-shirts and heavy leather gloves wrestled chunks of wood off a conveyor belt. Pulling green chain. Just before he took the next corner he realized that at least two of the men were in fact women. Affirmative action had caught up with Zellers Wood Products.

At the end of the mill property he hit Coffee Creek's only traffic light, put there three years earlier to help regulate shift changes. Coffee Creek was not, in the strictest sense, a company town. The Zellers family had never invested in real estate or commercial ventures like the café or grocery store. Most of the people in Coffee Creek owned their own homes. People who rented lived in a big trailer court across the river. But almost everyone's paycheck depended, in some way, on the Zellerses.

The downtown was fairly quiet, all the buildings locked up, even the two taverns that sat across from one another on Main Street. The location made tavern-hopping convenient for those so inclined. The fact that Main Street was actually Highway 32 made it a truly daredevil sport. A pickup nosed out of a side street ahead of Frank, made an unsteady turn, and moved along for a block before the driver remembered to turn the lights on.

Things had happened during the last few hours. Carver already knew that the rural ambulance had responded to the 911 call, scooped Tomasovic, and delivered him to the hospital in Eugene, where he had been pronounced dead on arrival. As soon as that was certain, Frank had picked up his car phone again to call his boss, Larry Hunsaker. The Neskanie supervisor had responded to the news with a single, succinct epithet.

"I agree," Frank replied.

"Christ, this is going to be a mess. The media will have it by morning. They'll be climbing all over us."

All over you, brother. Frank kept his thoughts to himself. He'd had only an hour's sleep, didn't expect to get more for a long time. Ward Tomasovic had died in Angus County. Sheriff Warren Holt would be in charge of the investigation. Frank already knew Holt's reaction to bodies—let someone else handle it. Preferably someone from another agency.

Hunsaker appeared to share that opinion. "Frank, we're going to want total damage control on this. Holt makes a move, you move with him. I want a personal report from you, twice a day, plus copies of all the paperwork. First thing in the morning we'll have Christina set up a press conference."

Christina Schnell was the Neskanie's PIO—public information officer. Hunsaker's first concern—and Frank couldn't blame him, really—was with public relations. The entire state was polarized over the spotted owl issue. Tomasovic's death could torch the whole thing like a match set to dry timber. A lot of people would be watching the Forest Service during the next few days, ready to rip in at the first sign of fumbling.

As soon as he set up the press conference and got Frank's initial report, Hunsaker would be on the horn to his own boss in the regional office. From there it would go to Washington, D.C., and echelons of officialdom so high that the typists outranked district rangers. But all that was Hunsaker's problem. As he made the dark, lonely drive from Longmont to Coffee Creek, keeping an eye out for deer and drunk drivers, Frank worried about something more personal.

Tomasovic had been dead before the EMTs got to him, and Ginny had watched him die. She'd heard the shot that killed him. She was tough, tougher than she knew, but it was no easy thing to watch a man die. Especially when your job was to protect him.

Pickup trucks and cars were pulled up along the fence at the edge of the school playing field, just past the ranger station. Frank made out a dozen or so figures standing among them. The sirens must have roused half the populace, but there couldn't have been much to see once the body was gone. Here and there a cigarette glowed. The playing field had been cordoned off with yellow ribbon, hanging still and ghostly in the dark. A flashlight moved across the ground at the far end, under the scoreboard.

Frank parked at the end of the line of vehicles and hopped out. His mouth tasted as though cattle had slept in it. He fingered the cigarette pack in his pocket. One left. He put it back and started toward the crowd.

Deputy Larkin broke off his conversation with two of the locals as he approached. Frank stuck his hand out. "Bill," he said, nodding. He had worked with Larkin once before, on a timber theft case in the south county. "I expect the sheriff's right behind me."

Larkin nodded. "He called in about half an hour ago. Not much happening here right now." The deputy gave Frank a brief report, saving the full description for his superior. After flagging off the scene, there hadn't been much to do except talk to the onlookers. Larkin had a list of people who had gathered to watch the EMTs at work, but none of them had had anything helpful to say.

"No witnesses," Frank said.

"Not a one, except that gal of yours. She's over there, with Bowers." He gestured to the end of the field, where the flashlight had been visible a few moments earlier. "She looks pretty wiped out, too. Ought to send her home."

"Maybe," Frank replied, guessing that Ginny wouldn't go willingly, any more than he would have. "Any word from the EarthAction folks?"

"Couple of them came by a while ago. I think they're at the ranger station. Your ranger's there, too. Said he wants to see you first thing."

Frank nodded. He wanted to see Ginny, talk to her, make sure she was okay, but it would have to wait. Protocol. No point in offending the district ranger. At least she wasn't alone, and Bowers was a good officer. As soon as he was done inside, though . . .

"Come light," Larkin said, "we'll have a full crowd." Frank watched him amble off, then turned toward the station.

Tony Bricca, the Coffee Creek ranger, was waiting for him. His curly hair was mussed and his rumpled green jacket might have come from the laundry basket. He greeted Frank with relief. Beside him stood a man and two women.

"Friends of Tomasovic's," Bricca said. "This is Frank Carver, the Neskanie's special agent. He'll be able to answer your questions."

Like hell. The man and the younger woman glared at Frank with undisguised hostility. The older woman offered her hand. "Gayle Wallace. We've talked on the phone."

Frank nodded, took her hand. Gayle Wallace had arranged for the Burnt Meadows campground. She had been a pleasure to deal with, friendly, well-organized, willing to accommodate Forest Service regulations.

"Glad to meet you," he murmured.

The other two didn't bother to introduce themselves. During the past week Frank had read dozens of articles and reports on Oregon's environmental movement. He recognized the dark, intense woman as Rachel Davis, a leader of the Eugene Environmental Coalition and a member of EarthAction.

"We want to know what happened," she demanded. "What was Ward doing out there, anyway? He was supposed to be at a party at Gayle's."

Frank stared at her. "Our PIO will have a statement in the morning."

"I'm asking *you*, right now." Rachel Davis glared, eyes flashing.

"And I'm asking you to get out of my way." Frank kept his voice level. "I've got an investigation to conduct."

The man stepped forward, muttering something. His sandy hair was pulled back into a thin ponytail, his faded down vest grimed with wear. Rachel laid a restraining hand on his arm. "Alan," she murmured.

Alan Breckenridge, self-style eco-saboteur. Frank had read the file on him, and the description matched. He had never seen a photo. As far as he knew, there were no photos.

He didn't have time for this. "Mrs. Wallace," he said, turning to Gayle, "thank you for coming down here. I'll want to talk to all of you a little later. Ranger Bricca can find you some coffee and a place to wait. Good night, Miss Davis."

He started down the hall, registering Rachel Davis's surprise that he knew her name. A cheap shot, perhaps, but one she deserved.

Tony Bricca hurried after him. "The Eugene paper's called already. I don't know what to tell them."

Another bureaucrat hung up on public relations. Frank kept going, heading for the back door. "Have them call Christina at the SO."

Bricca's legs were short. He hurried to keep up. "I'll do that. Bowers's office is right down here—but you know that. I've already arranged . . ."

Frank was no longer with him. He had found the door and was outside, striding across the grass toward Ginny and Bruce Bowers.

They were leaning against the fence, just inside the playing field. Bowers's hand was on Ginny's shoulder.

Christ. He'd never thought . . . He came to a stop, feeling as though someone had just clobbered him with a hammer.

Bruce saw him, dropped his hand, and straightened up.

"Okay, dammit," Frank growled. "This isn't the army."

Ginny gave him a tired smile. He studied her for a moment, noting her sagging shoulders and pale face. The yellow glare from the station's floodlights did nothing to improve her appearance.

Bowers, on the other hand, looked as alert and fresh as if he had just stepped out of the shower. He was talking now, running through the events of the past few hours. The ambulance had left about eleven-thirty. He had gotten a few photos before the medics removed the body, Ginny had marked the location on the grass, and then they had kept away from the area until it was light enough to see what was there.

"Good work, Officer. We'll start a grid search as soon as it's light. That is," he added, "if that's how Holt wants it done." He wasn't in homicide anymore, and wouldn't be in charge here, in any case. Holt would be showing up any minute, and he wanted to talk to Ginny in private before all hell broke loose.

Something was going on, and he didn't have to be a trained investigator to see it. Well, what did he expect? She was a damned attractive woman, Bowers was single, and he'd shoved them together himself.

Two could play at this game, though, and there were advantages to maturity. Being in charge, for instance. "Ten-six, Bowers," he said, using the code for standby. "Ginny." He gave her a gentle shove and led her back to the station. Once inside, he followed the smell of coffee into Dispatch. Tony Bricca was there, fussing with the coffeepot. He looked up as they came in.

"Hunsaker wants you to call him."

Frank glanced at the clock. "Christ, I just got here. What does he expect?"

Bricca shrugged and filled two mugs with coffee. He handed one to Ginny, the other to Frank. "Sheriff Holt called in, too. He'll be here in about ten minutes."

"Okay. Bowers is outside. He might appreciate some of this coffee."

Bricca nodded, filled another mug, and left, clearly glad to have something to do.

Ginny smiled. "First time I've seen a ranger fetch coffee." She wrapped her hands around the warm mug, raised it, and inhaled the sharp, bitter smell. Suddenly she swayed.

Frank reached out to grab her elbow just as she caught herself. "I guess I'd better sit down," she said weakly.

He watched as she lowered herself into a chair. A little color showed in her cheeks now, but her eyes still looked heavy, as though she needed to be tucked into bed. Frank's heart lurched, then started beating again. He sat down and took one of her hands in his. "Hey, Deputy, you okay?"

"I think so. It was a shock, but it's over."

It hadn't been that simple, of course. She had returned to the field just as the EMTs arrived, only to stand there feeling useless while they lifted Tomasovic onto a stretcher and loaded him into the ambulance. Bowers showed up, and then Larkin, who had been parked a quarter of a mile from the foot of Gayle Wallace's driveway. They were flagging off the playing field when she started to cry.

She kept stringing yellow ribbon along the fence while the sobs heaved slowly out of her chest. Maybe it was the lack of sleep. Time had somehow telescoped and she was experiencing two events at once—Tomasovic's death, and the day her husband had died.

She hadn't learned about the accident until Dale was already in surgery. She had been up Elk Creek that morning, sketching, while Rebecca picked flowers. When no one could reach her on the phone Craig Wheeler had driven out from the station. Together they drove to the hospital. Dale had died on the operating table. The last words she had said to him, as he left the house that morning, had been "See you tonight."

Deputy Larkin, on the other side of the field, hadn't noticed her distress, but Bowers was closer. She didn't realize she had stopped moving until she felt his hand on her arm.

"You okay, Ginny?"

She nodded, gulped, and then suddenly she was in his arms, crying against his shoulder. He held her gingerly, as though not quite sure what to do. After a moment she pushed him away. "I'm sorry, Bruce, I just..."

"You lost it. It's okay. Happens to everyone."

She took a deep breath, willing the sobs to stop. "My husband, Dale...he died a few years ago. It just all came back. I'm sorry, I just couldn't help it."

He didn't answer. His gaze seemed fixed on a point a little past her shoulder, with that air of abstraction she had noticed before. She could have sworn he was trembling.

"Bruce?"

He shuddered and shook his head. His eyes came back into focus as he seemed to register her presence again. "Right here. You okay now?"

She gave him a curious look. "I'll be all right. What about you?"

"Me? I'm fine. Little tired maybe."

She hadn't pressed it. If Bowers wanted to talk, she was willing to listen, but right now her own feelings were plenty to deal with. A few minutes later they were both flagging again, moving in opposite directions. Frank had shown up shortly afterward.

Now here she was inside the station. She lifted the mug with her free hand, hiding her face from Frank's searching gaze. The hot coffee seared her mouth. She lowered the mug, blinked.

"How did we let this happen?"

Frank paused, considering the question beneath the one she had asked. He chose his words with care. "Ginny, if someone wants to kill another person, it's just about impossible to stop them. We had no reason to anticipate this."

"But the letter? Those phone calls?"

He shrugged. "Threatening calls are a dime a dozen. There may be no connection."

She looked down at his hand, still holding hers.

"It's not your fault, Ginny. Someone was out to get him."

There was a commotion in the hall, footsteps, voices, and a moment later Sheriff Warren Holt blocked the doorway. Ranger Bricca's head was barely visible behind him, bobbing over Holt's hefty shoulders. The sheriff was built like a barrel, all chest and stomach set on narrow hips. He gave them a lopsided grin.

"Come on, Carver, get it in gear. We've got work to do."

Frank carefully set Ginny's hand back on her knee, determined not to let Holt fluster him. "You want to crawl around out there in the dark, Sheriff, be my guest."

"Nah, I borrowed a couple people from the state police to do that." Holt shouldered his way in, followed by Tony Bricca. "Some place we can set up around here?"

"The LEO's office," Tony said. "I've already arranged it."

"Phone?"

"Your own outside line."

A uniformed officer poked her head in. "Morris and Mahoney here, Sheriff. It'll be getting light pretty soon. Want to get started?"

"Yeah, I guess so. You coming, Carver?"

Frank got up. He was about to tell Ginny to wait when he realized she was up, tugging at her uniform to straighten out the wrinkles. He lifted an eyebrow.

She caught his look, and a sudden warmth took her by surprise, welling up from deep inside. Frank was looking out for her. She nodded. She was okay, and ready to go.

FIVE

DAWN SEEPED SLOWLY across the eastern sky as they stepped outside. A light breeze ruffled Ginny's hair and tugged at the men's jackets. Sheriff Holt paused to tuck his shirt more securely into his pants. "Gonna be a warm one," he murmured.

The playing field had been flagged off with yellow plastic ribbon, fluttering from the fence and from strips of lath Bowers had found in the station's warehouse. There was enough light to make out the patch of dark blood beneath the scoreboard. Ginny shivered, even though the breeze was mild.

Bowers joined them. He led the way through the fence, toward the scoreboard. Frank fell back to let Holt, the officer in charge, go first. The sheriff grunted an acknowledgment and motioned for them to follow.

There wasn't much to see. At least half-a-dozen people had already tramped through the area. The ambulance had pulled up to within a few feet of the body. In two or three days the bloody patch of grass would be almost gone.

As they talked a bright blue van drove slowly past the ranger station and parked at the edge of the playing field. KETV—the Eugene television station. Three people spilled out, two of them carrying video cameras. They started across the grass.

At a nod from Frank, Bowers left to intercept them. Holt continued to stare at the bloodstained grass.

"Can't tell much with the body gone," he muttered.

Frank nodded. The pictures Bowers had taken would help, but that had been after the EMTs had shifted the body. "How was he lying, Ginny? Do you remember?"

She gave him a look. Of course she remembered. She had been going over this for hours, had known they'd want a statement. Holt produced a pocket tape recorder. He fiddled with it for a moment, recorded the date and the people present, then let it run as Ginny pointed out where she had stood and described what she had seen and heard.

"You were standing at the door," the sheriff said. "Did something draw your attention to the scoreboard?"

Ginny hesitated. Had there been something? She closed her eyes and tried to remember. She had stepped outside for a breath of fresh air. The scoreboard dominated that end of the playing field, but it had been in shadow. Her eye had been drawn to the bright ribbon of the Milky Way, spangled across the night sky.

"I heard something," she said. "Voices."

"Voices? More than one?"

She shut her eyes, trying to remember. "Two. One a little louder than the other."

"More about the voices, Ginny," Frank said. "A man, a woman? How did they sound? Did you get any words?"

She concentrated again. "Just a murmur of voices. Back and forth, you could tell it was a conversation." She shook her head. "That's all I heard."

Holt sighed. "Well, if that's all we get, that's all we get." He switched the tape recorder off. "I'll send Larkin around to the neighbors, see if anyone noticed anything else."

They were joined by another officer and the policewoman Ginny had seen inside the station, who was now carrying a small video camera on her shoulder. The sheriff introduced them as Kim Morris and Steve Mahoney, Oregon State Police crime-scene investigators.

Bowers helped Kim Morris unload more equipment, including a metal detector, from the step van that served as a no-frills mobile crime laboratory. She moved toward the scoreboard and began to videotape the bloodstained grass. Bowers checked with the sheriff, then motioned to the reporters—the television crew had been joined by a pair from the Eugene newspaper—to move closer. For a few minutes they watched the novel sight of a video camera recording another video camera at work. The sun rose into a flawless blue sky. Birds sang from the stand of firs behind the ranger station.

"Not much to go on," Frank said sympathetically.

Sheriff Holt nodded, his face glum. "We'll find the bullet. Then we can start checking for handguns."

"Might not have been a handgun."

"At that distance, talking to the guy? You'd hardly have room to lift a rifle."

Frank shrugged. Holt was jumping to conclusions, but there wasn't any evidence to contradict him. They would just have to wait and see.

Holt surveyed the playing field, then motioned his people to come over. Bowers joined them as well. "Okay," Holt said, when he had everyone's attention. "I want Larkin to keep an eye on the crowd. The rest of you are going to search this field. Five-foot strips. Line out along the edge nearest the school, move through the scene, then circle back and grid the area under the scoreboard."

He produced a roll of string and handed it to Bowers. The four of them, Bowers, Ginny, and the two deputies, ran a line of string along the ground five feet in from the edge of the field. Each person searched one sector, with Kim Morris running the metal detector. When one strip was done, they set up a second line of string and searched between the

· lines. They leapfrogged the first line of string and started in again.

"This is going to take a while," Frank said, watching the team at work. "I've got some people waiting in the station I need to talk to."

Holt raised an eyebrow.

"Environmentalists. They knew Tomasovic. They were here when I arrived, ready to pick a fight."

"What about?"

"Anything, far as I could tell."

Just then a young cop came up, carrying a box. "Sheriff Holt?" he asked. "Eugene police. You wanted these?"

Holt nodded. "Thanks, son. Appreciate you making the trip out here." He hefted the box. "Tomasovic's clothes. Let's go inside."

They paused at the door while Holt surveyed the playing field one more time. The searchers were on their third strip. More cars had appeared. Well over fifty people stood idly just outside the line of yellow flagging. The sheriff turned to Frank.

"Larkin can handle the crowd, but I'm worried about those reporters. You say there's going to be a press conference?"

Frank nodded. "At the SO, probably in a couple of hours. I'll need to call our PIO pretty soon."

"Could you run that by me again, in English?"

Frank winced. "Sorry. Christina Schnell is our public information officer—PIO. She's setting up a press conference at the Neskanie headquarters in Longmont." He paused. "Bowers can deal with the reporters."

"Sounds good. When do you want to talk to your visitors?"

"Before the reporters get to them. Let's give the clothes a quick look-over first."

Bowers's desk in the law enforcement office was clear except for a telephone and a small African violet. Holt moved the plant, set the box down, and gently took out an assortment of bags, each tagged with an evidence label. One by one they spread the garments out and examined them. Frank found a pad of paper and a clipboard in the desk and took notes as they worked.

Holt held up a blood-soaked shirt, white, with subdued blue stripes. There was a small hole in the front, near the breast pocket, a larger one in the back. Tomasovic's lightweight blue jacket looked the same.

One pair of expensive running shoes, slightly scuffed. A wallet. They looked through it, finding the usual ID, ninety-three dollars in cash, and a photo of two children, a boy and a girl. They riffled through the pocket calendar. The Coffee Creek appearance was noted under yesterday's date, but nothing for Saturday. "Mom" had been penciled in under Sunday.

In the jeans pocket they found a scrap of paper, folded and refolded until it was only an inch square, the corners grimy from handling. Holt held one edge and used a pencil to open it up. The whole sheet was only four by six inches. ZELLERS WOOD PRODUCTS was printed across the top, the words bracketed by stylized trees. Below that was a message scribbled in blue ink: "Scoreboard, 11 p.m. Debbie."

The sheriff nodded with satisfaction. "Looks like we got a name for that other voice your gal heard."

Frank took the note down the hall to make a copy. When he got back, Holt was on the telephone. "You've got to be kidding," he said. "Okay, I'm on my way."

He hung up. "I don't believe this. There's been a two-car collision five miles west of Longmont. One fatality—a three-year-old girl."

"Shit."

The sheriff nodded. "Yeah, and there's more. They found a bag of coke in the other car. Shawn Michaels was driving."

Shawn Michaels, the nineteen-year-old son of the incumbent governor, had just finished his freshman year at Western Oregon State. He lived in one of the larger fraternity houses, one with a reputation for obnoxious behavior. The *Longmont Herald-Tribune* had devoted a number of column-inches to his activities during the past year. This was the first time, though, that Frank had heard about a drug connection.

"In my goddamn jurisdiction, too," Holt added.

"Anyone else in the car?"

"No, little Shawn was all by his lonesome. Don't know why the damn kid couldn't wait till he was inside the city limits."

"And the other car?"

"Mom and another kid in the hospital." Holt sighed. "And you think *you've* got publicity problems."

Frank looked up warily. "Now, wait a minute, Holt—"

"I haven't got a minute. What I've got is me, one under-sheriff, and six deputies in a county with over seventy thousand people. Every one of those deputies has got a full workload."

Frank glared.

"You want me to turn Tomasovic over to the state police? Not a bad bunch of guys, but not what you'd call cooperative, either."

"You can't just unload this—"

"Don't see why not. Your choice, Carver. I can get on the horn and have someone here within an hour. Don't think they're going to let you help run things, though."

He was right, damn him anyway. If the state police took over he'd be doing liaison, and strictly on their terms. That wasn't what Hunsaker wanted. Frank had no doubt that the forest supervisor would jump at the chance to have his own agent in charge.

He glared at Holt again. "You get back to that office of yours, you file some paperwork to make this legal."

"Ten-four. What's the matter, Carver? Getting fat and lazy working for the feds?"

"Screw you."

Holt chuckled. "You can have Larkin for a couple days. I'll talk to the team outside. See you mañana."

Frank took a minute to repack Tomasovic's clothing, grumbling to himself as he zipped up the plastic bags. The truth was, June 10—today, Saturday—was opening day for trout. So not only was he working homicide again, which he had taken this job to get away from, but he was missing the one true pleasure he still found in life.

He glanced at his watch. After six. He couldn't expect Gayle Wallace and her friends to wait much longer. The Debbie in the note, whoever she was, would have to keep.

One thing he could do, though, was arrange for a little company. Unlike most investigators, Frank rarely used a tape recorder during questioning. More than one district attorney had complained about his preference for written notes, but Frank clung stubbornly to his belief that a tape recorder inhibited both the subject and the interviewer. Besides, Ginny needed experience with this side of things, too.

He went outside to get her.

GAYLE WALLACE, the schoolteacher who had set up Tomasovic's appearance in Coffee Creek, was standing at the window of the district conference room. A woman Ginny knew must be Rachel Davis sat in one of the chairs, her back to the door. Timber sale maps and aerial photos covered the walls.

As soon as she heard their steps, Gayle turned and came forward. Her face was gray from lack of sleep, her hair straggling over her shoulders. She gave Frank a bleak, questioning look. "Ward is dead, isn't he?"

"Yes, Mrs. Wallace, I'm afraid he is." Frank sat down at the long table, motioning her to a chair. Ginny got her notebook out. The other woman continued to stare at the wall.

"Miss Davis, would you join us, please?"

She got up and moved stiffly to the table. Ginny stared. Rachel Davis was the younger of the two women she had confronted last night in the gym. The banner and the fiery defiance were gone now, the face wiped clean of emotion. She looked like a ghost.

"Where's your friend?" Frank asked.

"He left." Rachel's voice was as blank as her face.

"He said he'd give you a call, Mr. Carver," Gayle added. "He was pretty upset."

Frank guessed that Alan Breckenridge spent his life in a state of permanent upset, generally about one environmental devastation or another. He shrugged and let it go. Chances of getting a phone call from the man were zip. They'd have to track him down, sooner or later.

"Let's start with the last time you saw Tomasovic. Miss Davis?"

"Last night, at his talk." Her voice came out cracked and dry.

"You were in the audience?"

She glanced at Ginny. "You saw me there."

Ginny nodded. "She was with the EarthAction group, near the front."

"I see. Did you speak to Tomasovic after his talk?"

She shook her head.

"Did you have any plans to meet him, see him somewhere last night?"

She shook her head again.

"You were at the Burnt Meadows campground last night, weren't you?" A nod. "Your name was on the permit. What brought you down to the station?"

"Gayle came up about two, looking for Ward. We hadn't seen him. She said there was some sort of commotion in town, an ambulance, so we drove in to see what was going on."

"Deputy Larkin told us they'd taken Ward to the hospital," Gayle added.

Frank paused. "Miss Davis, did you know Tomasovic? Had you ever met him before?"

"Oh, yes. We'd known each other for years."

"Ah, so that's why you're here now. You were friends."

Her eyes flashed. "We were more than friends, Mr. Carver. We were comrades. We worked together. We did actions together. And we were lovers, until Ward let the bureaucrats co-opt him."

Frank rocked back in his chair. "I see. And when was this, that you stopped being lovers?"

Rachel's face had gone blank again. "Eighteen months ago."

"That would be about when Tomasovic went to Washington?"

She nodded.

"How did that happen? What made him go back East?"

"He got an offer from the National Environmental League. He was a fisheries biologist, you know. They wanted him to work up scientific support for fisheries legislation."

"And you didn't approve?"

"Ass-sucking, that's what it was." Her voice rose. "He did it for the money, the dirty, shitty money. He betrayed everything we were working for."

Frank let his chair down with a thump. "You make it sound like he was out there personally killing the fish. I thought the NEL had a good rep with you people."

Rachel glared at him. "I don't have to talk to you."

"No," said Frank mildly, "you don't. Not yet, anyway. We'll just get your address and phone number."

Ginny wrote these down while Frank considered Rachel Davis. The woman's intensity and sudden mood swings were unnerving. He could almost believe that she had broken with Tomasovic over a job. She had the commitment of a fanatic.

He turned to Gayle Wallace. "Had you known Tomasovic long?"

"Just a few days. I'd heard of him, of course. You know he grew up in Coffee Creek. People remember him. We moved here about five years after he left."

"What do they remember about him?" Frank asked.

"That he was stubborn, hotheaded, a good athlete. I guess he went to State in track his senior year."

"Anything else?"

Gayle frowned. "There was some kind of accident, a boy who was out fishing with Ward drowned."

"I didn't know that," Rachel murmured.

"I wonder how the boy's family felt about Tomasovic coming back," Frank said.

Gayle shrugged. "They're all gone. I don't remember the boy's name, but someone said they all either died or moved away."

"Any talk about why Tomasovic left town?"

"Something about breaking up with a girlfriend. I don't really know. He sounds like the sort of boy who would have left, sooner or later. Coffee Creek's not a very stimulating place."

"Are any of his family still in the area?"

"I haven't run into anyone with that name. I heard that his mother remarried and moved out to the coast."

Frank nodded. He needed to talk to someone in the family soon. There was an ex-wife in Longmont, but he didn't have an address. He continued with Gayle. "When did you last see Tomasovic?"

"Right after his talk. A lot of people had questions, and I wanted to get home before people showed up for the party. He said he'd be late, but should make it by twelve."

"He was staying at your house?"

She nodded. "I invited him to spend a few days, but he wasn't sure about his plans. He had a lot of people to see. He did plan to spend last night at our place, though. His sleeping bag and suitcase are still there."

"I'll send someone by to get them. You started worrying when he didn't show up?"

"About twelve-thirty. I'd invited a lot of people who really wanted to meet him. They were pretty disappointed."

Frank turned to Rachel. "Was he a punctual person? Would it be unusual for him to be late?"

She glared, but finally decided to respond. "He was incredibly dependable. If he was going to be late, he would have called."

Frank went on with his questions, filling in the picture of their movements the night before. Finally he leaned back in his chair. "That should do it for now. We'll get this typed for you to look over and sign."

"I don't have time for this," Rachel snapped. "We've got a hundred people at that campground. I need to get up there."

"Fine. I want you to stay in the area."

"I've got to be in Eugene tomorrow."

Frank fought down the urge to slap her across the face. That was probably what she wanted, so she could cry police brutality to the reporters outside. "Miss Davis," he said in his mildest voice, "you can either stay in Coffee Creek, or in the Angus County jail. I'll need to talk to you again."

"Go screw yourself," she snapped, eyes flashing. "This is a waste of time. I didn't kill Ward. Go talk to some of those goddamn rednecks with yellow ribbons on their log trucks. They're the ones who've got something to lose."

"Now, Rachel." Gayle Wallace laid a hand on her arm. "You can stay with us. I'm sure Mr. Carver won't keep you any longer than necessary."

Rachel shrugged Gayle's hand off, but she seemed to calm down. "Okay, okay," she muttered. "But I've got an environmental impact hearing in Portland on Tuesday."

"We'll see that you make it," Frank said. He let the pause lengthen. Ginny was watching Gayle Wallace.

"Do either of you know a Debbie?"

Rachel started, then gave a little shrug. If the name meant anything to her, she wasn't going to admit it.

Gayle seemed to be doing mental arithmetic. "Six, I think."

"All in Coffee Creek?" Frank asked in dismay.

"Oh, no. Only two of them live here. Debbie Kurtz and Debbie Brown. Debbie Brown was in my class last year."

"The first one you mentioned, Kurtz. How old is she?"

"She's in her late thirties. She's Charlie Zellers's daughter."

SIX

FRANK WALKED the two women out to the parking lot. They climbed into Gayle Wallace's car, an older station wagon with a Handicapped sticker on the bumper. After they left he turned toward the playing field, where the crowd had thinned considerably. The television news van was gone, too. He probably had Bowers to thank for that, and he was thankful. He had not been looking forward to seeing his own face on the screen.

He fished the battered pack from his shirt pocket and took out the last cigarette. Absolutely the last. He lit it (last time he would ever flick the lighter, last time he would watch the flame lean over as he sucked in the hot air) and went around the back of the station, looking for the LEO. Bruce was talking with Kim Morris, the video-toting female member of the crime team. She was a nice-looking blond in her early thirties, with a firm handshake and a calm, efficient air. About ten minutes earlier she had found the bullet.

She showed it to him, a small, misshapen lump of metal. Frank held it in the palm of his hand, studying it in the clear morning light. He was no firearms expert, did not, like many cops, take an avid interest in guns. He had, however, seen a lot of bullets. This looked like a .22 short cartridge. The sheriff had been right, then, about the distance. Beyond fifty feet a handgun would be wildly inaccurate, especially in the dark. That didn't absolve Holt from jumping to conclusions, but it wasn't likely to cure him of the habit, either.

Larkin and the other deputy joined them. They did not have much else to report. No casing, no tracks, no signs of a scuffle. Frank finished his smoke, dropped the butt, and stubbed it out with a twinge of regret. He looked through dozens of evidence bags containing cigarette filters mangled by mower blades, shreds of paper, a cat's-eye marble. It all looked like it had been there for a while.

"Where would you say the shot came from?"

Kim Morris pointed north, toward the spectators clustered along the highway. "I talked to the Lane County ME a few minutes ago. No lead dust on the body, no gunpowder. We'll want to examine the clothes too, of course, but the shot was probably fired from at least five feet away."

They were silent for a moment. "Holt tell you I'm taking over?" Frank asked.

She nodded. "We'll let the lab know. They can send our report directly to you." She looked at Bruce and, for the first time, smiled. "I've never seen Holt look more cheerful about arresting a VIP."

"The least dreaded alternative," said Bruce, smiling back. The sheriff's aversion to homicide investigations appeared to be common knowledge.

"We're pretty much done," she said. "How's the food at the café?"

"Heavy on the grease." Bruce shrugged. "Decent coffee, though."

Kim Morris talked it over with her partner. He wanted breakfast then and there, no matter how greasy, but they finally decided to pick up coffee and doughnuts and head back to Longmont right away. Bruce looked disappointed. He went inside for Tomasovic's clothes, helped them load up the van, then stood for a moment watching it drive off.

"Nice-looking gal," observed Frank.

Bruce nodded, then suddenly gave him a sheepish glance. "Sorry."

Frank chuckled. "Is the food really that bad?"

"I'm afraid so. The pancakes are okay, but the cook hasn't discovered fresh fruit yet."

"Let's get Ginny and head on over. I'm starved."

GINNY HAD A MESSAGE for him to call Christina Schnell ASAP. The Neskanie's public information officer answered on the first ring. Frank liked Christina, a friendly, talkative Mexican-American in her mid-thirties. Her husband, August, taught at the university. Christina knew almost nothing about forestry, but plenty about handling difficult people. This case looked as though it would bring a lot of them her way.

"Larry called me at six-thirty. Saturday morning. I walked in ten minutes ago and already I've got three messages on my desk, two from the regional office. If you're going to let people get knocked off down there, Frank, couldn't you pick someone a little less well known?"

"I'll keep that in mind next time," he said dryly. He gave her what little he had. "Look, Christina, I know you're busy, but could you try locating Tomasovic's former wife? I've got a Longmont address here in the file, 221 Northwest Jackson, no phone number. Her name's Teresa."

"And when I find her?"

Not if, Frank noted. When. "I'll want to talk to her right away. Chances are she'll have heard already. If not, well…"

"Not me, Carver, no way. I'll get her into my office and you can tell her. When are you coming back?"

"Later today, unless you reach her first. Keep in touch."

"Will do. Great, a camera crew just walked in. Time to check my makeup."

The phone clicked, disconnected. Frank smiled and shook his head. He looked up at Bruce and Ginny, standing by the window. "Hey, guys. Breakfast?"

They were almost out the door when one of the remote sensors, silent for hours, gave a beep. They all stopped in their tracks. A vehicle had entered the Burnt Meadows sale area. Bruce started counting seconds on his watch. Three beeps, close together. "Five seconds," he said. "They've passed the first spur." Silence. "They've stopped. Probably at that little meadow."

During the next few minutes the pattern of beeps repeated three times. Four vehicles, all stopped in the same place. "What are they doing up there?" Bruce muttered.

"Nothing they plan to keep a secret," said Frank. "They know the area's wired."

Ginny opened one of the files she had brought along and pulled out a schedule. "They had a prayer circle planned for sunrise, then breakfast. Tomasovic was supposed to give a talk at ten."

"Well, that's off," said Bruce.

Ginny glanced at him. "Yeah, I guess so." She went back to the schedule. "They're supposed to be having a nonviolence workshop about now."

The radio beeped again, this time the three tones first. "They're leaving," said Bruce. Four sets of beeps, four vehicles past the two sensors, on their way back down Prairie Mountain. "They're gone."

"Some of them could still be up there," Ginny said.

Frank nodded. "We aren't getting any action on the seismics inside the unit, though. If anybody did stay, they're keeping to the road."

"I don't like it," said Bowers.

"Neither do I. None of us is going to be happy until those people are out of there."

Ginny nodded. "Shall I go up?"

If Tomasovic hadn't died, that was where she would be right now. Frank considered. She hadn't had much sleep, but neither had he or Bowers. Since arriving in Coffee Creek five hours ago he had been promising himself the pleasure of having breakfast with her. But it was her shift, and aside from the three of them, there was no one else to send.

"I guess you'd better."

Tiffany walked in, carrying a box of doughnuts from the café. "Compliments of Fire Control," she said, setting them down. Bruce had scheduled her for eight hours, at time-and-a-half, minding Dispatch and the remote sensor receiver. Unlike the Galina and Sitkum districts, Coffee Creek had not planned a slash burn for the day, in spite of the perfect weather, so the station would be quiet. Frank suspected this was because the district fire management officer shared his feelings about the opening day of trout season.

Ginny filled her thermos from the pot of coffee Tony Bricca had made hours ago, grabbed a couple of doughnuts, and headed out. Frank picked out a cinnamon doughnut and took a bite, effectively ending his diet. He wasn't smoking now, of course, and no one could expect a man to give up two vices at the same time. He resigned himself to the inevitable. He wanted a real breakfast before tackling Debbie Kurtz, and Bruce Bowers was the only one left.

THE COFFEE CREEK CAFÉ did business in a picture-book house on the west edge of town. White clapboard, red roof, with morning glories climbing up a trellis on the side. Half-a-dozen little tables had been squeezed onto the wide porch next to window boxes filled with geraniums. The elderly couple drinking coffee at one of the tables watched their arrival with silent interest.

Bowers led the way inside. Conversation ceased as soon as they appeared. People paused with forks in midair, studied them for a moment, then resumed eating. A waitress who evidently knew Bowers came out of the kitchen and waved. He nodded to a few people as they made their way across the room to the only vacant table. They sat down. Conversations at the other tables picked up again, though more quietly than before. Frank caught Tomasovic's name in the drift of talk.

"Regulars?" he asked.

Bruce nodded. "Mostly. Some people here I don't recognize, but we've always got a few tourists. The fishermen are still out on the river. Won't see them till eleven or so."

Frank nodded, his face glum. The Jackson River, running only a few hundred yards away, was famous for trout. His own plan for the weekend, once Tomasovic was safely out of Coffee Creek, had included fishing the Little Bear, all the way from the end of the road down to the upper bridge. He glanced at the menu, but even the absence of tofu did not cheer him up. He was too filled with envy of each and every person who, at that very moment, was casting a line into running water somewhere in Oregon.

GINNY KEPT HER RADIO on the district channel as she drove up Prairie Mountain, just in case. Frank had a hand-held radio, and Tiffany could relay for them if necessary. Traffic was light for a perfect Saturday in June. She counted only four tents as she drove past the first of Prairie's two campgrounds. A family clustered around a picnic table, cooking breakfast on a Coleman stove. They looked up as the green Forest Service rig went past. She waved to the kids, got a wave in return. Friendly, open, always willing to talk things over, that was the role. She was a naturally friendly person, and she liked the role—patrolling campgrounds, giving directions, answering the phone. She liked dealing with the public, helping them find their way around what sometimes felt like her own backyard. And she liked the fact that the Forest Service gave that attitude its official sanction.

Not like the private companies, with their thousand-acre tree plantations, all the roads gated and posted. She had heard that Zellers wasn't as bad as some—they opened things up during deer season, left the gates unlocked, and didn't make you get a permit. Still, public relations was not a big part of what they did. Not that it had to be, of course. Zellers wasn't a public agency, didn't operate under congressional mandate, and didn't rely directly on tax dollars—though EarthAction would tell you (would be glad to tell you) that the government timber sales were a subsidy in all but name.

She passed the trailhead for the Prairie Mountain trail. No cars there, but it was still pretty early. Prairie was a good day hike, popular with people from Eugene. Her own district, Galina, did not have as much recreational development as Coffee Creek. Galina was the Neskanie's big timber district. That might be about to change, though. The endangered species act and the federal courts might just, between them, put forests like the Neskanie right out of the timber business.

With a little help from EarthAction. She passed the turnoff to the campground and continued up Road 1006, heading for the Burnt Meadows sale. When she spotted the boundary flags she radioed in to Tiffany, who told her she had just set off the first sensor. She cruised slowly along the road to the far side of the sale without seeing any vehicles or people. Tiffany let her know whenever she set off a sensor, so that by the time she turned around and drove out again she knew where all of them were. She made a few notes in her patrol log, then headed back down the mountain.

A few minutes later she turned north on Road 1010, then east on the spur leading to the Burnt Meadows campground. Friendly, open, always willing to talk things over. Her stomach knotted at the thought of talking things over with Rachel Davis.

She came to a stop in the campground parking lot, amid a collection of vehicles of all ages, mostly foreign-made, and plastered with environmental bumper stickers. The Burnt Meadows campground consisted of a picnic area near the parking lot, and then a half-mile loop with about fifty camping spots. The ones she could see were occupied by more small cars and vans and a scattering of tents. Later in the summer the campground would be filled with RVs, some as big as houses and just as expensive. The tastes of EarthAction members, and their budgets, ran to simpler arrangements.

Most of the people had gathered in the small open field off to one side of the picnic area where campers sometimes played volleyball or softball. Right now they seemed to be having a sing-along.

She slipped out of the truck, locked it, and walked slowly toward the gathering, feeling as conspicuous in her green uniform as a bear in a supermarket. A few people looked up as she came to stand on the outskirts of the group, then looked away again. No one approached her.

Three young women sat on a small raised platform beneath a fir tree. One had a guitar, one a drum, and one a flute. At the moment the flute was playing a solitary, sad tune. The audience swayed gently to the melody, some of them humming along. A woman close to Ginny nursed a baby in her lap, smiling dreamily into the distance. Two toddlers, one quite naked, clung to the moss of an old alder at the edge of the crowd, watched over by a bearded man in his twenties. The flute faded with a thin, reedy whisper.

She looked up to find Gayle Wallace at her side, with the older of the two women she had confronted over the banner the night before. They led her off a little way to one of the picnic tables and sat down.

Gayle introduced the other woman, whose gray hair was still braided with bright strips of ribbons, as Meg Nugent.

"What brings you up here, Ginny?" Meg asked. "Surely no one has complained about our singing." She fixed Ginny with a gaze so direct that she felt as naked as the little kid trying to climb the tree under its father's watchful eye.

"Just checking to see how things are going. You must have had to change some plans, rearrange your schedule..."

"Yes, we're having a memorial service right now. We've canceled the rest of the program for the day."

"Oh? What will you do instead?"

"We're not sure yet. Quite a few people want to hike through the Burnt Meadows sale."

Ginny straightened up.

"That wouldn't be a problem, would it?"

"I'll have to check with the district."

Meg Nugent nodded. "We've heard that Zellers plans to start cutting on Monday."

Ginny hoped her surprise didn't show. Did Frank know? And who at Zellers Wood Products would have told EarthAction? "You'd have to ask the timber sale officer, or someone at Zellers."

"Are they in today?"

"Probably not, on a Saturday. They won't start cutting *today*, though." She sure as hell hoped not. That was just what they needed. She hadn't seen any activity on her drive through the sale area. The whole forest was on early closure due to fire danger, so any fallers would be working hoot-owl, out first thing in the morning. Tomorrow was Sunday. The earliest Zellers would be likely to get started would be Monday. Now that the idea had occurred to her, it seemed more and more likely that the company would take advantage of last week's court decision to get a jump on anyone filing an appeal.

"If we go in," Meg asked, "do we need another one of those permits?"

"No, but we appreciate the courtesy of keeping us informed. We'd planned to have someone up here full-time today, but Tomasovic's death—his murder," she forced herself to say, "has changed that." There was a pause. "Has anyone been up to the Burnt Meadows sale this morning?"

Meg looked up, seeming to recall her thoughts from some distant place. "A few people drove up about eight. Why?"

"It's my job to keep tabs on people in the area. What were they doing?"

"Just looking around. They hadn't seen the area before, and of course it has quite a reputation now."

She wasn't lying—Ginny was convinced that this woman never lied. But she was certainly selecting which truths she was going to share.

"Sheriff Holt is investigating Ward's murder, isn't he?" Gayle Wallace asked. "Will he be coming up to talk to us?"

"Special Agent Carver is in charge now. He'd like a list of everyone who was up here last night, with addresses and phone numbers. He may be up later today. Everyone's going home this afternoon, isn't that right?"

"Well..." Meg hesitated. "That was the plan. Now I don't know. We'll have to play it by ear."

Ginny frowned. Would Frank want her to encourage them to leave, or to stay so he would have a chance to question them? She didn't know.

A drum had been beating slowly, insistently for the last few minutes. Now the tempo picked up. "That's Sequoia," murmured Meg. "I'll see about getting a list for you." She got up and walked away from the crowd, toward one of the campers parked nearby.

"Would you like to stay?" Gayle asked. "I've never been to a service like this before. It's, well, it's very moving."

Ginny glanced down at her uniform.

"No one will mind," Gayle said. "After all, you'd met him, too."

She did want to stay. She wanted to see more of these people, so different from most of her neighbors in Galina (though there was that old communal farm), and from the people she worked with. It was even possible she might learn something that would help the investigation. But mostly she wanted to stay because of Ward Tomasovic.

She followed Gayle back to the circle. The crowd was sitting up now, attention drawn taut by the beating drum. Sequoia, a slight, intense woman, began to chant. Her voice started low and quiet, filling in the spaces between the drumbeats.

"Earth our mother," she intoned. "We have raped you."

Ginny cringed. What was this? Some kind of feminist witchcraft?—she shook her head. All around her people were sitting up, listening, starting to join the chant. Sequoia threw her head back. Her voice took off in a high, keening wail, rising like a hawk over the beating drum. The chant grew louder. People started clapping with the beat.

No one else appeared to share Ginny's discomfort. She glanced at Gayle, sitting quietly beside her, eyes closed, absorbed. She took a breath and sat up straight. If a schoolteacher could handle it, so could she.

The whole crowd was chanting now, bodies swaying with the beat like a single organism. Ginny stiffened. She could have been an Episcopalian who had inadvertently walked into a church full of revivalists speaking in tongues. A few other people stood at the outskirts of the group, listening but not joining in. At least she wasn't the only one.

Then Meg Nugent was behind her, kneeling awkwardly, as though her legs no longer bent with ease. She laid her hands on Ginny's shoulders and kept them there while she swung to one side. Their eyes met. Meg smiled, and all her lines and wrinkles suddenly fell into place. The strips of ribbon in her gray braids flashed like birds on a rainy day. She settled back on her heels and began to gently knead Ginny's shoulders.

Her uniform was stiff and crinkly under Meg's hands, but her muscles yielded to the woman's touch, softened, and seemed to cry out for more. Ginny closed her eyes and let herself give way. Her intellectual protests faded beneath the repetitive beat of the drum. Meg's hands kneaded in time to the chant. Ginny started to sway as Sequoia's voice soared like a hawk on thermal drumbeats, fusing her with the group.

The music ended with a final, sharp cry. Meg's hands slid off Ginny's shoulders. She opened her eyes. All around her people sat quietly, waiting in expectant silence.

Rachel Davis stood up.

She turned to speak, and for the second time in twenty-four hours Ginny found herself listening to a speaker who could rivet a crowd's attention. Rachel spoke as someone who had known Ward Tomasovic well, who had admired and respected him, even through occasional disagreements. She recalled his commitment, his energy and above all his vision of wilderness, of free, untrammeled rivers filled with fish, hills shrouded again beneath blankets of trees.

At first Ginny was as mesmerized as the rest of the crowd. Rachel's speech was an eloquent testimonial, and as long as she was talking, Ginny found it hard to disbelieve. But when Rachel's voice dropped, then paused, Ginny's critical faculties took over again. Only a few hours ago she had heard the venom in Rachel's voice when she called her former lover's decision to work for the National Environmental League a betrayal. How could one person hold two such differing opinions at the same time?

She looked around. Gayle Wallace, still sitting beside her, seemed to have no trouble with Rachel's version of reality. Meg Nugent's eyes were closed, her forehead furrowed in thought. The morning's coolness had gone, and even at this higher altitude, halfway up Prairie, the heat was starting to build. Most of the children had moved off to the picnic tables at the far end of the campground, where a couple of adults were handing out snacks and getting some kind of circle game underway. Their shouts drifted softly over the waiting crowd.

Rachel was speaking again. A new stridency sounded in her voice as she built up to a call for action. A few people nodded in response, then a few more. Again Ginny thought of a revival meeting, this time of the call to come up and be saved. It's not enough to understand your sin and to see the vision of the New Jerusalem. You have to come forward, take action, commit.

Rachel Davis offered them a way to show that commitment. She wanted EarthAction to take over the Burnt Meadows sale and stop the logging.

SEVEN

FRANK STOOD on the porch of the Coffee Creek Café, watching Bruce Bowers's Forest Service pickup pull out onto the highway. Bowers was on his way back to the ranger station to relieve Deputy Larkin and give him a chance to get some chow. Over their own breakfast, Frank had lined out his limited resources. Larkin was to cover the local area, talking with anyone who might have heard or seen something unusual between ten-thirty and midnight the night before. Bowers would track down the threatening letter.

As for himself, he planned to talk to Debbie Kurtz. A few minutes ago he had called her home from the pay phone next to the café's rest rooms. A girl—middle school, judging from the giggles when he explained who he was—told him that Mom had gone into the office.

"On Saturday? Where does she work?"

A puzzled silence. "At the mill, of course."

Of course. Where else would the mill owner's daughter work? In a few minutes he would be talking to one of the possible Debbies, one who might have sent that note to Tomasovic.

Right now, though, standing outside the café, the big thing on his mind was cigarettes. For the past few years he had done most of his smoking out of doors, on porches, sidewalks, crammed under the dripping eaves with other members of the smokers' caucus. You couldn't smoke in a government office anymore. He'd stopped lighting up in vehicles, unless he was by himself. Ginny had known him over a month before realizing that he was hooked on nicotine.

The café, of course, had cigarettes, a nice display of them behind the cashier's counter. He almost stepped back inside, then forced himself in the other direction, down the steps, past his own rig, and across the highway. There he found a break in the barbed wire, with a narrow path threading its way across a pasture toward a line of alders. He kept walking. Once inside the trees he was hidden from the road. The cool, fishy smell of a big river hung in the still air. He paused, letting his eyes adjust to the green shadows. If there wasn't a fishing hole at the end of this path, he had no business calling himself an investigator.

Another hundred feet and the ground fell away in a steep bank to a small gravel beach about ten feet below. The path went almost straight down, a runnel of loose dirt lined with angling roots. At the end of it, two fishing rods stuck out over the water.

Frank came up to the edge and stopped. The rods were held by two boys, almost identically dressed in jeans and T-shirts so well laundered that their original color was nothing more than a guess. Bait fishing. One of them wore a baseball cap. The other's pale blond hair was cropped short, except for a tiny braid that clung to the nape of his neck. Frank had done more than enough fishing to get a little misty-eyed looking at them. That was when it hit him, really hit him, that Ward Tomasovic had grown up right here, in Coffee Creek, just like these boys. He'd probably put in a lot of hours fishing this very hole.

They were using bobbers. Frank watched the red-and-white plastic balls dip and weave with the current, always holding place. He had never met Ward Tomasovic. Everything he knew about him came from reports, newspaper stories, or gossip. Now, for the first time, he felt a connection. He didn't just know something *about* Tomasovic, he knew a part of him. And with that knowing came a little thrill of anticipation. Soon he would know more, then a little more, until finally, with luck and skill and perseverance, he would know who had fired that shot at eleven o'clock on a Friday night, and through luck, or skill, or even perseverance, had killed him. Sometimes a fishing trip started with that same anticipation. A homicide investigation could be a lot like a fishing trip, a thought that was not new to Frank but that always pleased him.

He shifted his weight and a pebble slid out from under his foot, rattling down the bank. The river noise and the boys' total absorption kept them from noticing. He watched for a few more minutes while he considered what to do next.

If Ginny had been an experienced officer, he would have assigned her to check out EarthAction, especially Rachel Davis's undisguised hostility toward Tomasovic. But she wasn't, and he couldn't ask an untrained Forest Service employee, not matter how intuitively good at it she had shown herself to be, to independently handle part of a murder investigation. For once, his personal inclinations and the demands of his job coincided. He would keep her with him as much as possible.

He glanced at his watch. Nine-thirty. Hunsaker was undoubtedly looking for him, probably Sheriff Holt, too, but he had given Tiffany instructions to relay only calls from Ginny, Bowers, or Larkin. His nicotine craving had subsided, for a while at least. It was time to pay a visit to Zellers Wood Products.

DEBBIE KURTZ LOOKED UP from the sheet of paper Frank had pushed across the table. "It's my handwriting," she said. "But I didn't write it."

He had expected a flat denial from this stylish blond woman who handled employee benefits for the family business. Instead she was looking him right in the eye and telling him two things that didn't make sense at the same time.

"Who did, then?"

She shrugged, eyes watching him, not giving anything away. She looked tired, too tired to be putting in overtime on a Saturday morning. He hadn't seen any work on her desk when the clerk led him through the empty personnel department to her office.

"You knew Tomasovic." It wasn't a guess anymore, even though she hadn't told him. "Did you see him last night?"

"I was at his talk. My husband was there, too."

"Did you see Tomasovic personally, speak to him?"

"No."

"Did you have an appointment, some sort of arrangement, to see him?"

She shook her head.

"How do you explain this note?"

"I don't explain it. Where did it come from?"

"It was in Tomasovic's pocket when he died. He was shot shortly after eleven, near the scoreboard."

Debbie nodded. "I see. I wasn't there, Mr. Carver."

"Someone was. Unless you can prove otherwise, Mrs. Kurtz, I'm going to have to assume it was you."

She slumped down in her chair with a little sigh. "Everybody in this town knows that Ward and I went together in high school. I've been married—happily married—for almost twenty years. I have three children, a lovely home, a satisfying job. Why would I risk all that for a man I haven't seen since I was sixteen?"

Frank shook his head. "I don't know. Tomasovic's speech ended about nine-thirty. Where exactly were you from ten-thirty until, say, midnight?"

"I suppose I have to answer this?"

"We'll be asking everyone we talk to, Mrs. Kurtz."

She thought for a moment. "Ed and Amanda and I went home after Ward's talk. We got back around ten, I'd guess. Amanda got right on the phone to one of her friends, and Ed made himself a sandwich. I went up to our room."

"Did you go to bed?"

She hesitated. "No, I went out again." Frank would have bet money she was telling him this only because her husband or daughter knew about it. "I was tired, but I couldn't sleep. Restless. Maybe seeing Ward again after all those years."

"Where did you go?"

"Out. Just drove around."

"You didn't stop anywhere?"

She shook her head.

"Did anyone see you?"

She shrugged.

"Where exactly did you go? Into town? Along the highway?"

"I just drove. I don't remember where I went. I got back about twelve-thirty."

"Did anyone see you come home?"

"Ed was up. We talked for a bit, then went to bed."

Frank shook his head. Until she could prove that she had not been at the school playing field at 11:00 p.m., he had to consider her a suspect—the only one he had, so far. His guess, based on her hesitation, her reluctance to talk, the subtle signs of recent, cosmetically repaired distress, was that she had in fact privately met, or planned to meet, Tomasovic during his stay in Coffee Creek. The interview was effectively stalled until they got that out in the open.

He'd have to talk to her husband and daughter. For the moment, though, he changed the subject by asking for a description of her car. A blue Chevy Blazer, two years old, with lots of extras. Debbie Kurtz rattled the description off as though she were writing an ad. He took it down. Perhaps someone had seen it last night.

He heard voices from the room outside the office, footsteps, and then caught the expression on Debbie's face as she looked up. Relief.

Charlie Zellers stood framed in the doorway. Frank had never seen him before, but he was instantly certain about the identity of this scrawny, white-haired old man. Zellers wore moccasins, suspenders, stagged pants—though Frank doubted that a seventy-year-old company president did much active logging—and wire-rimmed glasses so precariously balanced they looked like an afterthought.

"You okay, hon? Ed said you were down here, and then I heard the law was nosing around." He threw a hostile glance in Frank's direction.

"I'm okay, Daddy. Mr. Carver just had a few questions."

Charlie turned to study the interloper. "Any cops come on my property, Carver, I want to know about it."

Frank assumed his mildest demeanor, the one he could never believe anyone would fall for. "Just part of my job, sir."

"What are you doing down here picking on my little girl? Where's Holt?"

"Something came up that the sheriff had to attend to."

"Well, who the hell are you, anyhow? State police?"

Frank opened his wallet to show his badge. "Frank Carver, federal special agent for the Neskanie National Forest."

"Humph," Charlie grumbled. "You work for Larry, then?"

Just letting the peons know who's in charge. Frank refused to take offense. He nodded. Daddy, indeed. Charlie Zellers came on like a she-bear with cubs.

Charlie sat down. "Debbie didn't have anything to do with any of this. She hasn't even seen Ward for twenty years."

"Yes, she was just explaining that."

"He's got a note," Debbie said. "He thinks I arranged some sort of rendezvous last night."

Charlie jerked his head around to Frank. "What note?"

Frank handed him the sheet of paper. He glanced at it, then shoved it back. "This why you're here?"

"It's the immediate reason."

"Well, Debbie didn't write it."

"Your daughter has identified the handwriting as her own."

Charlie pursed his lips.

"That's where Ward was shot," Debbie said. "Under the scoreboard, just after eleven."

"Yeah, I know." He squinted at Frank, as though considering his chances. "I wrote that note."

"What!" Debbie stared openmouthed at her father. "Daddy, why would you?... You hated him!"

"Hush up, now." Charlie waved a hand in her direction. She closed her mouth.

"I wanted to talk to him. I knew he wouldn't agree to see me—you heard what Debbie just said. There was a lot of bad feeling between us when he left Coffee Creek."

"And?"

Charlie shrugged. "It was easy enough. See how she still makes a little circle on top of the 'i' in her name? She's done that since sixth grade."

"You figured he'd be willing to see Debbie, even if he wouldn't see you."

"Yeah, and I was right, too."

"You did meet him, then?"

"That's right." Charlie folded his arms and leaned back in his chair. "So you see, Debbie didn't have anything to do with it."

It was time to break them up. If Ginny had been along, he would have had her take Debbie into another room and find out everything she knew about Tomasovic's family while he worked on Charlie. He glanced at his watch. Ten-thirty. She'd been up at Burnt Meadows for a couple hours now.

"Mrs. Kurtz," he said. "I need to talk to your father privately. Could you wait outside?"

Debbie stood up, looking perplexed. Frank could hardly blame her, considering that he had just dismissed her from her own office. She gave her father a worried look as she went out. She was taller than she had seemed behind her desk, her long legs nicely filling a pair of well-cut jeans. The door closed softly behind her.

Frank studied Charlie. The old man still had his arms folded across his chest, and he was smiling. "Don't expect a Forest Service dick gets in on many murders."

Frank waited. He wasn't going to produce his credentials—which included ten years in homicide—for Charlie Zellers, not after that hint about being on such good terms with his boss.

After a minute or two Charlie's smile faded. He sat there, his level gaze meeting Frank's. "Hell," he finally said. "I'll blink. What do you want?"

"Proof that you wrote that note."

Charlie lowered his arms. "Okay. I know I'm not doing myself any favors, but I don't want Debbie mixed up in this. I wrote it yesterday afternoon, then gave it to the Sondheim kid to take over to the school."

"When was that?"

"About seven. I figured Ward would be there by then, but I didn't want him to get it too early. In case he ran into Debbie."

"No one knew you were doing this?"

Charlie shook his head.

"I'll want to talk to that kid."

"Eric Sondheim. Lives next door. Towhead. He's got one of those little braids the kids wear." Charlie fingered a non-existent lock at the back of his neck.

"Doesn't fish by any chance, does he?"

"Now and then. Saw him digging worms in his mom's flower bed this morning."

Frank nodded. He had a pretty good idea where Eric Sondheim was right now. "Tomasovic showed?"

"Yep. Eleven on the dot."

"You talked to him?"

"Yep."

"How long?"

"Maybe ten minutes."

Like pulling teeth. "And then what?"

"And then I left."

Frank leaned forward. "The shot that killed Tomasovic was fired at eleven-fourteen. You must have heard it."

"Didn't know you had the time down to the minute."

"Well, we do. Where were you when that shot was fired?"

"Halfway back across the field. I took a dive soon as I heard it. I could tell it was close. When I looked up I couldn't see a thing."

"Where was Tomasovic?"

"Don't know."

"You didn't look to make sure he was okay?"

"I figured he was gone. Then a minute or two later I heard a rig start up. Figured it was him."

"Okay, where was this vehicle?"

"Sounded like the school parking lot. I heard this morning, though, that Ward's van was still there."

Frank nodded slowly, visualizing the playing field. It was rectangular, the length running east-west. The ranger station was at the east end, the school parking lot at the west. Part of the school and a few houses straggled along the long south edge. The highway formed the north boundary.

"Where was your car parked?"

"Wasn't. I walked over. It's only a few blocks."

"Where did you enter the field, then?"

"At the end of Eighth, right by Dickerson's house."

"How did you get home?"

"Same way. I swear to God, if I'd known he was hurt I would have gone back."

He fell silent, studying his hands. They were tough hands, callused and deeply wrinkled. The tip of the left index finger was missing. When he spoke again his voice was strained. "I didn't hear a cry or nothing. I was almost home when the siren went off."

Charlie Zellers was hurting. There was more here than just the shock of realizing that someone you had talked to only a few hours earlier was now dead. Was it for his daughter? Somehow for himself?

"Your daughter says you hated Tomasovic."

Charlie's head jerked up. "He wanted to marry her. Hell, she was just sixteen, and I wouldn't have it. No, I didn't hate him. But to a young girl, in love like she was, it might seem like that."

Frank nodded, waited a moment. The siren Charlie heard had gone off about 11:25 p.m. The emergency dispatcher would have the precise time. "Okay," he said, "I've got no reason to disbelieve you. But you'll have to answer a couple more questions."

Charlie nodded. "Fire away."

"Do you own a gun?"

"Hell, yes. I must have half-a-dozen deer rifles."

"What about a handgun?"

"Couple of those, too."

"Licensed?"

"'Course they are. Come by my place and I'll show 'em to you."

They would be there. Clean, unfired, and no match for the bullet Kim Morris had shown him a few hours ago. There were too many ways to get unlicensed guns, and too many places to ditch them.

"Why did you want to see Tomasovic?"

Charlie looked up. "That's business between Ward and me, and it's over. It's done with."

"If you shot him, it's sure as hell done with."

"I didn't shoot him, Carver. I had no reason to want him dead."

He waited, but Charlie Zellers had nothing more to say. Finally he stood up. "Come over to the school and show me where you were when you heard the shot."

They left the office, Charlie leading the way. Debbie and the clerk who had let Frank in were both gone. Charlie locked up as they left the building.

They got into Frank's four-wheel drive. He flipped the radio on. "Coffee Creek, this is Carver. Any messages?"

There was a burst of static, and then Tiffany came on. "Trask called in about ten minutes ago, ETA Coffee Creek eleven-thirty. Hunsaker has called twice, urgent you contact him, ditto Holt, but he's only called once."

"Ten-four. Thanks. I should be there by eleven-thirty. Carver clear." No message from Christina Schnell, so she probably had not yet located Teresa Tomasovic. He was starting to worry about notifying next of kin.

He turned to Charlie. "You know anything about Tomasovic's parents?"

Charlie's head jerked up. "Why?"

"I need to notify next of kin, and so far we can't locate his ex-wife. Are his folks still around?"

"Nick Tomasovic died about ten years ago, heart attack. Used to do some contract logging for us. Ellen remarried three, four years back."

"You know her married name?"

"Jacobson. They live out on the coast now, Verona."

Verona was a town of about five thousand at the mouth of the Jackson River, thirty miles west of Coffee Creek. Ellen Jacobson shouldn't be too hard to track down.

Frank pulled behind the ranger station and hopped out of the truck. "Let's get going," he said, "before they find out I'm here."

Charlie gave a chuckle and followed him along the fence and onto the playing field. They talked for a moment, then Charlie pointed out where he had met Tomasovic. It was the same spot Ginny had heard voices coming from, a few feet from where Tomasovic had fallen. They moved to Charlie's approximate location when he heard the shot. Frank had him go through the same motions he had gone through the night before, timing him. After a minute they both walked briskly across the grass toward an opening in the fence on the south side, past a mailbox with the name Dickerson painted on it and down Eighth Street, an unpaved lane about two blocks long. Charlie took a left, then a right, crossed the bridge, took another right, and stopped at a comfortable-looking ranch house that backed on the river.

"This is it," he said. "I was just about here when the siren went off."

Frank checked his watch. Ten minutes. It didn't prove a thing. Charlie Zellers could have shot Tomasovic, then walked home just like he said, not even pausing as he dropped the gun into the Jackson River.

EIGHT

FRANK HADN'T BEEN BACK in the station more than five minutes when everything came unglued.

He had seven telephone messages, two of them from reporters. "Anyone who sounds like they work for a news agency," he told Tiffany, "just refer them to Christina Schnell."

"She called, too."

"Yeah, I see."

He took his messages into Bowers's office. The drawn venetian blinds and the houseplants made the room seem even cooler than it was. It felt good, though, after his excursion with Charlie Zellers. He returned Christina's call first, figuring he would get more information from her than from Holt or Hunsaker.

"We wrapped up the press conference about an hour ago," Christina said. "Got the Eugene and Portland TV stations, plus the newspapers. I asked them to lay off, Frank, and some of them will."

He grunted.

"They all want pictures, especially the TV crews. They got some good shots of the sheriff, but they want pictures with trees."

"The sheriff? Holt was there?"

"He's calling it a joint investigation. That's right, isn't it?"

"Christ, I guess so." As long as he had Larkin, it was technically true. "I thought Holt had his hands full with the Michaels kid."

"He was here. Look, I wondered if maybe we could bring a couple of camera crews down there, let them do a little taping."

"Christina!" he exploded. "This is a homicide investigation! Your job is to keep them out of here."

"Don't tell me what my job is, Frank Carver. Maybe that's how they do it in Seattle, but this is the Forest Service. I'm a public information officer. Public information. Everything we do is public."

"Like hell." He simmered down. "KETV had a crew out here this morning, taping our crime scene search. There's not much else to see."

"Okay, we'll drop it. For now, anyway. What have you got for me?"

"Not much. We're pursuing all leads."

Now it was Christina's turn to grunt.

"How are you doing on Teresa Tomasovic?"

"I've got an address and a phone number, but no one answers. Maybe I'll drive by."

"If we can't locate her today, I'll try to find Tomasovic's mother. She's supposed to be living out at the coast." He paused. "Larry's called twice. Do you know what he wants?"

"Information, same as me. You're not very forthcoming, you know."

"Tough, lady."

Christina chuckled. "He's at home now. You'd better call him. Andy Zellers and his lawyer were in here at nine o'clock this morning. They talked with Larry for almost an hour, real hush-hush."

"Give me a rundown on the Zellerses, will you? I've already met Charlie and the daughter."

"The other two are pretty tame, by comparison. Andy and Joe. They're both in their forties, both vice presidents in charge of something. We mostly see Andy around here—he comes in to drop off the bids and talk up the timber staff. Nice enough guys, both of them. Been to college. Married."

"Strictly a family business, huh?"

"No publicly held stock. Nice, well-run company. The kind you'd like to invest in, if it ever did go public."

"And if I had anything to invest. What did Andy want on a Saturday morning?"

"You'd better call Larry."

He didn't like the sound of that. Christina promised to call him after she checked Teresa Tomasovic's house. "I don't suppose we could get a shot of you in uniform," she added wistfully.

"Not alive, no."

If she had a retort to that, he didn't get to hear it. There was a tap on the door.

"Yo!"

Ginny's face appeared, eyebrows raised in question.

He hung the phone up. "Come on in. You got a report for me, Deputy?"

She sat down. "EarthAction is taking over the Burnt Meadows sale. They're moving people in right now."

THERE WERE SOME eventualities that twenty years on a big-city police force did not prepare you for. Frank stared at her as though he didn't quite comprehend. The half-dozen things he needed to take care of within the next thirty minutes prodded at the back of his mind. Suddenly he knew what Andy Zellers and his lawyer had been doing at the SO that morning.

Then twenty years of routine took over and gave him a kick in the butt. "Start from when you got up there," he said. "Tell me everything that happened."

Ginny told him. She told him about driving through the deserted sale area, about Meg Nugent and her suspicion that Zellers would start cutting on Monday. She told him about the crowd at the campground, and everything she could remember of Rachel Davis's call to action. The only thing she left out was her response to Sequoia's song.

Frank tapped his finger softly on the desk as he listened. The one thing clear so far was that they now had two full-time jobs.

"It's like they're doing it for Ward," she said. "Because he died."

"Great. The Ward Tomasovic Memorial Protest Action." He asked a few questions, but there was not much more to learn. After making the decision to occupy the sale area, everyone had kept out of Ginny's way.

"They didn't actually ask me to leave," she said. "But they sure stopped talking to me."

"Did you see any climbing gear?"

She shook her head. "Just camping stuff. You think they might get up into the trees?"

"That's their trademark." The Neskanie had not yet experienced a site occupation, but Frank had assisted at one just a few months ago, in March. That had been on the Willamette, up in the Oregon Cascades. He and two other Forest Service agents had been called in to help make arrests at the end of a two-week protest. Five demonstrators had gone to jail, to the accompaniment of much sympathetic publicity.

The whole thing had cost him a little soul-searching. Hell, one of the reasons for getting into this line of work was that you believed in resource protection. He appreciated a hike through a fine stand of timber as much as anyone, especially if there was a good trout stream at the end of it. In fact, that was where a good trout stream was likely to be.

Tomasovic's arguments in favor of protecting fish were not lost on Frank. Whatever else EarthAction might be doing, legal or illegal, there was no doubt that they were trying to protect a resource.

Protest demonstrations had been the main unofficial topic at the regional law enforcement conference last winter. Five of the region's twelve forests had been targets during the previous year. The Regional Office had even issued a few directives. He should be able to get plenty of advice.

What he needed, though, was warm bodies, and those were always in short supply.

He found the forest supervisor's home number in his address book, picked up the phone, and dialed.

Three rings, the click of an answering machine, and then his ears were assailed by max-volume rap music. He jerked the receiver away.

"Hold on a minute," said Larry Hunsaker, barely audible through the pulsing beat. The noise abruptly ceased. "Hello?"

"Carver here. This some new way to discourage telephone solicitors?"

"Kids. They control the phone. I've been trying to reach you."

"Yeah." Frank gave him a status report on the investigation. "We've got two suspects—Zellers and his daughter—which is more than we had at six this morning. We should have a lead on the threatening letter and the phone calls pretty soon." Then he told him about EarthAction.

"I was afraid of this," said Hunsaker quietly.

"Andy Zellers was in this morning?"

"Wanted an okay to send his fallers in on Monday."

"You gave it to him?"

He could almost see Hunsaker shrug. "The timber's his, the road's in, and the judge said go ahead. Yeah, I said okay."

"You couldn't talk him into holding off for a week?" Frank fumed, caught Ginny watching him, and toned it down. "This is a hell of a note, Larry. I've only got two LEOs."

"You want me to talk to Holt? Maybe he'll take the homicide back."

He almost laughed. "Fat chance. We can handle it, but we're going to need some help. Can Fire Control turn anyone loose?"

"How many bodies do you need?"

He did some rapid figuring. He'd have to put Bowers in charge at Burnt Meadows, bring in the Sitkum LEO to relieve him so they could run twenty-four-hour shifts. He needed two more people up there, and at least one to help with legwork on the homicide. "Three. If we make arrests, we may have to pull in personnel from off-forest."

"Okay, you've got them." Hunsaker's voice had turned crisp, decisive. "Tell Bricca you need someone from Coffee Creek. I'll round up two more and get them down there by tonight."

"Sounds good. Thanks, Larry."

He hung up and smiled at Ginny. "Well, Deputy, looks like we're going to be pretty busy."

THE FIRST THING was to get Bowers back. Tiffany raised him on the radio first try, with an ETA of twenty minutes. Frank reached Vince Paley, the Sitkum district law enforcement officer, and arranged to have him relieve Bowers that evening. Next he called Tony Bricca. Sooner or later he was going to have to tell the ranger that two of Coffee Creek's leading citizens were under suspicion of murder, but right now Burnt Meadows took his full attention. Bricca promised all possible support, starting with his own presence.

Ginny filled canteens and ordered three double lunches from the café. She was on her way out the door when the Burnt Meadows sensors started going off like popcorn in a microwave. She called Frank and the two of them stood there with Tiffany, counting beeps.

"Six rigs," Frank muttered. "God knows how many people."

"No one on foot, so far," Ginny said. The first of the seismic sensors went off. "Take that back."

Bowers came in, his expression instantly alert as he caught the sense of urgency in Dispatch. Frank started filling him in as Ginny left.

When she got back fifteen minutes later they were ready to go. Bowers was already in his truck. He had arranged to stop on the way to pick up Kenny McKinney, Coffee Creek's assistant fire management officer. Ginny handed him a sack lunch, stashed the other two in Frank's rig, and went inside.

"No need to keep monitoring traffic," Frank said. "We know where they are." He picked the sensor receiver up and added it to his gear, then turned to Tiffany. "How late can you stay?"

"As late as you need me. I love overtime." She was still working through the pile of magazines she had brought in that morning.

"Bricca's meeting us at Fish Hatchery Road. Got everything?"

Ginny nodded.

"We're out of here."

"AS I UNDERSTAND IT, there's a pattern to these things," Frank said. He slowed to take the first big turn on Coffee

Creek Road. "First there's a buildup. We've already seen that, the local opposition to the sale, the media attention, the letters to the editor. A group like EarthAction comes in and gets the locals motivated, helps them get set up. Most of these folks are amateurs, you know, but EarthAction has got a few professionals. Rachel Davis is one of them. She puts on training sessions on organization, nonviolent resistance."

"I'll bet she's good at it," said Ginny. She unwrapped a ham and cheese sandwich, handed half to Frank, and took a bite from the other half. Since dinner the night before she had eaten nothing but coffee and doughnuts. For a moment they both concentrated on food.

"Rachel Davis has been in the environmental movement since the seventies," said Frank. "That's practically all her adult life."

Ginny unwrapped another sandwich. "You should have heard her talk. By the time she was finished that crowd would have done anything she asked. She almost had me convinced."

"Almost, huh?"

"Except for what she said about Ward. That stopped me. According to Rachel, they never disagreed. Whatever Rachel wanted, Ward wanted too. They saw eye-to-eye on everything."

Frank snorted. "Didn't sound like that at six this morning, did she?"

"It made me mad," Ginny said quietly. "He hadn't been dead twelve hours, and she was using him."

They spotted Bricca's rig. Frank pulled up alongside and lowered his window. "Bowers is stopping to pick up Kenny McKinney. I thought we'd wait for them and go up together."

The ranger looked eager and ready to go. "Any idea what's happening up there?"

"We've got at least six rigs in the sale area. That's all I know right now."

A minute later Bowers's pickup took the turn and pulled in behind them. The three vehicles started up Prairie Mountain. Bricca stayed on the radio, full of questions and ideas about what to do next. Frank shook his head with annoyance. The Forest Service's new programmable radios were not that hard to come by. For all he knew, Rachel Davis and her friends were listening to every word they said.

They passed the Prairie Mountain trailhead, where they spotted a small pickup and a van. Bowers stopped to check them out and jot down the plate numbers. Frank took a quick detour down Road 1010 to check the campground. They found a few vehicles in the parking lot and a couple dozen occupied campsites. A gang of kids was eating lunch at the picnic tables. They looked up as the Forest Service rigs eased by, but no one waved.

The little convoy turned back out onto the main road. A few minutes later the monitor inside the rig beeped softly as they passed the first of the magnetic sensors. Then came the line of yellow flags that marked the boundary of the Burnt Meadows sale. So far they had seen neither vehicles nor people.

"They must be parked up at the landing," Frank murmured. Prairie Mountain Road, jointly maintained by the Forest Service and the county, ran right through the sale area, making it easily accessible to the public. The sale specifications included a large visual buffer along the road. Two of the three landings—flat areas for decking and loading logs—were completely out of sight. Zellers Wood Products had built them last winter, as soon as they had the sale and before the environmentalists had gone to court.

Ginny craned forward, peering out the windshield, not knowing what to expect. EarthAction must have heard them coming, must be expecting someone to show up. Frank eased the truck around a curve, and there they were.

Thirty people, give or take a few. They were a motley collection, some dressed for hiking, some in shorts and T-shirts. Quite a few had cameras or binoculars. They could have been a chapter of the Audubon Society, though a little more colorful and wearing less expensive jeans.

Except that they were standing, arms linked, in a line right across the road.

Frank came to a stop, with the other two vehicles behind him. "Don't get out yet," he said into the radio. He turned to Ginny. "Tell me who these people are."

During her two hours at the campground that morning, Ginny had formed a rough idea of who was doing what. She pointed out the people she knew by name, including Meg Nugent, whom Frank had not yet met. Gayle Wallace was there, looking uncomfortable but resolute. Next to her was a man in a motorized wheelchair. Ginny guessed he was Bill Wallace. Tiffany, who lived near the Wallaces, had said something about Gayle's husband having muscular dystrophy—that was one reason she had taken an early retirement. In his lap Ginny spotted a couple of radios and a scanner. She nudged Frank and pointed.

He nodded glumly. "I see." Thirty pairs of eyes were watching them. He sighed. "I guess we better talk to these people."

They both got out. The truck doors slammed shut like gunshots in the still afternoon. The line of demonstrators had been singing softly since their arrival. Now the voices grew louder, the words clearer. It wasn't a song Ginny knew.

Frank came to a stop, with Ginny off to one side, a few steps behind. The air smelled warm and resinous, with a trace of exhaust from the trucks. Frank looked up and down the line, meeting unfriendly stares for the most part. Gayle Wallace managed a small smile.

After a few minutes the singing stopped. Frank told them who he was, took out his badge, and held it up for everyone to see.

No response.

"There are some things you can do," he said, cranking his voice up, "and some things you can't. You can't block access to public land."

No one moved. Frank waited. "Who wants to be arrested first? Won't make much of a news story—no pictures or television cameras."

The line did not exactly waver, but people turned to look at one another. There was a brief murmur of discussion. Finally Meg Nugent stepped forward. She was wearing jeans and a T-shirt now, instead of a costume gown, but her hair was still braided with bright ribbons. Her trademark, Ginny decided.

"We heard that Zellers is going to start cutting this unit," she said. "We thought you might be the falling crew."

Frank glanced again at the radios in Bill Wallace's lap. Fat chance they didn't know who was driving up the road. Behind him another car door slammed shut. He looked back at Meg.

"We're Forest Service employees, up here in the course of our duties. You people need to let us through."

"Where are you going? What are you doing here?"

Tony Bricca joined them. Frank hoped he had enough sense to keep his mouth shut. "Well, now, that's really none of your business. But I don't mind telling you. We're going to post a couple officers, for security."

"We don't need any security."

"Maybe not. But some folks around here don't like what you stand for. Our job is to make sure no one gets hurt."

Rachel Davis broke from the line and stepped forward. "This sale is still in the courts, Carver. We're not going to let Zellers touch it."

"All the more reason I need a couple officers up here. Now, move your people and let us through."

There was a brief huddle, Meg and Rachel with half-a-dozen others. The line broke up and people moved slowly to the sides of the road.

Frank and Ginny walked back to their rig, with Bricca a few steps behind. "That's Bill Wallace, in the wheelchair," he said. "Is that one of our radios he's got?"

"Looks like it," said Frank. "I'd like to know who gave it to him."

"He's a ham operator. Their living room is stuffed with electronics. He runs communications whenever we've got a search and rescue."

"Great. Just what we need."

They got back into their vehicles and started up the road, past the cars and people on the main landing, and kept going. They drove completely through the sale area without seeing anyone else. Once they were past the yellow boundary ribbons, Frank pulled over, got out, and signaled the others—Bricca, Bowers, and McKinney—to join him.

"We have to assume that radio they've got can pick us up."

"What about the encryption mode?" Bowers asked.

"Bricca here says the guy is a ham."

"No shit?"

Frank nodded. "He'll recognize the encryption signal when he picks it up."

"He shouldn't be able to decode it, though," Bowers said.

"Let's hope not. Show Kenny how to encrypt, but watch what you say." Frank turned to Bricca. "Hunsaker says the fallers are coming in on Monday. That what you hear?"

Bricca nodded. "Zellers is anxious to get started."

"Well, this is going to slow them down. Have the fallers come in. We'll be here. Chances are EarthAction will try to block access, just like they did with us, except they'll be sure to have the media up here to cover the event. If they don't move, we get a supervisor's closure on the area. Once that's posted we can kick everybody out."

"Why not kick 'em out right now?" asked Kenny McKinney. Coffee Creek's assistant fire management officer was in his mid-thirties, clean-shaven except for a mustache. A wad of snoose bulged discreetly beneath his lower lip. At the moment he wore an expression that suggested they were fools to put up with this.

"They haven't done anything illegal," said Frank.

"They're sure as hell planning to."

"I don't get it," said Bricca, shaking his head. "I mean, when you see people who have every intention of breaking the law... We've got one hand tied behind our backs."

"It's frustrating," Frank agreed. "But they pay us to enforce the laws, not to make them. It's public land, and we can't move on these people until they break the law."

"They will," said Bowers. "Come Monday morning."

"Which gives us a day to get ready. Bruce, you're in charge up here, with Kenny for assistance. Vince Paley should show later this afternoon. He has instructions to relieve you at dark. Hunsaker's promised us more help, but who knows when that will arrive. Tony, could you ride back with us so Kenny can have your rig? They may need to split up. Bruce?" He signaled the LEO to join him.

The two of them walked up the road and stood talking, heads together. Tony Bricca moved his gear into Frank's truck. A few minutes later they were ready to leave.

Ginny looked out the window as they drove slowly down the road, past the landing full of vehicles and Earth-Actioners eating lunch, past the unit boundary, past the turnoff for the Burnt Meadows campground. Tony Bricca had lots of questions about surveillance and arrests, but finally seemed to notice that Frank wasn't answering them. He fell silent.

They reached Fish Hatchery Road. "What do we do now?" Ginny asked.

Frank brightened up. "Now we get back to our homicide investigation."

NINE

"YOUR PUBLIC INFORMATION officer called," Tiffany said, as soon as they walked into the station. "Christina Schnell. She's found the woman you're looking for."

Frank took the slip of paper she handed him and headed for the law enforcement office. Tony Bricca trailed along behind. "What woman is this?" he asked. "Does she have something to do with Tomasovic?"

"She used to be married to him," Frank said shortly. He stopped outside the door, afraid that if he let Bricca in he would never get him out again. How the hell did Bowers put up with it? Reluctantly, Frank realized he was going to have to find the ranger a job.

"Look, Tony," he said. "I've got my hands full with this homicide. I've put Bowers in charge up at Burnt Meadows, but I can't do much for him. He's going to need support. Are you familiar with this kind of operation?"

Bricca shook his head. "We've done some cooperative work with the sheriff's office before, but nothing like this."

Maybe that was why he kept butting in. As a district ranger, Bricca was used to running Coffee Creek the way a captain runs a ship. Now Frank was in charge of two of the biggest events in local history, and Bricca was reduced to trailing after him, trying to figure out what was going on.

He wished he had the Sitkum ranger to deal with, instead—a good manager, but unassuming, a little unsure of himself. Instead here was Bricca, wanting to run the show up on Prairie Mountain. He had enough problems dealing with Hunsaker and Holt. He didn't need this, too.

So he put Bricca in charge of liaison.

"The LEOs need room to do their job. What they don't need is Hunsaker, or Christina either, breathing down their necks, wanting every little detail. Plus, by tomorrow this place is going to be swarming with reporters, and none of us has time to talk to them."

Bricca nodded happily. It was the perfect assignment. He'd know everything that was going on. Frank briefed him on what was likely to happen at Burnt Meadows during the next few days and answered a few of his questions about the Tomasovic investigation. Bricca listened, offered some surprisingly good suggestions, and went away happy.

Frank sighed and finally opened the door to Bowers's office. The little room was in deep shadow, the sun having moved around a corner of the building. He twitched the venetian blinds open. Where was Ginny? She had disappeared right after they hit the station. He wanted her here. It wasn't reasonable, but it was what he wanted.

He sat down to make phone calls. Ginny came in just as he finished with Christina Schnell. "Where have you been?"

She gave him a surprised look. "I gassed both our rigs, got my stuff together, and rented us rooms at the motel for tomorrow. We're going back to Longmont tonight, aren't we?"

"Now, how did you know that?"

"You've got to see Teresa Tomasovic. The father of her children died over twelve hours ago, and she hasn't gotten any official notification." She paused. "She knows, doesn't she?"

He nodded. "Told Christina she heard it on the radio. We're meeting her at six."

"We'd better get going, then. It's after three now."

"That was a good idea, getting the motel rooms."

"Maybe all those people up on Prairie will go home and we won't need them."

He snorted. "Dreamer."

Before they left he filled her in on what Bowers had learned that morning. The Coffee Creek loggers and mill workers weren't as organized as Friends of Burnt Meadows, but there had been a few meetings in people's homes, and plenty of talk. Two of the biggest talkers had been Zellers's head faller and a sawyer at the mill. The sawyer was apparently out of town. Bowers had been on his way to talk to the faller when Frank called him back to help at Burnt Meadows.

"I tried both numbers before I called Christina," Frank said. "No one answered. We'll try to catch one of them tomorrow. I want to know who did that poster."

IT WAS A LONG DRIVE to Longmont, after a very long day. Ginny had used up her second wind hours ago, and now she fought to stay awake at the wheel. Frank, up ahead in his own rig, couldn't be doing much better. Tomorrow they could take turns driving. Tonight she'd get to see her daughter for an hour or two, and then sleep in her own bed.

They stopped in front of a modest stucco house at the south end of Longmont. A trumpet vine splayed across the front, drooping clumps of orange flowers over the bedroom windows. Geraniums bloomed in the brick planter beside the front door, and lobelia and marigolds alternated blue and yellow along the driveway. A tricycle lay on its side in the middle of the lawn.

Teresa Tomasovic opened the door. She was younger than Ginny had expected, a short, fine-boned woman who could almost have passed for a twelve-year-old. She looked them over and waved them in without speaking. The living room was small, with a few simple pieces of furniture. Another woman sat cross-legged on an oversized cushion in one corner, discreetly nursing a baby.

Teresa gestured Frank and Ginny to a futon folded up to make a couch. She pulled up a straight-backed chair for herself and sat down on the edge. Her dark, smooth hair was pulled back into a braid, leaving her face bare and unprotected. She looked as though she had been crying.

The silence was unnerving. Frank cleared his throat. "Frank Carver, Mrs. Tomasovic. I'm a special agent with the Neskanie National Forest. This is Ginny Trask." He paused. This was the one part of homicide he would gladly have turned over to someone else. A family's reaction to violent death was unpredictable, but always, in his experience, revealing. That was why he preferred to break the news himself.

"I know why you're here, Mr. Carver." Teresa Tomasovic's voice was quiet, controlled. "I was making lunch for the children when I heard the news on the radio."

"I'm sorry you had to find out that way. We had trouble getting your phone number."

"It's unlisted. Ward insisted on that, even after we split up. He didn't want harassing phone calls."

"Oh? Did he get many?"

She hesitated. "Not many."

Teresa Tomasovic was entirely too self-contained. Ginny tried to recall her own state of mind six hours after learning that Dale was dead, but the memories of those first few days of widowhood were jumbled, incomplete. Teresa, of course, wasn't a widow—she and Ward had been divorced. For all they knew, she had hated her ex-husband. Ginny didn't think so, though. Women who hated their ex-husbands didn't generally keep their names.

"When did you last see Ward?" Frank asked.

Ginny got her notebook out. The woman in the corner seemed preoccupied with the now-sleeping infant. Friend with baby present, she noted, after the date.

"On Wednesday. He came by to see the kids."

"How long was he here?"

"A couple of hours. I went shopping, stopped for a cup of coffee. I wanted to give them plenty of time together."

"Did he visit often?"

She shook her head and smiled, a slight, rueful smile. "Ward was very committed to his work, Mr. Carver. We've seen him only three times since he got back from Washington."

"You have two children?"

Teresa nodded. "Elisha's five, and Chad just turned three. They're sleeping now." She sighed, and suddenly looked much older. "I've told them that their father is dead, but of course they don't realize what that means. Chad thinks it's just another long trip."

Perhaps that was how she had explained Ward's absence to his children. Ginny turned a page in her notebook. A three-year-old might accept it, but by five a child would have questions, would sense that something was wrong. That might account for Teresa's apparent detachment, too. You wouldn't want to expect too much of a man who had managed to visit his children only three times in six months.

Frank asked more questions, filling in Teresa's background. She and Ward had both been students at Santa Cruz when they met, Ward working on his doctorate and Teresa majoring in psychology. The year their first child was born Ward had been offered a part-time position at Western Oregon State. The family had moved to Longmont. The year after their second child was born they had divorced, and Teresa had gone back to school for a master's degree in counseling. Six months ago she had started a part-time job with Children's Services.

"You knew that Tomasovic was speaking in Coffee Creek last night?"

She nodded. "It was in the paper."

"You didn't go?"

"Mr. Carver, I've heard that speech a hundred times."

"What did you do last night?"

"Stayed home with the kids. We ate dinner, made a batch of cookies, and then it was time for bed."

"Any visitors, phone calls?"

"Yes, Rose Marie called."

She glanced at the woman in the corner, who looked up and nodded. "I called about eight. I needed a phone number for the support group."

"We belong to a support group for single mothers," Teresa explained.

"You didn't go out after that?"

"Not with two little kids asleep in the house." She cocked her head and looked at him. "You're wondering if I drove down there, aren't you? I suppose that's your job, to wonder about those things. You might talk to Mrs. Schmidt, in the red house across the street. She'll tell you that my car was in the driveway all night."

Frank nodded. He would, in fact, talk to Mrs. Schmidt. He had every reason to believe Teresa was telling the truth, but at this stage he needed verified facts, as many of them as he could find. Facts like where anyone connected to Ward Tomasovic had been at eleven o'clock last night.

There was a pause. He drew it out, giving Ginny a chance to catch up with her notes while he considered where to go next. Teresa had relaxed a little—she was no longer perched on the edge of her chair, and some color had come back into her cheeks. Now was the time to get personal.

"You divorced your husband two years ago. Why?"

She glanced up, her face flushing brighter. "I changed, Mr. Carver, and Ward didn't. Did you meet him?"

Frank shook his head, but Ginny caught her eye and nodded. Teresa turned to include her in the conversation.

"You must have noticed how...how attractive he was. I was only twenty when I met Ward. I was naive, I guess, and romantic—he just overwhelmed me. He's ten years older, you know." She paused. "Was ten years older."

Ginny glanced at Frank, who nodded to give her the go-ahead. "He must have been active in the environmental movement even then," she said.

"Oh, yes. He and Alan Breckenridge practically founded the Santa Cruz EarthAction chapter. That was part of my romanticism—falling in love with a man who was literally going to save the world."

"Is that what you mean, when you say he didn't change?" Ginny asked.

She nodded. "That was one commitment he never broke."

"There were some, though, that he did?" Ginny asked gently.

"A lot of them. When there was a conflict, Ward always put his work first. Well, with two children, there were always conflicts. Sometimes we hardly saw him for days at a time. His position at the university was half-time, a contract that had to be renewed every year. We lived in a dump, with bad wiring and no yard. Those things didn't matter when I was twenty-two and out to save the whales and every other living thing, but they started to matter when you have kids."

She came to an abrupt stop. "I'm sorry." She shook her head and two tears spilled down her cheeks. Rose Marie got up, laid the sleeping baby on a cushion, and came to stand behind Teresa's chair, lightly rubbing her shoulders.

The way Meg Nugent had rubbed Ginny's shoulders. Teresa was going through hell, Ginny knew that, but suddenly she envied her. It felt like years since that kind of friendly, caring touch had been a part of her life. She had friends in Galina, good friends, and a wonderful sister-in-law, but now that Rebecca had passed the age of easy cuddles she could go for weeks with nothing more than a good-night peck on the cheek.

They waited, giving Teresa a chance to calm down. Frank glanced around the living room. A tiny dining area and part of the kitchen showed through an arched opening. Signs of children were everywhere; drawings plastered the refrigerator door and bins of toys were neatly stacked in a corner, beside a child-sized table and chairs. It was all neater and more organized than he remembered his own home when the girls had been little. The living room had a skylight and a small bay window filled with hanging plants. It was a small house, but nice. Nicer, in fact, than Teresa Tomasovic could probably afford.

She had stopped crying and was watching him, a little wary, ready for more questions. Rose Marie had returned to her baby.

"This is a nice place," Frank said. "Do you rent?"

"No, I bought it after the divorce."

Frank looked at her curiously. "How did you manage that?"

"It wasn't easy."

"Did Ward pay child support?"

"Oh, yes. After he went to Washington he started making double payments. Trying to make up for everything, I guess."

"And that was enough to buy a house?"

She stared at him for a moment, and then said flatly, "Ellen gave us the money."

"Ward's mother?"

Teresa nodded. "Ellen Jacobson. She remarried a few years ago."

"I see. Did she help you out when you were married?"

"Yes, more than once. God knows we always needed it. I was surprised when she offered to make the down payment, though. It was a lot of money."

"When was this, exactly?"

"Well, let me see." Teresa closed her eyes for a moment. "We bought the place a year ago, and I spent three months looking. So the spring of last year, I guess."

"You must be on good terms with your ex-mother-in-law."

She smiled. "We visit her a lot. The kids call her Nonny."

Frank got Ellen Jacobson's address and phone number, then went on with his questions. "What did she think about the divorce?"

"She was furious with Ward. Said he was acting like his father, and that she had raised him better than that." Teresa paused. "You see, Ward fell in love with someone else." She paused again. Making that admission had cost her something. "I couldn't figure out what she meant. I never met Nick Tomasovic—he died before Ward and I were married—but that's the only time Ellen's ever said anything against him. I got the impression they were pretty happy."

"Back up a minute," Frank said. "I thought you said you got a divorce because you had changed and he hadn't."

She gave a shrug. "It was all the same thing."

"Not quite," said Frank dryly.

"Human relationships are never simple, Mr. Carver. You must notice that, in your line of work."

Touché. Teresa Tomasovic wasn't as vulnerable as she looked. He felt better about asking his next question.

"Who did Ward fall in love with?"

She hesitated. "Do we have to talk about this?"

Rose Marie got up and came to stand behind Teresa's chair again. "Her husband just died," she said.

"Her ex-husband," said Frank shortly. "I'm trying to find out who killed him." He had a pretty good idea of who the woman had been, but he wanted Teresa's reactions.

She sighed. "Okay, I can see your point. I think it was Rachel Davis. I met her once or twice. Ward didn't talk about her, but that's what I heard."

Frank nodded. There was no intensity, no sign of suppressed hostility. Whatever else Teresa Tomasovic may have felt about her ex-husband, she had stopped loving him.

He went back to an earlier comment. "So your mother-in-law was on your side?"

"I don't like to see it as taking sides. Ellen has always been sympathetic. Even when I wouldn't take Ward back."

"He wanted to try again?"

She nodded. "Just before he left for Washington. He asked me to go with him."

"Why didn't you?"

"I just couldn't, even though the kids would be with their dad again. I could never trust him, you know?"

"I know," Frank said. He would have said it in any case, but in fact he meant it. When Minnie had asked for a divorce ten years ago, it hadn't been just so she could sell real estate. There had been another man, eight years her junior. He hadn't known. He'd been living with the woman all that time, and when she fell in love with someone else, he hadn't noticed. He still thought she'd made a fool of herself, but Minnie seemed happy enough. Happier than she had been with him, those last few years.

He wanted to learn more about Ward's background. He already knew that Tomasovic and Alan Breckenridge had been involved with EarthAction ten years earlier, when they were both students at Santa Cruz. He began asking Teresa about those days.

"Alan could be a lot of fun," she said, "but you never knew when something would set him off. He hated any kind of authority—in fact, he dropped out of school rather than take a required course he objected to. He was always more radical than Ward."

"Tomasovic finally left EarthAction, didn't he?"

Teresa nodded. "He couldn't support the kinds of things Alan and some of the others were doing. Ward believed in nonviolent civil disobedience. He wouldn't go along with actions that might hurt people. That," she added quietly, "was one thing I always respected him for."

Implying a loss of respect in how many other ways? Ginny would have liked to ask her, wanted to know more about the slow decline of her marriage, her disillusionment with Ward's charisma. Personal questions. She felt a personal connection with Teresa Tomasovic. They might have had friends in common, might have spent an hour over coffee, sharing their experiences with men, and children, and life.

Frank, though, was heading in a different direction. "Breckenridge disagreed with a nonviolent approach?"

"Not at first. But then—when was it? Soon after we were married Alan took a trip to the Southwest. He was different when he got back. He'd always been impatient, and daring, and quick-tempered, but now he couldn't seem to wait for anything. He got angry at Ward for filing court appeals, told him it was a waste of time. They had some pretty intense arguments. Then Alan disappeared. We didn't see him for a couple of years."

"When would that have been?"

Teresa thought for a moment. "About four years ago. We'd moved to Longmont when he turned up again."

"Where had he been?"

"I don't know. He might have told Ward, but not me."

Frank nodded. Breckenridge's file had a lot of gaps, but it was clear that he had been up to no good during those two years. A couple of arrests, one on a Colorado trespassing charge that was later dropped, one for interfering with an officer in New Mexico. He had served two weeks. The undocumented activities attributed to him include tree-spiking, demolishing heavy equipment, and "de-surveying" a planned logging road. He had become something of a legend within EarthAction.

"What kind of terms were Breckenridge and your husband on at that time?"

"I can't really say. Alan came to the house a few times. He seemed happier than I'd seen him in years. I was carrying Chad then—sort of a last-ditch effort to keep our marriage together. It wasn't an easy pregnancy. There were problems, and most of my energy was going to that. I didn't pay a lot of attention."

"Do you have any idea of Breckenridge's reaction to Ward taking the job in Washington?"

She looked up. "Yes, I do. Alan called and left a message on my answering machine. He evidently knew about Ward's job, but didn't know that we'd split up. It was... hateful. I have one of those machines that keep running as long as the caller talks. Alan talked for twenty minutes."

"About Ward's job?"

"And Rachel Davis. I guess they'd been living together, before she met Ward. She must have dumped him pretty hard." Teresa paused. "I knew, when I filed for divorce, that Ward was seeing someone else. It wasn't until that phone call that I knew who."

IT WAS ALMOST DARK when they left Teresa Tomasovic's house. Lights were on at Mrs. Schmidt's across the street, so they went over. She verified that Teresa had been home the night before. "I saw her pull the curtains in that front bedroom about, oh, ten o'clock. That's when she usually goes to bed."

"It couldn't have been a babysitter?" Frank asked.

"No, it was Teresa. Her car stayed right there in the driveway all night." Mrs. Schmidt shook her head. "Terrible thing, him getting shot like that. Can't say I agreed with him—my husband worked twenty years at the Willamette mill—but that's no cause to up and shoot someone."

Ginny was so tired she stumbled as they crossed the street. When they got to her truck she leaned against it with a sigh. "We've still got reports to write."

"Are you up for it? We're both pretty bushed."

"It's not quite eight. We can do it in an hour, and then they'll be done."

They worked in Frank's office, him on the typewriter and Ginny using the new PC. Forty-five minutes later Frank laid a copy of the day's report on Hunsaker's desk, where he would see it first thing in the morning.

When he got back to his office, Ginny was asleep at his desk. He gently shook her awake.

"Are you still driving out to Galina tonight?"

"Forty minutes there, pick up my car, and another twenty minutes to get home." Her voice was flat and groggy with exhaustion. "Guess I better get going."

"Ginny."

She stopped.

"It's past nine o'clock. We need to hit Coffee Creek early tomorrow." He seemed to be having trouble putting his words together. Probably as wiped out as she was. "Are they expecting you home tonight?"

"No, I told Susie I might not get back till Sunday."

"Look, why don't you just stay at my place? I've got an extra bedroom, even has a bed. Save you a lot of driving. You're in no shape to drive, anyway."

Her fatigued brain moved slowly, figuring it out. She could call home, talk to Susie and Rebecca, tell them she might be gone for a few more days. She had a clean change of clothes in her pack, along with shampoo, a tooth-brush—everything she needed, really. And she wouldn't have to drive.

That clinched it. Frank was right. She couldn't stay awake for another hour. She nodded.

"Good." He smiled. "Are you hungry?"

She shook her head. "Too tired."

"Okay, then. Let's go home."

SHE WOKE UP in the middle of the night from a dream of darkness and overwhelming space. She lay there for a moment, not quite sure where she was. Her own house was full of familiar nighttime noises—the humming refrigerator, the ticking of the dining room clock that had been a wedding gift from Dale's mother. Frank's apartment was silent. He lived in a town house on the new west side of Longmont, part of a complex tucked away among trees at the top of a gentle hill. She was in the smaller of the two sparsely fur-nished bedrooms. A light breeze came through the open window.

She shivered and tucked her legs up, trying to warm her-self. The bed had enough blankets for a mild June night, but the dream had left her feeling cold. Cold and lonely, with the memory of a dark land under a vast, starless sky. If she'd been at home, she might have gotten out of bed and gone upstairs to Rebecca's room. Rebecca was a fine sleeper, her ten-year-old mind apparently untouched by night anxieties. Sometimes Ginny sat by her bed, watching her sleep. If she was still wakeful after that she might warm some milk and drink it at the kitchen table. That usually did the trick.

Milk wasn't what she wanted tonight, though. She wanted to touch someone, to feel another body close to hers.

What would Frank think if she climbed into his bed? What did she want him to think?

She sat up and swung her legs over the side. The carpet was soft under her feet. She had on one of Frank's pajama tops—it came almost to her knees. The apartment was dark, but she managed to make it to his room without tripping over anything. Frank was sleeping on his back, stretched out on one side of the double bed.

That was a funny thing about double beds. She slept on one side of hers, too, though Dale had been dead for over five years. She still thought of the other half as his.

Frank came awake as soon as she touched the mattress. "Ginny?" His voice was low, surprised.

She sat on the edge of the bed. "Hm."

He lifted the covers. She slipped underneath, and then his arms were around her, pulling her into the warmth of his body. It felt like coming home.

They lay for a while without speaking. She dozed off, waking once or twice just to enjoy the closeness, the feel of his arms around her. She thought he fell back asleep, too, but when she moved to stretch her legs she felt him tense. He was probably as unused to sleeping with someone as she was.

His lips brushed across her forehead. "Do you want to make love?" he murmured.

She wasn't sure. She told him so.

"It can wait," he said. "We have lots of time."

He kissed her hair. Just before she fell asleep again she realized that *he* wasn't wearing pajamas at all.

TEN

SHE WOKE UP the next morning to the smell of coffee. Frank was gone, though his side of the bed was still warm. She opened her eyes. The drapes had been pulled back to reveal a square of sunny blue sky, but the room itself was cool and dim. From the bathroom came the sound of showering. Six a.m.

She snuggled back into the covers. When she woke up again Frank was sitting on the bed, dressed, smiling at her.

"Hey, Deputy, you want a shower?"

She pushed herself up. The pajama top, already loose, slipped down on one shoulder. It had been years since she had made a serious attempt at seducing a man. She smiled back.

Their eyes met and held. Frank's breath came raggedly. She reached out and ran her hand along his cheek, down the side of his neck. He gave a little gasp, then pressed her face against the light cotton of his shirt, burying his hand in her hair.

A moment later he released her. They looked steadily into each other's eyes. Finally Frank sighed. "What do you think you're up to?"

"You can't tell?"

He chuckled. "Ms. Trask, we are on duty, and we are leaving here in half an hour. Scrambled eggs for breakfast."

She leaned forward and kissed him on the cheek. "Okay, if you insist." She practically waltzed into the shower. She couldn't remember the last time she had felt so damn happy.

DEBBIE KURTZ and her family lived about two miles out of Coffee Creek, in a large and obviously expensive house. Three vehicles were parked in the driveway: a new passenger van, a beat-up truck, and Debbie's Blazer. The family, presumably, was at home.

They rang the bell. A young girl with crimped blond hair and china-blue eyes opened the door.

"Amanda Kurtz?" Frank asked.

She gave a little gasp. "How did you know?"

Frank smiled. "We talked on the phone yesterday. Is your father home?"

She nodded and gestured for them to come inside. "Dad!" she called out. "Someone's here."

They were in a little foyer, empty except for a small table holding a bouquet of garden flowers. Sounds came from within—dishwasher noises in the kitchen, a radio, a blow-dryer running somewhere upstairs. Amanda waited with them, one ear cocked toward the living room. If she had been a little older, and if her father had not been about to walk in, Frank would have started grilling her about her mother's whereabouts on Friday night. He would wait, though, until he had parental permission. The seconds passed in awkward silence. Finally they heard footsteps. Amanda gave them a relieved smile. "Here he comes."

Ed Kurtz was a big man, over six feet, with heavy shoulders and a thick, muscular neck. His hair, black going gray, was cropped into a crew cut that had been out of style so long it was almost back in again. He peered at them from under dark, bushy eyebrows—an assessing look, not hostile, but not friendly, either.

Frank introduced himself and Ginny.

Ed looked skeptical. "Didn't know the Forest Service had cops."

He produced his badge.

Ed studied it, then looked up. "You the guy talked to my wife yesterday?"

"Yes. I need to verify her movements on Friday night, and ask a few more questions."

"Okay. You might as well come in. Mandy, go tell your mom this Carver guy's here. The two of you finish getting ready. We're still leaving in twenty minutes."

Amanda took off up the stairs. "Church," Ed Kurtz explained as he led them into the living room. "Expect we're going to hear more about Ward—the prodigal son, most likely."

Frank revised his initial impression of Ed Kurtz. He was shrewder than he looked, and capable of sarcasm.

Ed gestured for them to sit on the couch, while he took an overstuffed chair on the other side of the coffee table. "Now, what can I do for you?"

Ed's use of Tomasovic's first name gave Frank a clue. "Did you grow up in Coffee Creek?"

Ed nodded. "Lived in the valley all my life."

"You knew Tomasovic, then?"

"Sure, I knew Ward. He was a couple years older, so we were never in the same class in school, but I knew who he was. Good runner. A great runner, in fact."

"I heard he took State in track. Heard a couple other things, too."

"Yeah?" Ed asked warily.

"There was some kind of accident, when Ward was sixteen? A kid drowned?"

Ed Kurtz looked relieved. "The Ney kid. Ward took him out in his dad's drift boat. Kid fell overboard, river was fast and high, he never had a chance."

"Tomasovic wasn't at fault?"

"Hell, no. It was an accident, pure and simple."

Frank paused. "I've heard about him and your wife, too."

Ed's eyes grew hard. "I expected that. Some people in town just can't let go, once they get their teeth into a piece of gossip."

Gossip was exactly what Frank wanted, but it seemed unlikely he would get it from Ed Kurtz. "It puts your wife in a difficult position. She's known to have had a relationship with the victim in the past—a close relationship—and now she can't adequately account for her whereabouts at the time he died."

Ed stared at Frank, then ignored the first half of his statement. "Where does she say she was?"

"Driving around."

"Then that's what she was doing."

"Let's just go over Friday night. You and your wife and daughter went to hear Tomasovic."

"Yeah. Kevin had a date in Longmont, so he didn't come."

"Kevin is?"

"Our boy. Starting at Western this fall."

"That his pickup outside?"

Ed nodded. Frank led him through an account of the family's movements on Friday night, which tallied with Debbie's version. They had arrived home shortly after ten p.m. Debbie had gone upstairs for a few minutes, while Ed made a sandwich. About ten-fifteen she had gone out for a drive.

"Why?" Frank asked.

Ed shrugged. "Felt restless, I guess."

"You didn't think this was unusual, going for a drive alone at night?"

"I go for a drive sometimes, when I start feeling cooped up. There's not a hell of a lot to do in Coffee Creek after dark. Especially if you're not a drinking man."

"So it wasn't out of the ordinary for your wife to take off for a few hours?"

"She's done it before."

"You didn't think that perhaps she was meeting Tomasovic?"

"Dammit, no, I didn't think that." Ed Kurtz clenched his fist. His fingernails were grimed, his knuckles permanently creased with black. "Half the town probably does, if you've been snooping around with questions like this, but I trust my wife. It might have upset her a bit, seeing Ward again, but she sure as hell didn't have any rendezvous with him. And she sure didn't shoot him, either."

"What time did she get back home?"

"Twelve-thirty. I was awake."

"Were you worried about her?"

"A little, sure I was." He fell silent, his eyes lowered, studying the coffee table. After a moment he looked up. "I want to make one thing clear, Carver. Debbie was a virgin when we started going together. I don't care what anyone else says. Who's going to know better than me?"

It was not what Frank had expected to hear, and it posed a whole new set of questions—questions he doubted Ed Kurtz would willingly answer. After a pause he returned to Friday night. Ed claimed that he and Amanda had not left the house after arriving home. Andy Zellers, Debbie's brother, had called about ten-thirty.

"What for?" Frank asked.

"He was looking for Charlie. Something about the Burnt Meadows unit—said it was urgent." Ed shrugged. "I just do my job. The family doesn't talk to me much about management."

"What is your job, exactly?"

"Head mechanic. Someone's got to keep all that machinery running." Footsteps shuffled on the carpet outside the living room. Ed glanced at his watch. "Time for us to go."

Frank stood up as Debbie and Amanda came in. "I appreciate your time, Ed. We'd like to talk to your daughter for just a moment."

"Alone?"

"I'd prefer that. I just have a few questions."

Ed Kurtz glanced at his wife. Neither of them looked happy about it, but they agreed. A few minutes later Frank and Ginny were talking to Amanda on the front porch, under the watchful eyes of her parents, who waited in the van.

"This must be pretty exciting," Frank suggested, "having your mom's old boyfriend show up."

Amanda's eyes lit up. "It's like one of those romantic novels."

"Is that why you had to get right on the phone the other night, as soon as you got home?"

She giggled. She had, in fact, called her best friend to discuss every detail of Ward Tomasovic's appearance. "He was really cute. I loved his beard."

No apparent reaction to his death. Had the family even discussed it? There was no one, Frank mused, as innocently self-centered as a spoiled and pretty young girl.

"How long were you on the phone?"

"Fifteen minutes. I have a time limit."

"And then your uncle called. Did you answer the phone?"

She nodded. "He wanted Grandpa."

"Did your dad talk to him?"

"No, I just left a note in the kitchen saying he'd called. Mom and Dad make me write notes, too."

"Where was your father?"

She shrugged. "Downstairs, I guess. I could hear the television."

"Then what did you do?"

"I went to bed."

"Without saying good night to your dad?"

Amanda gave him a look.

"Okay, you went to bed." He paused. "So you thought Ward Tomasovic was pretty cute, huh?"

"Oh yes," Amanda gushed. "A lot better looking than Dad."

"I wonder why your mother didn't marry him."

She looked surprised. "Didn't you know? Grandpa broke them up. Mom was only sixteen, and everyone was afraid they'd elope. Grandpa sent her on a trip to Europe. When she got back, Ward was gone."

"I see. Did your mom tell you this?"

"Oh, no. My sister did. We just found out last year. I mean, we'd heard stuff, but we didn't put it all together."

Ginny had been doing some calculations in her head. "How many kids in your family?" she asked.

"Three. Becky, Kevin, and me."

"How old is Becky?"

"Twenty-two. She's in England this summer. I hope I get to do something like that when I'm in college."

From the van came an impatient tap on the horn. Amanda looked at them questioningly.

Frank glanced at Ginny, who nodded that she was done. "You'd better go," he said.

Amanda climbed in behind her parents. Ed Kurtz didn't leave immediately, though. He waited until Frank and Ginny got their truck started, then followed them down the driveway, speeding up to pass only when they were completely clear of his property.

When they were gone, Frank pulled over to the side of the road to call Bowers on the mobile phone. The LEO answered on the second ring, his voice groggy with sleep. Vince Paley, the Sitkum law enforcement officer, had relieved him and Kenny McKinney at about nine o'clock the night before. Vince had called an hour ago to report that things were quiet at the Burnt Meadows sale, with about twenty protesters present, most of them eating breakfast. Bowers planned to join him up there before noon.

"We've got another errand to run," Frank said. "I'll swing by Burnt Meadows early this afternoon, see how things look. You heard from Bricca?"

"Christ, yes. Why did you have to sic him on me?"

He laughed. "If you're nice to the ranger he might put you up for a merit award. Well, you better catch up on your beauty sleep."

Bowers snorted. "Fat chance. By the way, I talked to Larkin last night. He didn't come up with anything from the neighbors. You might want to give him a ring."

Deputy Larkin wasn't the only person Frank needed to call. He replaced the receiver, wondering how long he could put Hunsaker off. During their conversation yesterday afternoon the forest supervisor had requested twice-daily briefings on both the homicide investigation and Burnt Meadows. He was no doubt expecting one of those briefings within the next hour, and he wasn't going to be satisfied with Frank's statement that nothing of importance had happened.

During his twenty years with the Seattle police, Frank had worked for a number of men—and one woman—with a variety of supervisory styles. The one thing they had in common, though, was that they were all career cops. They all at least knew what Frank was *supposed* to be up to. Larry Hunsaker, who had a degree in forestry and another in administration, knew zip about law enforcement. During his year on the Neskanie, Frank had learned that his new boss also hated to delegate responsibility and took an inordinate interest in the details of Frank's job. It was not a happy combination.

He owed Hunsaker one phone call a day, Frank decided. If the supervisor got too antsy, he could grill Tony Bricca about Burnt Meadows. Maybe that would keep both of them happy.

He turned to look at Ginny. "You've been pretty quiet over there."

"I've been counting."

He raised an eyebrow.

"Look, Debbie Kurtz is thirty-eight."

"How do you figure that?"

"Because she was sixteen when she broke up with Tomasovic. He left Coffee Creek right afterwards. His press releases say that was the year after he finished high school, so he would have been eighteen. Two years older than Debbie. He was forty when he died, so Debbie must be thirty-eight."

"Okay, you can add and subtract. Where does that get us?"

"Her oldest child is twenty-two. Debbie couldn't have been more than sixteen when that child was born."

"You think her first kid might be Tomasovic's?"

"No, I don't, because Ed Kurtz obviously doesn't think so. He can probably add, too. But look, she must have married Ed within a year of breaking up with Ward."

"Love on the rebound?"

Ginny shook her head. "Charlie Zellers broke them up. No sixteen-year-old is going to stop being in love with someone—especially someone like Ward Tomasovic—just because her father says no. That's likely to make her more determined."

"Probably why Charlie shipped her off to Europe."

"Right. Then she comes home and immediately falls in love with Ed Kurtz? After Tomasovic? No way."

"I'll grant that Ed isn't real exciting, but Debbie seems satisfied."

Ginny shook her head. "You heard Amanda. 'Way better looking than Dad.' Debbie probably sounded just like her, at that age. Ward was older, a track star." She looked up. "I met him, Frank. He was a damned attractive man. I'd bet money that Debbie was still in love with him, all these years later."

"You think she went to meet him Friday night?"

"I do. And he didn't show."

"Charlie was on the right track, then, writing that note. I wonder if he did it to prevent their meeting. It wouldn't surprise me. Charlie still treats her like a little girl."

"And how does she respond?"

"Like a little girl." He paused. "I still don't see where it gets us, though."

"Maybe nowhere. But look, why didn't Charlie want his daughter mixed up with Tomasovic?"

"Wrong side of the tracks," said Frank promptly. "Twenty-two years ago the Zellerses were the big honchos in Coffee Creek, just like they are now, and Tomasovic's dad was a backwoods gyppo logger."

"Yeah, that's what I'd been thinking. But look at Ed Kurtz. Which side of the tracks did he come from?"

"Good point."

"Why would Charlie reject a young man as promising as Ward—you've got to admit, Frank, he must have been promising—and then settle for Ed Kurtz?"

JUST BEFORE THE JACKSON River bridge Frank turned off onto a short street that could have been lifted from any landscaped suburb in America.

"We're looking for a young man who likes to fish," he said, peering at the names on the mailboxes. The Sondheims' was mounted on a post beside Charlie Zellers's. He parked, hoping that Eric's family was not as regular in its Sunday devotions as the Kurtzes.

Mrs. Sondheim answered the door. She looked puzzled at Frank's request, but invited them in. They waited in a living room comfortably strewn with the Sunday paper while she went upstairs to track down her offspring.

Eric came in a few moments later, followed by his father. It took only one glance to see where the boy got his fair skin and white-blond hair.

"Aaron Sondheim," the man said, offering his hand. "You want to ask my son a few questions?"

Frank explained their business. "We understand that Eric was running an errand for your neighbor, Charlie Zellers, and may have seen the victim that evening."

Aaron Sondheim nodded. "Eric, tell the man whatever he wants to know."

Frank turned to Eric with interest. Kids of this age, he had found, could often make excellent witnesses. Free of adult motives and prejudices, they were likely to describe events and objects just as they appeared. Besides, he liked the kid already.

"Mr. Zellers says he gave you a note to deliver on Friday afternoon."

Eric nodded.

"What time was that?" Frank led him through the circumstances surrounding the note. Charlie had given it to him about seven o'clock, with instructions to deliver it to Ward Tomasovic at the high school. Charlie had paid him two dollars, and cautioned him not to tell anyone what he was doing.

"And did you tell anyone?"

"No, sir. Dad didn't even know until now."

Frank glanced at Aaron Sondheim, who nodded. "Charlie often pays Eric to do odd jobs."

Mrs. Sondheim came in with a coffeepot and a tray of mugs. She cleared a place on the coffee table and began pouring, while Frank watched with a mixture of dismay and relief. They really didn't have time—it was already past ten-thirty. On the other hand, though he would have given one of his arms just then for a cigarette, coffee would do. Besides, it was a pleasure to interview people who seemed genuinely helpful. He glanced at Ginny. She handed him a mug full of coffee.

She wouldn't have done that yesterday. He smiled to himself. It had been a long time since a woman had pre-empted these minor decisions for him. He still liked it.

"So you got to the school a little after seven?"

"Yes, sir. There were a lot of people, but Charlie had told me that Mr. Tomasovic would be backstage. So I went back there and asked for him."

"Who did you ask?"

"Mrs. Wallace. She was the only person I really knew. I had her for fourth grade."

That would be Gayle Wallace, and it made sense that she would be there. "Did you find Mr. Tomasovic?"

"No. Mrs. Wallace said he had asked to be left alone for a few minutes before his talk. Charlie told me not to tell anyone about the note, so I didn't know what to do. Then I saw the cop."

"The cop?"

"The Forest Service cop, the new guy who just moved here a few months ago."

"Bruce Bowers?"

"Yeah, that's his name. He came to our school just before summer vacation. Anyhow, I gave the note to him."

"But if Charlie told you—"

"I know," Eric interrupted. "But what could I do? If I took the note back to Charlie, the guy wouldn't get it before his talk. Mr. Bowers said he'd see he got it in time."

Frank shook his head. One of his own officers had inadvertently helped put the victim in the wrong place at the wrong time. He would check with Bowers. Frank generally did not share all the developments in a case with one person—Bruce didn't know about the note they had found in Tomasovic's jeans. He probably hadn't thought twice about it since Friday night.

"Tell me more about this note," he said. "Was it folded up, in an envelope, what?"

"It was in an envelope, one of those plain white ones." Eric got up, went to a desk near the window, and came back with a regular letter envelope. "Like this, only sealed shut."

"Any writing on the outside?"

Eric shook his head. "Just a plain envelope." He looked worried. "I didn't do anything wrong, did I? I heard Mr. Tomasovic talk, and I thought he was right on. It's just awful that someone killed him."

"It is awful," Frank agreed. "And no, you didn't do anything wrong. In fact, the information you've given us will be a big help."

Eric flushed and glanced at his father, who nodded his approval. Frank finished his coffee. The nicotine urge was fading, but still hard to ignore. He set his cup down and asked a question that had rarely seemed relevant in Seattle, but had become standard in the predominantly rural area that now made up his beat.

"Did you folks grow up around here?"

"Oh, no." Aaron Sondheim shook his head. "We're from California. Moved up about three years ago. I'm an accountant for Zellers Wood Products." He nodded at his wife. "Melanie teaches half-time in Eugene."

Melanie Sondheim set her own cup down and looked at Frank. "Mr. Carver, I want you to know that not everyone in Coffee Creek hated Ward Tomasovic. We supported what he was trying to do, even though Aaron works at the mill. We're not all a bunch of timber beasts."

"Tomasovic was right," Aaron Sondheim added, spreading his hands. "The timber companies, including Zellers, have been overcutting for years. We're going to run out of trees, even without the spotted owl."

"A lot of people around here don't want to face reality," added Melanie. It was clear that this was an old discussion, one they had had before.

"You said not everyone hated him," Frank observed. "That sounds like a lot of people did."

Aaron nodded. "I'm afraid so."

"There's been talk," said Melanie.

"Wild talk," Aaron agreed. "A few meetings, too, though we haven't gone to any."

"Threats?" Frank asked.

The Sondheims looked at each other over the head of their son.

"Eric," Melanie said.

"Aw, Mom, please? It's not like I don't know somebody killed him."

"That's true," Aaron said quietly. He got up, went out of the room for a moment, and came back with a sheet of paper.

Frank and Ginny moved closer to get a good look. It was a copy of the letter—poster was perhaps a better word—the

Forest Service had received earlier in the week. Tomasovic's features looked up at them from the shredded photo.

"This was on the bulletin board at work," Aaron said. "I
brought it home to show Melanie."

"May I keep it?" Frank asked.

"Sure, if you think it will help."

He set it down on the table, careful to touch it by the
edges only. "Where was this bulletin board?"

"The employee lounge in the main office. There must be
a dozen bulletin boards around the mill, in one place or another." He glanced at the poster. "Probably a dozen of
those, too."

"Any idea where it came from?"

Aaron shook his head. "You know how things are.
Someone makes a copy of a joke or a cartoon, and suddenly it's everywhere. I first saw this one on Wednesday, I
guess. I brought it home on Friday."

The original had arrived at the Neskanie SO on Wednesday. The postmark had not been much help—all Coffee
Creek's mail was now postmarked in Eugene. It had probably been mailed on Monday.

Frank sent Ginny out to the truck for an evidence bag.
The chances of turning up a usable print were slight, but it
was worth a try. What he really wanted, though, was a professional opinion on whether or not this copy had been
taken directly from the original, or from another copy. Once
copies were made, anyone could make and post more copies—as Aaron Sondheim said, a joke or cartoon could suddenly show up everywhere. A copy of the original, though,
would have to come from the person who had created the
thing in the first place.

The photo in this one was reasonably clear. Frank thought
it was a copy of the original. If so, that narrowed the suspects down to someone connected with Zellers Wood Prod-

ucts. The suspects for the threatening letter. As for Tomasovic's murder—he was keeping an open mind.

He caught Ginny's eye and gave her a nod. It was time to pay a visit to Zellers's head faller.

ELEVEN

THEY LEFT THE HOUSE and walked back to the truck, taking their time. The day was perfect, warm enough for shirtsleeves but not too hot, with cotton-puff clouds pinned to the sky. The river was very close. Without a word they kept going, past the truck, toward the sound of rushing water.

They stopped at the edge of the bank. Water swirled below, where the river's channel narrowed beneath the bridge. Frank dropped his hand and let it hang awkwardly at his side. Ginny smiled to herself. She let her own hand brush his and, sure enough, his fingers curled around hers. She glanced quickly over her shoulder. The short street of houses was out of sight from this spot.

After a moment they looked at each other and smiled. Frank leaned over and kissed her on the forehead.

She closed her eyes. "Mmmmm."

This time he kissed her on the mouth.

He had worked with women before, had even had one as a partner for the last year before he left Seattle. Mary Rawlings her name was—thirty-six, plump, nice-looking. Married, with two teenage sons. She'd sent him a card last Christmas. He couldn't imagine kissing Mary Rawlings.

What he could imagine, all too vividly, was explaining to Hunsaker why he had to disqualify himself from the selection committee for the Galina LEO position. How long would the supervisor's secretary keep that one under her hat?

"Mmmm, indeed." He gave her hand a squeeze and reluctantly let it go. They continued to stare at the river. "Nice folks, the Sondheims," he finally said.

"Friendly, too." She stuck her hands into her pockets. This was nice, working together and starting to have these feelings. Not like dating. More like it had been with Dale. She had been nineteen when they married, and they had worked together from the start—getting Dale through his last year of school, the first job with the Forest Service, the promotion and transfer, buying the house, having a baby, building a life together. And then, suddenly, nothing.

Most of the time, now, it didn't hurt. Now there was just an emptiness, a great, yawning sadness. She was, she guessed, getting on with her life—wasn't that what widows were supposed to do? Her mother kept saying so, as did Alice, her sister-in-law. She glanced at Frank, suddenly aware that she wasn't seeing him from the outside anymore. She no longer saw a disgruntled, middle-aged cop with grizzled hair and crow's-feet embedded beside each eye. She saw a person, a man—a man she was starting to like very much.

They walked back in silence, enjoying the sun after the coolness of the river. They came up to the truck on the driver's side. Ginny opened the door and looked in, then glanced at Frank.

"How about if I drive?"

He raised an eyebrow. The Forest Service had unwritten rules about who drove and when. "You know where we're going?"

"Mel Barnhart's. Did Bruce give you directions?"

"Yeah, he did." He got into the passenger's side and buckled up.

She climbed in and got comfortable, running her fingers over the various knobs and levers. She was used to driving a different rig every day. GS-5's were low on the district totem pole and got stuck with the vehicles no one else wanted. Once she had taken a tanker out to do a fuels inventory. Frank's truck, though, had controls she had never seen before.

"Winch," he said helpfully, as her fingers grazed a switch. "Red and blue flashers, siren's over here. Spotlight."

She started up.

"Take a right at the corner." He settled back to enjoy the ride.

The truck handled nicely, a real pleasure after the tubs she usually drove. She turned out onto the highway and pushed it up to fifty-five. After a couple of minutes she glanced at Frank. His eyes were closed, but she didn't believe for a minute that he was asleep.

She knew the rules. The crew boss drives, or delegates the driving. Not just in the Forest Service, either. Look at any collection of people—a family, a group of friends. If you want to know who's top dog, look for the person with the keys. She cranked the window down another notch, letting the breeze run through her hair. She had never, in her five years as a dispatcher, asked for a turn at the wheel. She felt pretty damn good.

MEL BARNHART LIVED in a nice little two-story house just off the highway. A chain-link fence ran around the front yard, protecting a plot of grass and neatly tended beds of petunias and roses. Ginny pulled into the driveway. Beyond an uncluttered carport they could see a motor home and a small boat covered with tarps. The house was closed up, though, and no one appeared to be home.

"Tidy fellow," Frank observed.

"Well-paid, too," Ginny said dryly. It was a standing complaint among Forest Service employees that loggers

made two to three times what they did. They all knew that
logging was harder—and a lot more dangerous—but still, it
was something to complain about.

"Should have called first," Frank said. "At least we
know they're not out boating."

"Unless they've got two. What about the other guy, Ricky
Adams?"

"Yeah, let's give him a try." He pulled out his notebook
and checked the address. "Adams lives about three miles
farther down the highway. We turn off at Elk Creek. Left."

"Want to call first?"

"Naw, let's take him by surprise."

RICKY ADAMS was surprised, all right.

Zellers's sawyer was home, and he was not pleased to see
them. About five-foot-ten, slim, well-built, with dark hair
and neatly trimmed beard, he glared at them from the door
of his double-wide mobile home.

Surly, Ginny thought. That was definitely the word. She
stood a half step behind Frank on the wood deck. The trailer
was one of a group of four about a quarter of a mile up Elk
Creek. Kids had been playing in the ragged weeds of the
yard next door when they pulled up. Now they were clustered around the tailgate of Adams's shiny black four-wheel
drive, watching every move up on the deck.

Frank explained their business. "We need to ask you a
few questions, Mr. Adams."

"Ask away," Adams growled.

"May we come in?" Frank glanced back at the children.
"You seem to have a lot of neighbors."

Adams considered, backed away, and let them in. The
trailer was deep in gloom, all the curtains drawn. Adams
grabbed an ashtray off the coffee table on his way through

the living room, switched on a lamp, and headed back toward the kitchen.

Ginny almost tripped over a pair of shoes as she picked her way across the rug. She sat down. The couch was massive, a frame of dark wood filled with velvet cushions. Empty beer cans and drifts of ash littered the coffee table.

The coffee table. Frank caught her eye and glanced down. At first she didn't see it. The end of a joint, neatly clipped into a roach holder. Adams must have missed it when he cleared the ashtray.

Their host had disappeared into the bedroom. There was a murmur of voices, the distinctive sound of urine cascading into a toilet, flushing water.

Ginny swallowed unhappily.

"Hey," said Frank.

She looked up.

"Think about what you'd do if you were here by yourself."

She nodded. If she got the LEO job, she would sooner or later find herself alone in these situations. She got her notebook out—by way of looking professional—and started arranging her thoughts. What did they want to know? First, who was responsible for the threatening posters. Second, was there a connection between the posters and Tomasovic's death. Finally, she guessed that Frank would want to explore any knowledge—or guesses—Adams might have about who hated Tomasovic enough to kill him.

If she had been on her own, and had managed to get this far—she wasn't sure she would have asked to come in— she'd start by getting the guy comfortable. Get him talking about something that interested him. His job, for instance. She waited to see what Frank would do.

Adams came back and sat down. His beard glistened with water and his hair was combed. He looked marginally

friendlier. Frank eyed his man. He wished to hell that Mel
Barnhart had been home. From what Bowers said, Barnhart would have been easier to deal with. Always talk to the
least hostile witness first. But sometimes it didn't work out
that way.

Just to make things worse, Ricky Adams found a crumpled pack of cigarettes on the table, fished one out, and
lighted up. Frank watched him suck the flame in, take the
first draw, relax, and settle back in his chair. Every cell in his
body cried out for nicotine. The pack wasn't empty, and it
was all he could do to keep from reaching for it.

If I live through this, he promised himself, I'll... But what
could he promise? The only thing his body wanted was nicotine. Hell, if he lived through it, he'd buy a pack of cigarettes. One wouldn't kill him. And he sure as hell wasn't
going to bum a smoke from Ricky Adams.

Once they got started, the interview itself wasn't so bad.
Ricky Adams's truculence seemed to spring at least partly
from having his Sunday morning interrupted—it had been
a female voice in the bedroom. Frank left the roach untouched, in plain sight on the coffee table. Perhaps he
wouldn't need to use it.

First he asked Adams about his job. Like most people,
Adams enjoyed talking about his work. It was a good way
to establish rapport.

"It's all computers now," he said. "Used to be the sawyer was right out there with the logs, spitting sawdust. Not
anymore. I'm in a little room chock-full of computers. Glass
all around, so I can see the rig. It's all automated now. A lot
safer."

"Not as much fun, though?" Frank asked.

Adams chuckled. "I guess not. To tell the truth, I never
worked an old-style head-rig. Shit, I started pulling green

chain when I was eighteen, and I'm only thirty-two. By the time I got to be a sawyer, the computers had taken over.''

A woman came out of the bedroom and moved into the kitchen behind Adams. Her brown hair hung loose, brushing the shoulders of a pink-and-turquoise cowboy shirt. She got out a frying pan and opened the refrigerator.

"You making coffee, Irene?" Adams asked.

She didn't reply, but a moment later she started fiddling with the coffee maker on the counter. The machine burped a couple of times, then began to drip steadily. The smell of coffee drifted into the living room.

It was time. "About Tomasovic," Frank said. "We've heard there were some strong feelings against him at the mill."

"Damn right. Sucker deserved what he got."

"Were you in the gym Friday night?"

Adams shook his head. "Had a date with Irene."

"I'm surprised you missed Tomasovic's talk."

"You hear that, honey?"

Irene came into the living room with a mug of coffee. She handed it to Adams. "Ricky wouldn't dare stand me up," she said, without a hint of a smile. She went back into the kitchen.

"Where'd you go?" Frank asked.

"Let's see, we had oysters at Joey's—that's in Verona—then walked around Old Town for a bit. Ended up at the Lost Pelican. They had a band."

"You remember the band's name?"

Adams looked at him. "You're going to check this out, aren't you? Jimmy's Hot Licks."

"We check everything out," said Frank easily.

"We know the drummer," added Irene from the kitchen. "Allen Lonsdale. He'll tell you we were there."

"When did you leave?"

"After midnight."

"Twelve-thirty," said Irene. "We were back at my place by one."

Ginny took it all down, the drummer's name, Irene's address. Adams seemed cooperative enough. Irene was frying bacon in the kitchen. Ginny's stomach growled softly.

"The guys at Zellers talk much about Tomasovic?" Frank asked.

"Hell, yes. Wouldn't you talk about a guy who was doing everything he could to destroy your way of life?"

"That's how folks there see it? A threat to their way of life?"

"He wanted to lock up the woods, didn't he? Those EarthAction types won't be happy till every logger in the state is out of business. How are we going to make a living then? Coffee Creek would die with Zellers, and Zellers is going to die without logs."

"I thought Tomasovic was looking for a compromise, something that would keep the timber towns going."

"Naw, that's just a front. Those environmentalists are all in it together. They've got a hidden agenda—that's what Mel calls it. They just talk that way so people will think they're reasonable. They want to shut us down totally, for good."

"I can see how that would get people upset."

"Hell, yes. A lot of people got upset."

"Upset enough to make threats?"

Adams suddenly looked wary. "What kind of threats?"

"Well, we heard about some posters at Zellers." Frank took a sheet of paper from his pocket and unfolded it. "We even got a copy at the Forest Service."

"Yeah, I saw those."

"Mr. Adams, do you think the person responsible for that poster killed Tomasovic?"

"Hell, no! I mean, talking is one thing, but killing a man? No way."

Frank didn't reply. In the kitchen Irene lifted bacon out of the frying pan and set it down on a paper towel. She turned to watch them, one hand resting lightly on her hip.

"Listen, Ricky," Frank said. Adams lifted his head. "I'm a cop. My job is to find out who killed Tomasovic. You know, and I know, that the guy who did that poster might not have had anything to do with the shooting. It might be he wasn't even in Coffee Creek that night."

Adams nodded slowly. His eyes came to rest on the roach on the coffee table. His lips moved silently, but Frank didn't need to hear the words. Ricky Adams had just realized that he was caught between a rock and the deep blue sea.

"But because I'm a cop," Frank went on, "and because that's my job, I've got to know who did that poster. If the man's got an alibi, I just cross him off the list and go on with my investigation."

Adams had closed his eyes.

"Tell him," said Irene.

He sighed. "Okay. I made the poster."

"By yourself?"

"No, there was three or four other guys, too. We did it a couple weeks ago, when we heard Tomasovic was coming here."

"Who were the other guys?"

In the kitchen, Irene started cracking eggs into the frying pan. Ginny noted down the names as Adams gave them.

"They all work at Zellers," he said miserably. "Mel wasn't there, but he liked the idea. He's the one who made copies and handed them out."

"And the phone call to the Forest Service?" Frank asked.

"That was me. Had to borrow my neighbor's saw—mine wasn't running."

Ginny got the neighbor's name, too.

Frank asked a few more questions, clarifying times and places. Ricky answered them all, apparently relieved that the worst was over. The Coffee Creek antienvironmentalists sounded vocal but unorganized. Perhaps you didn't need organization when you were the vast majority.

"One more thing," Frank said. "Do you have any idea who might have killed Tomasovic?"

Adams closed his eyes again. He shook his head. "I'd be lying if I said I'm sorry he's dead. Most folks I know probably feel the same." He opened his eyes. "Some of the guys might go off half-cocked sometimes, get in a fight, do something stupid. Not kill a man, though, not like that, picking him off in the dark."

They left a few minutes later. The kids were gone, but they could hear a radio playing inside the neighbor's mobile home.

"Wish I had some of that bacon and eggs," Frank said.

"Me, too. Don't you keep anything to eat in that truck?"

Frank looked at her. "Tough guys don't keep snacks in the glove compartment."

"That's why you're so lean and mean, huh?"

"Okay for you, partner. You just march right up to that trailer and find out if Adams really borrowed a chain saw."

She marched. The neighbors, a couple in their twenties, verified Adams's story. He had borrowed the saw earlier that week and still had it.

"No problem, though," the man said. "I'm always borrowing stuff from Rick. Glad to do him the favor."

A few minutes later they were back in the truck, heading down Elk Creek toward the highway. "Do we really check *everything* out?" Ginny asked.

"As much as possible. Sometimes you just can't get verification. But remember—anything we do might end up in court. And with homicide, we're literally talking about life and death. Are you ready to swear in the witness stand that Ricky Adams was in Verona on Friday night?''

"It could take a lot of time, tracking down that drummer."

"Your time, I might add."

"I had a hunch you'd say that."

TWELVE

THIS TIME FRANK GOT the sandwiches. Pallid slices of ham, processed cheese, and too much mayonnaise on limp white bread.

He took a bite. "No mustard, either."

"At least it's food."

"Technically."

They were in Dispatch, where Ginny had found the makings for coffee. Frank spread out the front page of the Sunday paper he had picked up at the café. He had seen the cigarettes, too, but had managed to get out without buying any. One thing about making promises to yourself, you could break them later, when sanity returned.

"Here's what's keeping the sheriff busy," he said, pointing to a headline. "'Governor's son arrested in traffic fatality.'"

"They arrested him?"

"Didn't have much choice, with drugs in the vehicle." He glanced through the article. Shawn Michaels had told a reporter the coke must have been planted in his car. After that his lawyer got hold of him and shut him up. The governor had issued a statement expressing his condolences and deep regret. Sheriff Holt had his hands full, all right.

He crumpled his sandwich wrapper into a ball and tossed it at the wastebasket. "You get anywhere with that drummer?"

She shook her head. "It's a local band. I got home phone numbers for three of them. Lonsdale, the drummer, doesn't answer, but one of the other guys says he turns his phone off when he's sleeping. They had another gig last night, so that's probably what he's doing."

"Well, he's got to get up sooner or later."

"It's two-thirty now. He must sleep all day."

"Not a bad idea." Frank finished his coffee. "I'd better check in with the chief. See if you can raise Bowers—tell him we'll be up ASAP."

Hunsaker had left two messages on the law enforcement office's answering machine. Sheriff Holt had been calling, too. Frank tried the sheriff first, but he was out. It wouldn't surprise him if they spent the day returning each other's calls and leaving messages.

The forest supervisor, however, was in. "What's going on at Burnt Meadows?"

"We've got two people up there, twenty to thirty protesters. No activity reported."

"You haven't been up yourself?"

"Not yet." He was damned if he was going to explain himself. The silence lengthened. "We do have a homicide investigation."

"I thought that was almost wrapped up."

"No, sir, not that I'm aware of." He could have quoted Ed Kurtz. *And who would know better than me?*

"Look, Andy Zellers called this morning, pretty hot under the collar. He's been talking to his lawyer. I outlined the game plan for him."

Frank groaned inwardly. He hated game plans, and people who mistook themselves for coaches. "What plan is that?"

"I worked it out last night with Christina and Tom." Tom Laeger, the Neskanie's timber staff officer, would be the person the Zellerses dealt with most often. "Zellers plans to send a falling crew in first thing tomorrow. The Earth-

Actioners have already alerted the media, arranged to have cameras and reporters up there.''

"How did they know tomorrow's the day?"

"Andy Zellers would like an answer to that question, too. He thinks someone at the mill told them."

"So why not just wait another day? Or even a week? The timber's not going anywhere."

"Well, we suggested that, but Andy wasn't buying. The environmentalists are probably going to file a new appeal on the sale. Zellers wants to get it cut before some judge has a chance to slap on another injunction."

"So now we get to play referee."

"We want it peaceful, Frank. No arrests, if you can help it—and if you can't, call in the sheriff and let him make them."

"Wouldn't want the Forest Service to look like bad guys."

"That's right," said Hunsaker agreeably. "We'll let the EarthActioners get their pictures in the paper, maybe a couple shots of loggers leaving. Then we'll put a closure on the area."

It was the tactic advised by the Regional Office. After the reporters were gone, the protesters could be quietly arrested for violating the closure order.

"How long will it take to cut the unit?"

"Andy figures a couple weeks."

Longer to yard the logs out, but getting it down was what counted. "You realize EarthAction might not go along with all this?"

"What they want is publicity. We'll let them have plenty of that, then get them out of there."

Frank thought they wanted more than publicity. They wanted the trees left standing, the creeks unsullied by mud and debris, a halt to all old-growth logging. It was hard not to feel a certain sympathy. "What about Zellers?" he asked.

"They're willing to cooperate, for tomorrow at least."

"And after that all hell breaks loose."

"Not if we can stop it, Frank. That's your job."

He hung up and stared morosely out the window. It all sounded neat and tidy the way Hunsaker laid it out. The forest supervisor had never met Rachel Davis, though, or Alan Breckenridge. Somehow, Frank just didn't believe it was going to stay neat and tidy.

The telephone beeped. He picked it up.

"Andy Zellers is on his way to you," Ginny said. "Pretty ticked off."

An instant later the office door slammed against the wall and Andy Zellers stood before him. "Listen, Carver, what are you going to do about those assholes up at our timber sale?"

He was taller than Charlie, his father, but just as wiry and pugnacious. Sandy hair, blue eyes, and a scowl to make children run. Frank tipped back in his chair, taking his time. "Well, now, I thought you'd just been over that with Hunsaker."

"Yeah, yeah, I talked to your boss." Charlie Zellers had said something similar yesterday. Evidently the whole family was on close terms with the forest supervisor.

Another man edged into the office and stood beside Andy. About the same size, three-piece suit, thinning hair, glasses. "We've been in close contact with Mr. Hunsaker," he said. "We've always worked well together in the past."

"And who are you?" Frank inquired.

"Bob Blanchard, attorney representing Zellers Wood Products."

He reached into his vest for a business card, but Zellers brushed him aside. "Larry thinks those jerks are going to leave after they get their pictures in the paper. I don't believe it, and I want to know what you're going to do."

"Mr. Zellers, as long as your company has a legal right to log the sale—"

"Oh, yes, we certainly do," mumbled Bob Blanchard.

"—the Forest Service will make sure you have access."

"Hell, yes, we've got a legal right," Andy Zellers sputtered. "We bought the damn thing, and no bunch of nuts is going to keep us out!"

Frank hoped fervently that Andy Zellers was not going up with his fallers tomorrow morning. On the other hand, he wouldn't mind seeing Zellers mix it up with Rachel Davis. That would be quite a show.

"You bought the timber," he said shortly. "The land is still public. They've got a right to be there. When—and if—they break the law, we'll get a closure order and your crew can get to work."

"They're up there right now, breaking the law. Spiking trees, setting booby traps, God knows what. You better get them out, Carver."

He turned and stamped out, almost tripping over Bob Blanchard, who followed his employer down the hall without another word. A moment later the outside door slammed shut, the noise reverberating through the empty station.

Frank took a couple of deep breaths. When he looked up Ginny was standing in the doorway, a worried expression on her face.

"Did you catch all that?" he asked.

She nodded.

"Now there," he said quietly, "is a man it would be a pleasure to arrest."

"CHRIST, I'M NOT LOOKING forward to this." Frank turned the truck onto Fish Hatchery Road. They were on their way up to the Burnt Meadows sale, where Frank planned to touch base with Bowers and Kenny McKinney, the Coffee Creek employee assigned to help them with security. The afternoon was warm and still, without even a breeze to stir the dusty leaves of the alders lining the creek. To their right loomed Prairie Mountain, its summit hidden by the stands of firs marching across the lower slopes. The air coming through the open windows smelled of warm asphalt.

"I am," Ginny said. "At least we'll be outdoors. This is a nice truck, but I'm getting pretty tired of it."

"Yeah, you've got to say one thing for EarthAction. They choose some beautiful spots to break the law." He was quiet for a moment. "Trouble is, I'm starting to agree with them."

"You?" She turned to him. "Frank Our-Job-Is-to-Enforce-the-Laws-Not-Make-Them Carver?"

"Yeah, me."

She fell silent. Her own feelings were far from clear, but she had taken Frank as some kind of steady beacon. As long as he was sure they were doing the right thing, she could believe it, too. She wasn't prepared for moral qualms on his part. Suddenly she didn't want to hear them. She turned away and stared out the window, remembering the time Dale had cried.

They had been married about a year. Dale was struggling through his final courses in the forestry program. He was a good student, pulling steady Bs, but not an intellectual giant. She was doing pasteup for the local paper, making minimum wage. Money was tight. Dale's grant was running out. The night before an important final she walked into their studio apartment to find him sobbing on the bed.

She had never seen a man cry. She was only twenty, and she came unglued. She sat down and burst into tears herself. The evening ended with Dale holding her, kissing her hair, his own feelings pushed aside so that he could take care of hers.

Later, she regretted that night. She should have let him cry, let him lean on her. She could have been the strong one for once. But by then it was too late. She never saw him cry again.

She turned to look at Frank. He had slowed down behind a station wagon full of kids. It swung in at the fish hatchery, but he didn't speed up. The truck crept along at twenty miles an hour. A few more miles and they would turn onto the road up Prairie Mountain.

"Tell me," she said. "Tell me what you agree with."

He sighed. "Well, I agree that there's been too much logging. I'm not a professional forester, but hell, I'm not sure I need to be, to see that. Besides, a lot of the professionals are saying it, too."

The road left the creek and started to climb. They rounded a curve and found themselves confronted with a view. Frank pulled over at a turnout. Below them a plantation of young trees fell away down the steep slope. In a few more years they would form a wall of green along the road. Most views were temporary in the Coast Range, created by logging or fire, then gone as the hills greened up again.

"Look," Frank said. "You can see part of the Burnt Meadows sale from here. Tony Bricca says it's the last uncut drainage on this side of Prairie. That little creek down there still has a wild cutthroat run—the Forest Service's own fisheries biologist found fingerlings in it last spring. Gayle Wallace and her friends think it's spotted owl habitat. If it is, and the Forest Service lets Zellers log, then who's breaking the law?"

"They sent the owl callers in?" The Neskanie had started a spotted owl survey about a year ago. Wildlife technicians spent the night in the woods, imitating the bird's distinctive call. A reply counted as a hit. Sometimes they even saw one of the rare creatures.

"Yeah, last winter. They thought they had something, planned to go back up. Then the sale got pushed through."

"They wouldn't call on a sold sale."

He nodded. "Could open up a breach-of-contract suit. And who knows? Maybe there aren't any owls up there. And maybe if there are, they're on private land."

"It's not all Forest Service?" She was surprised. Most of the remaining stands of old growth were on public land.

"No, it's one of those checkerboards."

Checkerboard was a good description. Years ago the federal government had granted the railroads alternating square miles of land along their routes. Most had been sold to timber companies, some had returned to federal ownership, but the old pattern of private and public sections still showed on the maps.

They fell silent, gazing out at the wooded ridges and draws of the Burnt Meadows sale. The timber near the top, at the edge of the grassy bald that gave Prairie Mountain its name, was second-growth, about a hundred and twenty years old. The first settlers had found the area black and smoldering. Lightning, they had guessed, and called the area Burnt Meadows. Below that, though, the stands of old-growth towered untouched—Douglas fir, grand fir, noble fir at the higher elevations, red cedar along the creeks, with shade-tolerant hemlocks pushing up beneath the older trees.

"I never had this problem in homicide," Frank said, half to himself. "Maybe that's one reason I don't want to deal with it right now. I'd rather keep going on this murder. I don't have any doubts about murder."

"They're so sincere," Ginny murmured. "How could you arrest someone like Gayle Wallace?"

"At least she'd come along. Rachel Davis, now, is another story. So's Breckenridge. They're both fanatics. They'd kill to save those trees."

She was quiet for a moment. "I've been wondering if they'd kill Tomasovic."

"Yeah. So have I."

"But it doesn't make sense. He was on their side."

"Rachel doesn't think so."

ALAN BRECKENRIDGE PULLED Rachel Davis back and glared at Bruce Bowers. "You touch her again and—"

Rachel jerked her arm out of Breckenridge's grasp. "Shut up, Alan. I can take care of myself."

That stung, and his expression showed it. He turned back to Bowers. The LEO crossed his arms over his chest and stood firm. He had caught sight of Frank and Ginny, and now he waited, fuming, at the edge of the road, surrounded by protesters.

Frank saw trouble as soon as he stopped the truck. There was some sort of scuffle, then the group broke up and Bowers backed off, his uniform sticking out like an exclamation point among the jeans and T-shirts. Kenny McKinney, the wad of snoose tucked inside his lower lip, looked glad to see them.

Frank motioned for Ginny to come along and walked slowly toward the group. Through the years he had pulled over hundreds of cars, and each time it had been like this. The pounding heart, the adrenaline rush. You never knew. Most stops were ordinary, law-abiding citizens who had made a mistake. Sometimes a dealer, or a burglar with a van full of hot electronics. Once in a thousand, maybe a million, but often enough to scare the crap out of you, an armed psychopath with nothing to lose. You never knew.

His heart slowed as he took in the scene. The only weapon in sight was safely holstered on Bowers's belt. Tension hung over the small crowd like an electric charge, but no one moved. Rachel Davis watched him approach. Alan Breckenridge's eyes were still on Bowers. His angry glare was gone, and he looked almost puzzled. Bowers stood stiffly, his face flushed, his eyes fixed on the nearby trees. A half-rotted log, one end still buried in the brush, stuck out a couple of feet into the road.

"Problems?" Frank asked softly.

Bowers cleared his throat. "They were trying to block the road."

"And?"

"I stopped them."

Frank grunted. Rachel turned to Breckenridge and started talking in a low, vehement tone. The crowd began to murmur, their voices rising. This was just what he needed—and just the kind of thing Hunsaker didn't want. Bowers was, most likely, completely in the right, but at the moment his presence was causing more problems than it solved.

Frank was about to send him back to the truck when Gayle Wallace stepped out of the crowd. Good. The former teacher from Coffee Creek had had a calming effect on Rachel Davis once before. Perhaps she could manage it again.

Gayle put her hands on her hips. "That's not true, Rachel, and you know it. The officer didn't threaten anyone. He was just doing his job."

The crowd—including Rachel Davis—fell silent. They could have been a class of fourth-graders, reprimanded for fighting on the playground. In fact, Frank realized, most of the protesters were young enough to have had Gayle Wallace for a teacher.

"We agreed to certain things during our training," Gayle went on. "What good is it going to do to get yourself arrested now? The officer isn't cutting any trees."

Rachel's eyes flashed. She cast a meaningful look toward the four Forest Service employees. "This is no place to discuss tactics."

"Then let's go somewhere else."

The crowd broke up and moved off down the road, everyone talking at once. Alan Breckenridge was one of the last to go. He still looked puzzled, and for a moment Frank thought he was going to speak to Bowers. Then someone called his name. He gave a little shrug and hurried after the others.

"Now," Frank said, "what was that all about?"

Bruce finally uncrossed his arms and relaxed just a little. "We were patrolling the road when we found some of them dragging this out of the woods." He glanced at the log lying on the shoulder, its end almost to the pavement. "They've been trying stuff like this all afternoon."

"First it was rocks," said Kenny McKinney. "By the time we get one mess cleared up, they've started another somewhere else."

Frank nodded. "Keeping you busy. Now, what was going on with Rachel Davis, just before we got here?"

"That bitch," Kenny murmured.

Frank raised an eyebrow. "She really must have done something to get your goat."

"Yeah," said Bruce. "She says the Forest Service killed Tomasovic."

THIRTEEN

"RUN THAT BY ME AGAIN?" said Frank.

Bruce shrugged. "She says the Forest Service killed Tomasovic."

"Oh? Who does she think fired the shot? You? Me, maybe? Ginny?"

"You'll have to ask her."

"I think I will," said Frank. "Now, what was going on just as we pulled up?"

Bruce flushed unhappily. "They were dragging that log out into the road—"

"We'd just finished clearing up the rock," Kenny McKinney interrupted. He shifted the wad of snoose and turned to spit discreetly to one side. "Took almost an hour. We were pretty ticked when we came down here and saw that log."

"I told them to stop," said Bruce. "They didn't. Rachel was the closest, so I grabbed her."

"First mistake," murmured Kenny.

"She started yelling, hitting me, so I let her go."

"Second mistake."

"Then everyone else showed up, and it turned into a regular circus."

"Calling us names," said Kenny. "It got pretty personal."

"You didn't return any of these insults, did you?"

There was an unhappy silence.

"You realize that she does these things to goad you into overreacting?"

"Yes, sir," said Bruce.

"It works, too," added Kenny.

"I can see that." Frank sighed and glanced at his watch. Three-forty-five. He had planned to drive out to Verona to interview Tomasovic's mother, but that was going to have to wait. Unless—he looked at Bowers. Maybe he could take care of two problems at once. "Bruce, I've got a job for you." He explained what he wanted. "Call Ellen Jacobson first, make sure she's home. Tomasovic had a note on his calendar to see her on the tenth."

"That's today."

"Yeah, I guess it is. Pretty tough on the old girl." Bowers knew he was being relieved, but Frank couldn't tell how he was taking it. Well, the drive out to the coast would give him time to cool down and think.

"Do we know when the funeral is?" Ginny asked. It was the first thing she had said since their arrival at Burnt Meadows.

Frank shook his head. "Haven't heard."

"I'll ask Mrs. Jacobson." Bruce turned and walked away toward his truck. He started it up, gunned the engine, and drove past them with a perfunctory nod.

Trouble there, Frank noted. He turned to Kenny. "You're on standby for now. Wait here."

"Ten-four." Kenny gave him a mock salute.

"Wise guy." He turned to Ginny. "Okay. Let's go talk to Rachel Davis."

THEY FOUND the EarthActioners gathered on the main landing beside a couple of cars and a battered VW bus. Frank shook his head. Twenty years ago those hippie buses had been the symbol of a whole subculture. Now you hardly ever saw them—most of their owners had graduated to pricier imports. This one had air scoops improvised from a plastic tub and a bunch of feathers hanging from the rear-view mirror. The side door was pulled open, revealing an interior with that lived-in look. Alan Breckenridge sat just inside, his legs dangling over the edge. Rachel Davis was beside him. Another half-dozen people—mostly in their twenties—sat nearby.

Rachel got up as soon as they approached. Alan said something and, to Frank's surprise, she sat down again. There was a brief discussion, then Gayle Wallace stood up. The designated spokesperson, Frank guessed. He liked Gayle—maybe that was why they'd chosen her—but he didn't feel especially friendly at the moment.

"You people know you can't block a public road."

"We're sorry about what happened with Officer Bowers," said Gayle.

"You can't block a public road," Frank repeated.

"We know it's against the law. We just think that saving trees is more important."

He closed his eyes. Ten years ago he had had conversations like this with his teenage daughters. There is a morality above the law. To break the law in defense of (fill in the blank) is no crime. He had been around long enough that sometimes—just sometimes—he could almost buy it. There were plenty of stupid laws. Breaking them, though, was not the way to get them changed.

He opened his eyes. Gayle Wallace was still there. She looked pretty stubborn.

"If you block the road, we're going to arrest you."

"We know that, Mr. Carver," Gayle said softly, her eyes filled with sympathy. He had seen that look before, near the start of his career, on the face of an antiwar protester being dragged off to jail. Forgive them for they know not what they do. He kept his eyes front, face blank. Like Ginny, he didn't want to arrest Gayle Wallace.

Alan Breckenridge got out of his bus. "We're going back to camp, anyway."

"We're allowed to do that, aren't we?" Rachel Davis asked. She looked keyed up, tense, her eyes too bright.

"I want to talk to you first. You and Breckenridge."

"Do you, now?" Her tone was withering.

"Yes, Miss Davis. I want to know what you meant when you told my officer that the Forest Service killed Tomasovic."

"I didn't say that."

"What did you say, then?"

There was an uncomfortable silence, broken by Gayle Wallace. "That is what you said, Rachel. We all heard you."

Frank smiled to himself. Gayle didn't miss a beat when it came to truth and responsibility.

"You didn't protect him!" Rachel blurted. "It was your job to keep him safe. Now he's dead, and who knows what they'll do next? Look at us, we aren't armed. Who's going to protect *us* if a bunch of loggers come up here with guns?"

He did his best to hide his astonishment. Rachel Davis afraid was the last thing he had expected. Was she acting? He wasn't sure.

"Miss Davis, I've been on this investigation for almost forty-eight hours, and I've found no sign of a loggers' conspiracy to kill Tomasovic. You've roused a lot of anger in those people, but I don't believe they would try to kill you, or anyone else."

"Ward's dead!" she screamed. "He's dead, and you didn't stop them!"

"Rachel." Alan reached out to touch her, but she pushed him away. "I've seen those posters, and I've heard them talk. They hated him, hated him, even though he was born here. And they hate us, too."

"Rachel." Gayle looked her in the eye, her voice calm and steady. "Officer Carver and his people are here to prevent violence. You know that."

"A lot of good they've done! Following him around all day, but he's still dead." Suddenly she burst into tears and turned to Alan, burying her face against his shoulder. He wrapped his arms around her. They stood together, rocking gently back and forth. The woods were quiet except for Rachel's muffled sobs.

"We'll go back to camp, Mr. Carver," Gayle said. "We'll go, but we aren't leaving."

"No, I don't expect you are."

That seemed to take care of it. The half-dozen protesters started talking, moving around, getting into their vehicles. Rachel left with Breckenridge, her face hidden by her long dark hair. A few minutes later the landing was empty except for Frank and Ginny.

"What was that all about?" Ginny asked.

"Diversion." He was quiet for a moment. "That's not quite true. Rachel seems to be genuinely scared."

"You think Ricky Adams and his friends might try something?"

"They might come up here for a little harassment. I wouldn't put it past them. But I don't think they're going to shoot anybody."

She looked at him. "Who *do* you think killed Tomasovic?"

"I don't know. I'm a cop, and I don't know until I see evidence. But right now I see only one person who has directly benefited from his death."

"And that is?"

"Alan Breckenridge. He's got the girl."

"That's right," she said softly. "They'd been living together, hadn't they?"

"Before she met Tomasovic. Remember what Teresa said? Alan called and left a message on her answering machine. I wish we had that tape."

"But how? The shooting, I mean. Charlie would have seen him."

"I've been thinking about that. Holt's sure the shot came from nearby, and the crime lab seems to back him up. But it could have been long-range. There weren't any powder marks on the body—the technicians are going on the bullet alone. And it could have come from a .22 rifle." He thought for a moment. "To use that bullet with a rifle, you'd either have to know enough about guns to do it on purpose—which suggests that Charlie was set up—or you'd have to be pretty ignorant, and do it by accident."

"Does Breckenridge know about guns?"

"Oh, yes. He knows plenty." In Colorado the police had found two rifles and a handgun in Breckenridge's bus. All legal and registered. He'd have to check the report and see if any of those had been .22 caliber.

"Charlie heard a rig start up," Ginny said.

"Those old buses make a pretty distinctive sound. I wonder if he could identify it."

"And if he does?"

"We'll get a warrant to search the bus, and we'll have a long talk with Mr. Breckenridge. Let's give Charlie Zellers a call."

They returned to the truck. Frank picked up the mobile phone and punched in Charlie Zellers's number. He let it ring ten times before hanging up, then tried the mill. Zellers ran a Sunday shift, but no one seemed to be in the office. On the off-chance, he tried the Kurtz household.

"No, he's not here," said Kurtz. "This is Carver, isn't it? Listen, Carver, you talk to my daughter again and I'll see your ass in court. You got that?"

Frank got it. He pulled a face and cradled the phone as though it might bite him. "I guess he didn't care for our interrogation technique."

"What if Breckenridge takes off?"

"I don't think he will. Did you see the look on his face while he was holding Rachel? He's not leaving until she does, and she's not leaving anytime soon."

"It's hard to believe, but it does make a certain kind of sense."

"He's devious enough to set it up. Head of major timber company murders environmentalist. What a circus that would be."

"So we just wait?"

"We'll keep trying Charlie. He should be home around dinnertime. Meanwhile, we've got EarthAction to think about."

"Yeah. What did you mean about a diversion?"

"They're up to something. EarthActioners don't just walk away. You made those motel reservations?"

She nodded.

"I want you to get plenty of sleep tonight. I've got a hunch things are going to start early tomorrow."

"Where are you going to be?"

"Up here. I've got a sleeping bag. I'll call Vince, ask him to bring me some dinner."

"But, Frank—"

"You can ride down with Kenny. Type up your notes from today, add Bowers's report when he gets back. Hunsaker will want them on his desk tomorrow morning." He suddenly remembered that he hadn't asked Bowers about

Charlie Zellers's note to Tomasovic. Too much going on. "I'll give you a call about nine tonight."

"I could stay up here with you."

He smiled and touched her cheek. "Call your daughter. She's probably wondering if she'll ever see you again."

He got out of the truck while she used the phone. That was nice, offering to stay. He'd been looking forward to having dinner together, then—well, anyway. Another time. Meanwhile, he wanted to move the seismic sensors—the ones that detected foot traffic—to the lower edge of the unit. The fallers would start near the creek, laying the timber down in the crisscross pattern favored in a high-lead show. It was the obvious place for EarthAction to put people up in the trees.

GINNY FINISHED the last french fry, took a final swallow of Coke, and waited for a moment to see if her stomach had any comment. She was in the law enforcement office, typing up the day's report on Bowers's computer terminal. It was getting late, past seven, but she could still see sunlight out the window. The Coffee Creek Café's hamburgers, she decided, were marginally better than its sandwiches. Susie and Rebecca, fifty miles away, were having salad from the garden and lemon meringue pie. She missed Susie's cooking almost as much as she missed her daughter.

One of the lines on Bowers's telephone started blinking. Out at the front desk the phone was ringing into emptiness. She picked it up.

"Who's this? Ginny? Where's Carver? I've been trying to reach him for hours."

She recognized Tony Bricca's voice. "He's up at Burnt Meadows. Shall I try to get him on the radio?"

"Yeah, right away. I'll hold."

The ranger was obviously upset. She went into Dispatch to call Frank. No response. That didn't surprise her, if he was still down in the unit.

"I can't reach him," she told Bricca.

"Keep trying. Does he know about Charlie Zellers?"

"Know what?"

"I've got to talk to him. As soon as you get him, have him call me. I'm at home." Bricca hung up.

She frowned. If the ranger wasn't going to tell her what had happened, she had better get hold of Frank. She'd try again in about ten minutes.

On her way back to the law enforcement office she passed the planning room, where they had questioned Gayle Wallace and Rachel Davis that first night. Maps and aerial photos still covered the walls. The foresters and techs working on the district could probably have identified many of the photos, but to her they were simply a montage of clear-cuts and timber. Burnt Meadows was unlikely to be there, anyway. These were photos of sales currently being planned, not sold and ready for logging. What she needed would be somewhere in Timber.

Coffee Creek's station had been built about the same time as the one in Galina, apparently from similar plans. She found Timber and stood for a moment just inside the door, orienting herself. Finally she saw what she was looking for, pinned to the back side of an orange room divider—a map of the north end of the district with roads, boundaries, and ownership information. Planned and current sales were traced on overlays and pinned on top. Now all she had to do was find Burnt Meadows.

She traced Fish Hatchery Road, found the turn. Lacking the landmarks she would have used on the ground, the map was hard to read. Burnt Meadows, though, was clearly marked as a current sale. And sure enough, a black section line ran right through the middle of the drainage—USFS on one side, private on the other. And the other side was marked "ZWP—Zellers Wood Products."

Zellers already owned a full section—six hundred and forty acres—of prime old-growth. Probably a bit more than that, she thought, studying the map. The property boundaries did not follow the drainage, so it was hard to form a clear picture. Still, that was a lot of timber.

How much was six hundred and forty acres of old-growth worth? Millions. Tens, hundreds of millions. Numbers a lot bigger than any she would ever see on a bank statement.

The outside door at the end of the hall opened and softly closed. She lifted her head. Someone else was in the building. She'd locked the door, so it had to be someone with a key, but the idea spooked her anyway. Lucky she hadn't turned on the lights. Holding her breath, she moved quietly back to the doorway just in time to see Bruce Bowers turn the corner, heading for his office.

She let her breath out and stepped into the hall. As soon as he saw his desk, Bruce would know she was in the building. She slipped into the women's rest room, flushed the toilet, and turned on the tap. That ought to announce her presence.

When she came out Bruce was standing in the doorway of his office. "I wondered where everyone was." He gave her a thin smile. "What do you think? Did Carver get me out of the way because he was afraid I'd spoil the big moment?"

"What?"

"Come on, he cooked up that little errand in Verona just to get rid of me."

She must have still looked puzzled, because he went on. "You mean he got rid of you, too? Maybe he can't stand to share the glory."

"What are you talking about, Bruce?"

"You really don't know, do you? They arrested Charlie Zellers this afternoon. I heard it on the news just now." He shook his head. "He snookered both of us, didn't he?"

FOURTEEN

IF THE BURNT MEADOWS SALE had had a roof, Frank would have gone right through it.

He had just hiked out, twenty minutes up from the bottom with two stops to catch his breath, and he was winded. He came over the top and stood at the side of the landing, a few feet from his truck, blowing like a horse. Christ, much more of this and he'd have a heart attack. Circles of sweat spread under his arms, staining his shirt. He took his hard hat off and ran a hand through his hair, damp and sticky with more sweat. After a moment he looked up.

Twilight had settled among the massive trunks and patches of brush. Creamy white dogwood blossoms gleamed like votive candles in the shadows. He lifted his eyes to the canopy, two hundred feet above, where the tips of the trees still danced in golden daylight. Birds still called up there, bright notes dropping like jewels into the dusk, while nearby a pair of doves cooed back and forth.

At least he guessed they were doves. He had his breath back now and could think again. The only birds he really recognized were pigeons and vultures. The first because he'd seen so damned many of them in Seattle, the second because they were hard to miss, cutting their slow, gruesome circles through the summer skies.

His heart rate had just settled down to something he'd be willing to admit to a doctor when the radio went off. It was Ginny, with the news about Charlie Zellers.

"Holy shit. When did they do this?"

"Sometime this afternoon. All we know is what Bruce heard on the radio."

"What does Holt think he's doing?"

"You didn't know about it?"

"Hell, no. But I plan to find out. Carver clear."

He cradled the mike and sat for a moment. He was ticked, good and ticked, but there was no point in going off half-cocked. Sheriff Holt must have a good reason for making the arrest. Maybe they had found the gun. Maybe there *had* been a witness, or maybe Charlie had confessed.

He put the call through and reached Holt on the second try, at his home. The sheriff sounded pleased at his accomplishment. "We nailed the Michaels kid, too. We may see him in jail yet. I've been trying to reach you all day."

Frank grunted.

"Finally we decided to move on Zellers."

"On whose authority?"

There was a pause. "Mine."

"Damn it, Holt, you turned the case over to me."

"Joint investigation, that's what we said."

"Not anymore, brother. It's all yours. You've stuck your foot in shit, and you can have it."

"Now, wait a minute, Carver—"

"Oh, no. Not me. I'm a busy man. We've got a couple dozen EarthActioners up here."

"Listen, damn you! That's what Hunsaker said. I thought you wanted the case off your hands!"

"What the hell has the forest supervisor got to do with it?"

"He's been pushing for an arrest all day, since your goddamn ranger spilled his guts on the morning news."

"Whoa! Wait up. What ranger? Bricca?"

"Where the hell have you been? Bricca knew you'd fingered Zellers as a suspect. A reporter cornered him last night and pumped him dry. He is in deep shit, let me tell you."

How could Bricca—? He couldn't have seen the report they'd left on the supervisor's desk last night. And then he knew. "Okay, okay," he sighed. "I've been trying to reach you, too, you know. You better back up and fill me in."

Holt was still simmering. After hearing his story, Frank understood why. He also understood that he had helped set the train of events in motion himself. He was the one who had asked Tony Bricca to coordinate information on EarthAction. All he had wanted was to get the ranger off his back. He hadn't counted on the man's need to run every show on his district. Bricca had evidently decided to work liaison for both the protest action *and* the homicide investigation.

And Frank himself had told Bricca that Charlie Zellers was a suspect. At the time it had seemed like a simple courtesy. After all, Bricca was going to have to handle the local fallout if they made an arrest. Two hours later, Holt explained, a pair of TV reporters had cornered the ranger, ostensibly to ask him about the Burnt Meadows protest, and picked his brains. By ten o'clock that night, while Frank and Ginny were getting ready for bed, the first brief stories had appeared on the nightly news.

The reporters had been busy ever since, collecting responses from the usual bunch of media-conscious environmentalists. By Sunday morning they were talking about a Forest Service cover-up, and by noon Hunsaker was fielding calls from the regional office, demanding some kind of response. That was when he called the sheriff.

"Said you were tied up with the protesters," Holt said. "Well, I read your report and felt we had enough to justify an arrest. Zellers admits he was there, won't say why, and there's nothing to suggest another suspect."

"You can't make an arrest without evidence."

"Or a witness."

Frank fell silent. "Who've you got?"

"Your gal, Ginny Trask."

Had he missed something? He didn't think so. "I questioned her myself. She can't make an ID."

"She heard two people talking, she's real clear about that. Not three, not four. We know who those two people were. One of them's dead. It's pretty simple, Carver, even for a federale."

"Zellers didn't do it."

"Come on, Frank."

"First of all, it could have been a long-range shot—"

A snort from the sheriff.

"Damn it, Holt, you show me a motive! Tomasovic wasn't a threat to either Zellers or his company. He was a moderate. Charlie would have been better off plugging a real rabble-rouser like Rachel Davis."

"Maybe she was next on his list."

"You didn't talk to him." It was the way Charlie had said he would have gone back if he'd known Tomasovic was hurt. There had been something in his voice, in his face. Of all the people Frank had talked to in the last two days, only Charlie Zellers seemed genuinely grieved by Tomasovic's death.

"Okay," Holt said reasonably. "Who *did* shoot him?"

"I don't know yet. Maybe if I didn't have to deal with these damn protesters I'd have time to find out. You don't have any physical evidence linking Zellers to the crime?"

"He's not stupid, Frank. He would have tossed the gun. We're planning to drag the river tomorrow, just below the bridge."

"Have you checked his handguns? He says he's got two, both licensed."

"And he's going to use his licensed gun to kill someone, right?"

Frank didn't have any reply to that. He'd already figured the gun was gone, untraceable, no matter who had fired it. There wasn't much more to say, and after another minute or two they hung up.

Night had fallen, though the sky to the west still held a few streaks of light. Frank sat in the truck, contemplating his next move. It was frustrating, having so few people to work with. Right now he wanted to interrogate some EarthActioners, one by one, in the privacy of his own office. With the Zellers fallers scheduled to show up in the morning, though, he didn't dare leave Burnt Meadows unprotected for even an hour. He twisted around in his seat, grunting (the steering wheels in these new rigs seemed to stick out a lot more than the old ones), and rummaged around until he found a small tape recorder. He eyed it with distaste. Too many gadgets these days. He punched the record button, counted to ten out loud, then played it back. Damned thing seemed to work.

The radio squawked, and Vince Paley came on. The Sitkum officer was on his way up. A few minutes later headlights showed around the bend. Vince pulled his unmarked pickup alongside Frank's truck and rolled the window down.

"Brought you some coffee and sandwiches. Planning to make a night of it?"

THE EARTHACTIONERS gathered around the fire at the Burnt Meadows campground were not expecting company. Frank drove his truck right into the parking lot, slewing the high beams across the tents and picnic tables, picking out startled faces frozen like statues by the lights. Sometimes it helped to be a real asshole, and he was ready.

He left the lights on and got out, regretting for once that he was out of uniform. He did have his gun belt, the butt of his Smith and Wesson showing above the holster. He walked up to the campfire, keeping the lights behind him.

Three or four people got up, moving forward to block his path. He stopped.

"Where's Breckenridge?"

"Why?" Rachel Davis stood with her hands on her hips, her face white in the glaring headlights.

He was in no mood to answer questions. "Where is he?"

"Not here. He's gone."

Breckenridge's face was not among those Frank could see, and his van had not been in the parking area. He glanced at the half-dozen tents, legally off-limits without a warrant. Not that Breckenridge was likely to be there. He could be holed up in any one of a thousand places, all within a mile or two, where he would be safe from everything but a full-scale search.

Chances were he was somewhere near the bottom of Burnt Meadows, hauling climbing spurs and a safety harness, looking at trees. Maybe Paley would pull him in.

He was fed up with Rachel Davis, and didn't expect she'd tell him what he wanted to know in any case. He looked over the assembled faces again, putting names to the ones he recognized. When he saw Meg Nugent, he knew he'd found what he wanted.

The regional office had a file on her, compiled through the years from newspaper clippings and interviews. She had been active in the environmental movement since the seventies, starting with the Sierra Club and moving leftward ever since. She frequently testified at public hearings, and had served on a couple of advisory committees when Region Six was putting together its new management plans. Three or four years ago she had started showing up at EarthAction rallies. He knew something else about her, too. She had been born in Pennsylvania, into a Quaker family, and she still held to Quaker beliefs. Nonviolence and adherence to the truth were bred into her bones.

Perfect. If she would talk.

She wasn't going to talk to an asshole.

And he'd been looking forward to it, too.

Frank sighed. There were cops who lived by the motto, never admit to making a mistake. Well, he'd made plenty of mistakes in his career, not to mention his personal life, and he'd always found it better to set them right. Now he turned, walked back to his rig, and shut the headlights off.

The talk that had sprung up as soon as he turned his back stopped abruptly when he returned. He hunkered down just inside the circle of firelight and looked at the assembled faces. Even by the flickering orange flames he could see that most were in their early twenties, eager to save the world but probably too young for what he wanted. Gayle Wallace wasn't there. He wasn't surprised—Bill Wallace probably needed some help getting around with that wheelchair. Gayle hadn't known these people long enough for what he wanted, anyway.

He fished his badge out of his pocket and held it out for Meg Nugent to see. "I'm investigating the death of Ward Tomasovic. I'd like to talk to you."

No one spoke. He had taken them by surprise, their minds on tomorrow's confrontation, not murder. Meg looked at the badge for a moment, then at him.

"I'll answer questions about Ward, but not about what's going on here."

"We can talk in my truck. I've got a tape recorder."

Meg balked. "Out here. There's a place back by my tent."

Frank shook his head. "I'll leave the dome light on, so everyone can see us. But it's going to be private."

She thought for a moment. "All right, with the light on."

Frank led the way, threading among the picnic tables piled with cooking gear and food. Back at his rig he held the door for Meg, then got in himself. He flicked the dome light on. Meg Nugent was about his own age. Her gray hair was pulled back at the neck, revealing soft wrinkles and a pair of alert brown eyes. She was a bit overweight—another resemblance—and looked comfortably solid in jeans and a striped Guatemalan blouse.

Frank opened the thermos Vince Paley had brought up with his dinner. When the smell of coffee hit his nostrils he reached automatically for the cigarettes in his pocket. Empty. Damn. Ambushed by his own habits.

"Coffee?" he asked. "It's black."

Meg shook her head.

He poured himself a cup, shook in two packets of sugar, stirred, and spoke into the recorder. "This is Frank Carver interviewing Meg Nugent." He added the time, place, and date, and got his notebook out. You couldn't trust machines.

"Now, Mrs. Nugent—may I call you Meg?"

"I don't see why not. May I call you Frank?"

"Fair enough. Now, Meg, what I really need is background information on Ward Tomasovic. How long had you known him?"

"Almost ten years. We met in Santa Cruz. He was in graduate school. My husband was teaching there, and I was doing volunteer work for the Sierra Club."

"Did you know Breckenridge then, too?"

"Oh, yes. And Teresa Buchannan, the girl Ward married. She used to come to the Santa Cruz Friends meeting. We weren't close, you understand. They're all quite a bit younger. I'd met them through Sierra Club projects, and we just gradually got to know one another.''

He had struck pay dirt—someone who had known Tomasovic's circle before it broke up. "You say your husband was teaching at Santa Cruz. Was he one of Ward's professors?"

"Oh, no. Jim teaches psychology. He did have Teresa in a few classes, but I knew Ward through the Sierra Club."

They had met at meetings about a proposed dam. Alan Breckenridge had been there, too. "I think they hadn't known each other long. Ward was in the doctorate program, living in a co-op house with some other grad students. Alan was a biology major. An OTA—older-than-average student. He'd been in the military—the navy—I think, and then gone to a community college."

"How did they get along?"

"As though they'd known each other forever."

They had been friends, buddies, partners, and they had succeeded in halting the dam project. Breckenridge had dropped out of school shortly afterward to work full-time on environmental causes. He had put pressure on Ward to do the same, but Ward had married Teresa by then, and was committed to finishing his doctorate. Alan swung more and more toward radical environmentalism, moving out of the sphere of Sierra Club projects. In 1984 he left for a prolonged stay in Arizona. "That's when he met Rachel. He came back full of talk about monkeywrenching."

Monkeywrenching—monkey around, throw a wrench in the works. The terms came from an Edward Abbey novel, and had helped spawn groups like EarthAction.

Frank nodded. "So you knew Rachel Davis back then, too?"

"I didn't meet her until we moved up to Oregon. But I'd certainly heard a lot about her."

That was what Frank wanted, but once again Meg Nugent balked. "Most of it is just hearsay. I've known her, personally, for only a few years, and she's changed. I don't know that it serves any purpose to bring up all that old stuff."

"Did Rachel have a major effect on Ward's life?"

"Oh, yes."

"Then I need to know. I'd rather hear it from you, because I trust your judgment. You're mature, reflective—"

Meg chuckled.

"Yes?"

"I like 'mature.' It's so flattering."

"Should I ask someone else? One of those youngsters over at the campfire? People she works with in Eugene?"

Meg sighed. "You've got a point. Rachel has a lot of enemies. I'm sure she'd rather you heard it from me than from them."

"Why does she have enemies?"

"Because she's such a bitch."

The term startled him, coming from Meg. She noticed his reaction. "She's the first to admit it, you know. I don't think Rachel has ever been a very happy person." Her political awakening had occurred in high school, in upstate New York, where she had started a feminist group during her senior year. Eager to get as far from home as possible, she had enrolled in the University of Oregon in Eugene, where she had quickly embroiled herself in the feminist and radical left communities. Her relationships with both men and women tended to be intense, manipulative, and abrupt.

"She'd break up with a political group or a man, and in a few weeks she'd be all wrapped up in something new, a new cause or lover or housemate. She's notorious in Eugene. A lot of people, women especially, are afraid of her."

"How does she manage to keep going, then? Why do people put up with her?"

"Because when she's working on something, it's one hundred percent. If Rachel's on your project, your project will get everything she's got, and that includes money. I don't know how big her trust fund is, but she doesn't seem to have made any major dents in it yet. She's good at organization, motivating the troops, environmental law—you know she's been to law school. She's got the golden touch. Almost everything she works on succeeds."

"But if she's so destructive—"

"You've got to understand, she's not vindictive. She doesn't hold grudges. She'll screw up someone's life and then walk away without fully realizing what she's done." Meg nodded, almost to herself. "She's a very unusual woman—committed to all the right causes, but personally amoral."

"What about your own relationship with her?"

"Oh, that."

Frank waited.

"I guess it's no secret. She had an affair with my husband."

"And you're still working with her?"

Meg shut her eyes. "Frank, I really believe in what I'm doing. I want to stop all the logging on public land. So does Rachel Davis."

"And she has the golden touch."

"She's also a human being." Meg opened her eyes. "When human beings act the way Rachel does, it's because something inside is wrong. Maybe someday she'll find what she needs to make it right."

"Meanwhile, an affair here, a wrecked life there—"

Meg shrugged unconvincingly. "It didn't last long."

They were silent. Frank opened the thermos. Again the rich, bitter smell of coffee filled the truck, but this time he didn't reach for his empty pocket.

"I'll take some of that now," Meg said.

He reached behind his seat and rummaged around until he found another cup. Holding it up, he eyed Meg. "You a fanatic about cleanliness?"

"Only about trees." She sounded glad to change the subject. "Besides, that coffee smells as though it has germicidal properties."

He filled the cup and handed it to her. "Tell me about Rachel and Tomasovic."

"And Alan. You can't leave Alan out of it." She took a sip of coffee. "All those old stories are recirculating, since Ward came back to Oregon. People can't leave it alone, they've got to talk."

"Someone's been doing more than talking."

She looked up. "I know. That's why I'm sitting here, repeating gossip to a cop. It's not the sort of thing I usually do."

"I appreciate that, Meg."

"Good." She paused. "Alan met Rachel sometime in '84, in Arizona. He came back to Santa Cruz long enough to pick up the boxes he'd stored in our garage, and then he moved up to Eugene. Rachel has a pretty nice house there, you know. She always has a roommate or two, though she doesn't need the money. Company, I guess. Alan moved in with her. It lasted for about a year."

"And then?"

"Ward finished his doctorate and was offered an assistant professorship in Longmont. Well, it's only forty miles from Eugene. Of course, he looked Alan up. And then, of course, he met Rachel."

Fireworks, from the way Meg described it. "We'd moved back to Oregon by then, too. Jim had contracts for a couple of books, and we were glad to get out of California. I'd begun to move away from the Sierra Club myself. I wanted more of a commitment to direct action. I joined the Eugene Environmental Coalition, and suddenly I was in the middle of this major situation with Rachel and Ward.

"They were completely engrossed in each other. I don't know how Ward managed to keep his job. Within a month he was practically living with Rachel. Alan was still there, too, and at first we thought it was a ménage à trois. Perhaps it was, but that didn't last long. Alan and Rachel had an incredible fight, at the coalition office, just so no one would miss it, and then he was gone. No one heard from him again for over a year."

She paused. "Poor Teresa. There she was, stuck in that run-down little house in Longmont, taking care of one baby and then pregnant again. I used to visit her every couple of months. She must have suspected something was going on, but she never talked about it. I think she found out just before Chad was born. She filed for divorce when he was about four months old."

"She seems to have done okay."

Meg raised an eyebrow. "You've seen her, then. How's she taking Ward's death?"

Frank shrugged. "She had a friend with her."

"She's always had friends, good friends. She'll make it."

"What happened after the divorce?"

"Ward moved in with Rachel and started commuting to Longmont to teach. He'd gone half-time by then, was spending most of his time working for the coalition. Then I guess he heard about the job with the National Environmental League and put in an application."

"What did Rachel think about that?"

"She didn't know, until he flew back East for the interview. She was furious. I almost have to say hysterical, and that's a word I don't care for. You see, she'd wanted to marry him."

"And that stopped her?"

"Oh, yes. Rachel despises bureaucrats. She hated him, after that." Meg fell silent. "There was more to it, of course. By that time Ward had cooled off a bit. Rachel runs her life at a pretty high pitch. It can wear on a person."

"I can imagine."

Meg chuckled softly. "Yes. That might be one reason he applied for the NEL job. Also, I think he missed Teresa and the kids."

Frank nodded. Teresa had said Ward wanted her back, had wanted all of them to go to Washington together. He wondered if Rachel had known that.

"So he left."

"He left. Three weeks later Alan Breckenridge was back in town, staying at Rachel's. He's been there, on and off, ever since."

"What happened when Tomasovic came back?"

Meg took a moment to answer. "I don't really know. I'm pretty sure Rachel saw him, at least once. He was trying to distance himself from EarthAction, to come across as a moderate so he would have credibility in places like Coffee Creek. But I can't imagine that Rachel would let him ignore her. You see, she was still in love with him."

"A few minutes ago you said she hated him."

"Yes. She's obsessed with him. That kind of obsession can take the form of love or hate, or even both at the same time."

Frank nodded. He had seen relationships like that before. Sometimes they ended in murder.

"And Breckenridge?"

Meg shrugged. "Poor Alan. We disagree about a lot of things, but I can't help feeling sorry for him."

"In your opinion, could either of them have shot Tomasovic?"

"I've wondered."

"You know these people, Meg. You must have done more than wonder."

"Violence is always difficult to understand."

Frank waited. Meg seemed lost in thought. After a moment he broke the silence. "Meg, I need help."

She looked up, her eyes wide, almost luminous. "Oh, yes. We all do."

Was she going to talk about Jesus? He braced himself.

She smiled. "I'd rather have my job than yours anyday."

"Oh? What's your job?"

"Loving that of God in every person."

"Even murderers?"

"They need it the most, don't you think?"

FIFTEEN

EVERYONE AT COFFEE CREEK Ranger Station knew the big moment had come. At seven-thirty that morning, just an hour ago, Mel Barnhart and three other fallers had driven past, their Zellers crew cab loaded with chain saws, wedges, and jerry cans of gas. The KETV crew had been spotted ordering doughnuts and coffee at the café a little earlier. Now people were starting to drift in Dispatch, where Tiffany had turned on the Forest Service radio and a CB turned to the Zellers channel. Ginny, sitting in the law enforcement office, listened to the talk from the hall.

"Ten on the table says Barnhart leaves without laying his saw on a single tree."

"You're on. You don't know Mel. He never walked away from a fight."

"You betting, Henry?"

"No way. I don't bet on a rigged game."

"Come on."

"Mel's crew is going to stick around long enough to get their pictures in the paper, then go home. They won't start cutting until tomorrow."

"Ten on the table says they start today."

"I'd be ashamed to take such easy money."

Their voices faded as they turned the corner into Dispatch. Ginny had a radio, too, tuned to the law enforcement frequency. So far she hadn't heard much. Frank was up there with the two LEOs, Bruce Bowers and Vince Paley. Holt was supposed to be there too, but at the last minute he had been subpoenaed to appear in court in Longmont at eight in the morning. Deputy Larkin was somewhere down in the south end of the county, presumably on call if needed.

And she was sitting in the Coffee Creek station, typing up a report for the forest supervisor. It was grossly unfair.

"He wants a daily report," Frank had said that morning. "He's the boss. We give the boss what he wants."

"Since when?" she asked.

"Since right now."

"But I'm going to miss everything!"

"Your problem is, you got too much sleep last night. Those motel beds must be pretty comfortable."

Frank had looked like he could use a good night's sleep himself. They were eating breakfast at the café, about 6:00 a.m. Things had been quiet enough at Burnt Meadows that he had felt all right about slipping away for an hour. "I don't expect it to last, though."

He dropped her off at the station, where she settled down at the word processor, ready to decipher Bruce's notes of his interview with Ellen Jacobson.

In the end, it turned out pretty much as Henry, who wouldn't take the easy money, had predicted. Barnhart and his falling crew were on their way off the mountain by ten o'clock, saws untouched. Frank made a formal request for a closure order and expected to have it by the next day. People drifted out of Dispatch and back to their offices. There wasn't much to do except wait.

She was just finishing up the report for Hunsaker when the telephone beeped. It was the receptionist. "We've got a lady out here looking for Bruce."

She went out to the front desk. The lady was in her sixties, tall and straight-backed, her hair a soft frizz of white. She was wearing a dark, softly draped dress and looking out the window. Ginny knew who she was even before she turned around.

"Officer Bowers isn't in right now," she said. "May I help you?"

"I talked to him last night. I'm Ellen Jacobson." She seemed to falter, then went on. "There were just one or two things..."

"I've been reading through his notes," Ginny said, ushering her down the hall. "We've both been working on your son's death."

"Oh. Well, I can tell you, then, I suppose." They stepped into the law enforcement office. Ginny pulled a chair up and shut the door.

Ellen Jacobson glanced around unhappily. "I'm on my way to Eugene, to see about the funeral. It's scheduled for tomorrow, you know, and with Harold laid up, there's no one else to do it."

"Harold's your husband?"

She nodded. "Harold Jacobson. He had a stroke a couple months back, and isn't really over it yet."

Ginny waited.

"I'm afraid the officer upset him last night. Didn't mean to, of course, but Harold's always been protective. He liked Ward."

Bowers's questions had mostly been about Tomasovic's plans at the time of his death. Who he had expected to see in Coffee Creek, where he had expected to go next. Ginny couldn't see why that would upset anyone. "What exactly did he ask, Mrs. Jacobson?"

"Bringing up that old business with Debbie Zellers." Ellen Jacobson looked straight at Ginny, her blue eyes sharp and clear. "Charlie Zellers did what he had to do, and I never blamed him. I want to tell you something, miss. Charlie never shot Ward. You've got the wrong man in jail."

Ginny's head was starting to spin. "Wait a minute, Mrs. Jacobson. You're going too fast for me. Officer Bowers asked if your son had plans to see Debbie Kurtz?"

"That's right. That's what got Harold so upset. Thought he was protecting me, I guess. He always liked Ward a lot, was real proud of him."

Ellen Jacobson came to an abrupt stop. Her eyes filled with tears. After a moment she wiped them with a hankie from her purse and went on. "You see, back when he was in high school, his last year, Ward fell for Debbie. She was pretty as a picture, and just turned fifteen. Ward fell hard, too. Couldn't help himself, just like his dad. Charlie practically drove him out of town. Harold's never forgiven him for that."

Ginny finally got everyone sorted out. Harold was Ward Tomasovic's stepfather. She already knew that Debbie Kurtz had been Ward's girlfriend, and Charlie, of course, was Charlie Zellers, Debbie's father.

"Now, you told Officer Bowers that Ward didn't mention any plans to see Debbie."

"That's right. He never *said* anything, but I'm not so sure. You see, Ward came over quite a bit this spring. Harold and I were both surprised. He'd show up, have dinner, spend the night. He was always a little vague about his plans. I think he was probably meeting Debbie."

"This was just a few months ago?"

She nodded. "Started about February. He just had this look about him."

"What makes you say that Charlie Zellers didn't shoot your son?"

Ellen Jacobson hesitated. "If I drive up to Longmont, will they let me see Charlie?"

"I think so. Would you like me to check?"

"If you would."

Ginny got on the phone and called the county jail in Longmont. Visiting hours were from three to five that afternoon.

"I'll go see him, then," Ellen said. She had not answered Ginny's other question.

Ginny tried again. "Why are you sure Charlie didn't shoot your son?"

"I've got to talk to Charlie," she said and gathered up her gloves and handbag, but then made no move to leave.

"Is there anything else I can help you with?" Ginny asked.

"Officer Bowers seemed like a nice man."

"Yes," Ginny replied cautiously, "I believe he is."

"You don't know where he's from, do you?"

"No, I don't. He was up in Portland before he started with the Forest Service."

Ellen Jacobson shook her head. "Portland, that wouldn't be right."

"What is it, Mrs. Jacobson?"

Ellen set her handbag down again. "He reminded me of someone. A friend of Ward's." She shrugged. "Well, there's probably nothing to it. They've been gone a long time."

Now Ginny was curious, too. Bruce had never mentioned his family. "Someone Ward knew when he lived here?"

"Billy Ney. He died, drowned, just a young boy. Ward was there. Took him a long time to get over it."

Ginny nodded thoughtfully. She had heard this before, but where? Someone she'd talked to within the past few days.

Ellen gave a sigh and picked up her handbag again. "Bill had a little brother. I used to cook down at the school, and I remember them coming through the line at lunch. I always gave them something extra. You could tell they needed it." She got up. "I'd better get along. Just wanted to clear up that bit about Ward and Debbie. I hope it helps."

"Every piece of information helps," Ginny said, getting up. She walked Ellen down the hall and through the reception area. They paused at the door. "What happened to the little brother?"

Ellen looked puzzled for a moment. "Oh! Sorry, I guess I was thinking about the funeral. The mother was divorced. She remarried soon after Billy died. They moved, I'm not sure where. Eastern Oregon, or maybe Idaho."

"Well, I'll have to tell Officer Bowers he has a look-alike."

Ellen nodded, her mind clearly somewhere else. Ginny watched her walk out to her car, her back still straight and firm. Then she turned and went, not to the law enforcement office, but to Timber. The room was deserted, the reconners and cruisers out in the field. The sales map covering the north end of the district was still pinned up on the orange room divider. Once again she traced Fish Hatchery Road, ran her finger along the turn up Prairie Mountain, found the Burnt Meadows sale and the privately owned section marked "ZWP, Zellers Wood Products." Underneath, on the map itself, not the overlay, someone had penciled in "The Old Ney Place."

She shook her head. If Bruce was Billy Ney's brother—if he'd spent part of his childhood in Coffee Creek—why hadn't he said so? It was a pretty stable community. Surely he would know at least a few people—old teachers, friends of the family. It didn't make sense. After a few moments she went back to the law enforcement office, sat down at the word processor, and started typing in their interview with Ellen Jacobson.

BRECKENRIDGE COULD HAVE done it. He had motive, means, and opportunity. Frank spun out the possibilities as he worked his way through the timber on the east side of Burnt Meadows. Last night he had planted two seismic sensors at the bottom, and so far he hadn't heard a peep from either. Maybe no one was down there, but he didn't believe it. The climbing gear he'd spotted at the Earth-Action camp wasn't just for show. More likely he'd somehow screwed up the sensor deployment. So he was going down to see for himself.

He shouldered his way through a clump of vine maple, searching for another of the yellow ribbons that marked the sale boundary. They weren't easy to spot, dangling in the sunshine in the green and yellow brush. Every so often he came upon yellow signs tacked up on trees, helpfully explaining that they faced the sale area. He caught sight of the next ribbon, six feet up on the edge of a huckleberry thicket. The timber crew had swamped a line through the brush when they put the boundary in, three years earlier. It was barely visible now, just a few sawed-off stubs below the new shoots, lying in wait to jab the unwary foot.

He clambered over a downed log, skidding on the loosened bark, and thought about Breckenridge some more. Say he'd waited outside the gym, maybe in the parking lot. No, Bruce and Ginny would have seen his van in the parking lot. More likely he parked somewhere close, but not obvious—along the highway, for instance. Sooner or later Tomasovic would come out to his own van. Breckenridge usually carried a couple of guns in his rig. Chances were one of them was a .22 rifle.

But when Ward left the gym, he didn't go to the parking lot. He cut off across the playing field, toward the goalposts. Frank imagined himself standing beside the beat-up Volks, watching Tomasovic disappear into the night. Another figure moved in the darkness, across the playing field. Frank knew it was Charlie Zellers, but what would Breckenridge think? He'd want to know what was going on. He glanced into the van, and something caught his eye. The .22 he always kept in back—and then Frank had it. An infrared scope. He could keep his distance, see what was going on, and possibly even identify the second person. He could almost see Breckenridge grab the rifle and take off.

He'd walk up the highway, keeping parallel to Tomasovic. Frank stopped, shut his eyes, concentrated. Coffee Creek didn't have much in the way of streetlights, but the town wasn't absolutely dark. The school was lighted by three of those orange sodium jobs, mounted on poles. Floodlights surrounded the ranger station. From a stretch along the highway, say maybe a hundred yards, those floodlights would silhouette the goalposts—and anyone standing near them.

Crouch, aim the scope, press the button to send the infrared beam shooting into the dark. Breckenridge would want to know who Ward was meeting so secretively. And when he realized it was Charlie Zellers? Breckenridge already hated Ward, already considered him a traitor. What would he do when he saw him dealing with the enemy?

Frank started forward again, dodging through a clump of alders. He was almost at the bottom. A minute later he came to a corner marker. Three of the yellow signs, a bunch of flashers, and enough yellow ribbon to decorate a log truck, all pinned to the side of a tree. He'd come this way yesterday afternoon, hauling those damn sensors, which weighed a ton in spite of what the manufacturer claimed. The boundary took a sharp left here, running along a little break about a hundred feet up from the creek. This left a buffer, about three trees wide, between the creek and the clear-cut. Not enough, the environmentalists complained. Too much, the loggers replied. Thank God he didn't have to settle that quarrel.

The boundary line ran through salmonberry, dense and thick down here by the creek. The pink blossoms were mostly gone now, grown into the tasteless orange berries that gave the stuff its name. He'd talked to Mel Barnhart that morning, just before the fallers headed back down the hill. Mel had walked the unit already, a few weeks earlier, and knew just where he planned to start. There weren't that many choices, really, and Frank figured the Earth-Actioners had walked the unit, too. He'd set the sensors up in the most likely spot.

Not that they'd be a hell of a lot of use. All you had to do was read the "deployment considerations" that came with them. "Select areas where the walking surface is firm or hard... avoid roots or heavy surface vegetation... choose a location where walking is likely to be continuous, not start-stop or extremely cautious... avoid extremely rough terrain." Right. Perfect. Just the sort of place he was going to find on the side of a hill in the middle of the Oregon Coast Range.

Somewhere around here. He was in a small clearing, opened up a few years ago when a Douglas fir had toppled downhill. Weathered branches stuck up from the decaying trunk. Foxgloves straggled along one side, purple and white spikes stretching to the sun. One of the sensors was buried a few yards into the timber, the location marked by an inconspicuous bit of white ribbon. Frank climbed up on the downed tree to get a better view. White was even harder to see than yellow.

He scanned the brush, passing quickly over a couple of trees, then stopped and came back. An end of rope dangled along one of the trunks, just above eye level, barely visible against the deeply furrowed bark.

He moved his gaze up the rope, past a small folding saw dangling from another rope, past the climbing spurs sunk deep into the bark, past the boots and blue jeans, the safety belt pulled taut around the trunk, and up to the face. Alan Breckenridge. His head resting against the bark, his mouth agape, his eyes wide open and staring at the ground.

There was no way he could be alive.

SIXTEEN

AN HOUR LATER the area was crawling with people, in spite of Frank's efforts to keep them out. A half-dozen district employees stood guard in the woods, fending off Earth-Actioners and sightseers from Coffee Creek. It was amazing how accessible those few square yards at the bottom of Burnt Meadows had suddenly become.

They spent the rest of the day getting Breckenridge's body out of the tree. Frank's first thought was to call in a chopper, but a quick conference with the district's air support crew dissuaded him. The body was only fifty feet up. That left a hundred feet of canopy, all of it in the way. They ruled out the helicopter.

Kenny McKinney, the Coffee Creek fire officer helping with surveillance, suggested climbing gear. "We get a couple climbers up there, rig up some ropes, and rappel him to the ground." He fished a snoose tin out of his pocket, took a pinch, and tucked it into his lower lip. "Piece of cake."

"You've done this before?" Frank inquired.

That was when he learned that, among his other talents, Kenny was considered Coffee Creek's most daring (foolhardy, someone interjected) tree climber. Every few years, when the crop was particularly good, he spent most of August a hundred feet up in the air, picking cones.

"A body's a little bigger than a pine cone," Frank observed.

"Fir," Kenny said. "Around here we pick fir cones." He turned serious. "Two years ago we lowered a climber.

Branch broke while she was on it. She had a busted-up shoulder and a head injury."

Frank winced. "That must have hurt."

"She was unconscious. We had a hell of a time getting her down. She was way up in the canopy, lots of branches in the way."

There was a pause. "And?"

Kenny shrugged. "She's okay. In fact, a couple weeks ago she asked about climbing again this summer."

Frank gazed at the lifeless body, still slumped against the tree. Blood, dark and sticky looking, stained the dirty T-shirt. He'd seen enough, through binoculars, to guess that Breckenridge had died of a bullet wound in the chest. He knew he was missing a lot, though. He wanted a closer look before the body was moved. Doc Jarvis and the sheriff weren't expected for another hour, and the medical examiner sure as hell wasn't going to climb up there.

"You've got the gear?" he asked.

Kenny nodded. "Back at the station."

"Go get it, then. Bring some extra spurs and a belt."

"Ten-four. Couple more guys, too. You ever done any climbing?"

Frank nodded. "Yeah. Looks like I'm going to do some more."

In the army, when he was nineteen. He'd missed the Korean War by a few years, so it had been a peacetime army. He'd been disappointed at the time. Funny how those things changed. Anyway, they assigned him to communications. For two years he monkeyed around with crystal sets, installed telephones, and strung wire across the countryside. That had been thirty years ago, and he hadn't worn climbing spurs since.

While they waited for Kenny to return, Frank and Vince Paley searched the area Frank had flagged off around the tree. Usually such searches turned up a fair amount of material, most of which proved to be unrelated to the crime. This search was unique in Frank's experience in that any evidence of human activity would probably be significant. The dry, duffy ground, however, revealed only a few scrapes, most likely left by Breckenridge's spurs as he approached the tree.

"Looks like he was alone," Frank said, studying the scrapes.

Vince Paley nodded. "Don't climbers usually work in pairs?"

"Supposed to, but Breckenridge wasn't what you'd call safety-conscious. Whoa, what's this?" He picked up a pencil stub, only a couple of inches long and stained with blood.

They both looked up at the body hanging grotesquely above them. The pencil had been directly beneath.

An hour later Kenny McKinney was back, with two more climbers and a mountain of gear that included a light stretcher. Holt and Doc Jarvis had arrived by then, along with an ambulance from Longmont. Frank grumbled unhappily as Kenny helped him get into a belt and spurs. Climbing up there was going to be bad enough. He didn't need an audience.

"Keep your feet pointed out, so the spurs will dig in," Kenny said. "The bark's thickest near the bottom. About ten feet up you should start biting into wood."

Frank cinched the yellow climbing belt up around his crotch, strapped the spurs on, and hobbled awkwardly toward the tree, the two-inch spikes sinking into the duff. Kenny helped him knot the climbing rope, then ran it around the trunk and clipped the other end on with a D-ring. As the trunk narrowcd, Frank could pass his second rope around the tree and shorten the first one at the knot.

He kicked a spur into the bark, about two feet up. Not deep enough. He yanked it out and jammed it in again until it held. He kicked the other one in, flipped the rope up the tree, and was off the ground. He paused for a moment, letting his knees and calves adjust to the strain. The tree had a bit of a lean. He stayed on the uphill side, easing his body back so that the rope took his weight. The furrowed bark in front of his face showed chips and gouges. Breckenridge had gone up the same way. He pulled a spur out, lifted his foot, and sank it in again a little higher. Then the other spur. He flipped the rope again and grunted as he pulled his weight up the tree.

Twenty feet off the ground, he stopped to adjust the rope. Following shouted instructions from Kenny, he braced himself on his spurs, leaned into the tree, and awkwardly tried to swing the second line around the trunk. He had to grab it, blind, with his other hand, and he kept missing. The rough bark scraped his face, and all he could smell was pitch. Finally he got it, pulled it around, and clipped it to his belt. Then he unknotted the rope, took in about a foot, and tied it back on. He leaned back to let it take his weight before releasing the second line. Sweat beaded along his forehead and rolled down his sides beneath his shirt. He yanked a spur out and started up again.

Finally he was as close as he could get without disturbing the body. He worked his way around until he was almost underneath, his rope cinched up about a foot beneath the dead man's spurs. He jammed his own spurs in, leaned back, and paused to catch his breath. Now that he wasn't moving, his calves began to tremble. After a moment they stopped. He let his weight settle in the belt and looked down.

The spectators stood away from the tree, held back by the ring of yellow ribbon, their bodies strangely foreshortened from his new vantage point. Most of them were looking up at him. Holt stood with his hands planted on his hips, his paunch making him look like one of those dolls with the rounded bottoms that can never be knocked over. Doc Jarvis stood beside him, peering up through his glasses. The ambulance crew waited next to the two Coffee Creek climbers, a man and a woman who stood coiling rope as they studied the situation.

He twisted his body until he could reach Breckenridge's dangling hand. It was cold, but not stiff. He had died, Frank guessed, sometime within the last twelve hours. Chances of anyone making a decent shot in the dark narrowed it down to sometime after 5 a.m. Tomasovic had been shot at night, though. If they were dealing with the same killer, the dark didn't seem to bother him.

He lowered a line so that Kenny could clip on a small bag with his camera. As he waited he studied the grisly scene just above his head. A bullet appeared to have entered the body below the ribs, tearing a gaping hole in the chest. The exit wound would be on the other side, near the shoulder. Frank looked down, judging where the assailant would have stood. Probably within the area he had flagged. He called down, pointing the spot out to Vince Paley, who moved over to search it again. Frank didn't think he would find anything.

Breckenridge couldn't have lived long. Blood loss would have been severe. Ten minutes, maybe, and part of that unconscious. At least Frank hoped he'd been unconscious.

Kenny gave a tug on the line, signaling Frank to haul the camera up. He worked his way around the tree, snapping the shutter. He had just finished shot number twelve when he saw the notebook.

It was caught between Breckenridge's body and the trunk, a few inches below the victim's left hand. Frank snapped the shutter a couple more times, recording its position, then reached out and gingerly pried it loose. A pocket-sized, spiral-bound notebook, the kind you could buy in any drugstore. Blood had smeared across the top sheets of paper. Beneath the blood was writing.

Four letters, faintly traced in pencil, the outlines sloppy and uneven. F-R-E-D. Frank looked at it again. There was only one reason Breckenridge would use his last moments of life to spell out a name. But Fred? He'd gone over the list of EarthActioners present at Tomasovic's talk, and another list of those at the campground. No Fred had appeared anywhere in the investigation.

He pulled a Baggie out of his pocket and carefully sealed the notebook inside. A few more pictures and he was done. He lowered the camera and the Baggie and began his descent.

Coming down was harder than going up. Twice his spurs slipped, and he had to scrabble for a foothold. Finally he jerked them out for the last time and set his feet on solid ground. His arms and legs felt as drained as if he had run a race. He unclipped his rope, pulled it around, and hobbled away from the tree. What a performance. He felt like a retired clown, pulled back into service to make people laugh.

He knelt to unbuckle his spurs. When he stood up Kenny McKinney flashed him a grin. "That was great! I hope I can do that when I'm your age."

How old did he think he was, anyway? Frank glanced around, and saw that Kenny wasn't the only one smiling. Holt and Doc Jarvis, the ambulance crew, even the two climbers—who looked like teenagers—had grins plastered across their faces. It took him a moment to realize that they weren't making fun. They were proud of his accomplishment, pleased that he had pulled it off.

He looked back at the tree, ran his gaze along the trunk. It was a long way up. He hoped to hell he would never have to climb another one, but now he couldn't help smiling. He'd shown them what an old man could do.

The climbers were ready. Kenny went up first, twice as fast as Frank had done, the rope slapping against the tree as he flipped it up. Frank stayed long enough to watch him work his way above the body, using two ropes. Twenty feet higher he stopped to cut a couple of dead limbs out of the way, then moved up to the first live branch. He hooked his safety line to the trunk, dropped the rope, and started rigging up a rappel.

It could take hours. Frank turned to Sheriff Holt.

"Glad you could make it."

"No problem. Didn't know you were half squirrel."

Frank chuckled.

"You think we're dealing with the same guy here?" Holt asked.

Only a few hours earlier he'd convinced himself that Breckenridge was a murderer. Now Breckenridge was dead, and he wasn't sure he was competent to form an opinion. It was possible that two killers were at work, but he didn't think so. He nodded slowly.

"You want to stay on the case?" Holt asked.

Frank looked at him in disbelief. "It's my case."

"Joint investi—"

"Bullshit. You keep your nose out of this, Holt. Two days ago it was just another hassle, and you didn't want it. You're not going to horn in now that it's getting to be fun."

Holt's mouth almost twitched into a grin. Frank saw it and glared harder. "Okay, okay," the sheriff said. "Anything my office can do, just let me know."

Frank snorted.

"What did you find up there, anyway?"

He gave the sheriff a wary, guarded glance.

"What do you want me to do," Holt asked, "beg?"

"Yeah."

This time he did grin. "Okay, I'm begging."

Frank showed him the notebook, the bloodstained page visible through the plastic Baggie, and the pencil he had found earlier. The sheriff studied them for a moment. "Fred," he murmured. "There's old Fred Canning, out Verona way." He shook his head. "Got yourself a bit of evidence there, I'd say. Any idea what it means?"

"No more than you," Frank said grimly. He didn't like having his prime suspect knocked off under his nose, and he planned to do something about it.

THE SILENCE at the Burnt Meadows campground had a strained, eerie feel. In the middle of a June afternoon the place should have been bustling, with kids running among RVs, tripping over tent pegs, and dodging new arrivals. Instead, only three campsites showed signs of occupancy. Bruce Bowers's pickup was parked near the picnic area, and Bruce himself sat at a table a few feet away.

He got up as Frank pulled in and walked over to report. "Most of them left about an hour ago."

"Any problems?"

"No, they were anxious to go, especially the ones with kids. This second death really shook them up."

"Anyone see or talk to Breckenridge?"

Bruce shook his head. "He left camp before dinner, about four. Didn't say where he was going, but that wasn't unusual."

"What about Rachel Davis?"

Bruce jerked his head toward one of the tents. "She's in there. Won't talk to me. Won't talk to you, either."

"Oh?"

"She wants Ginny."

Shit. It was as though a hand had come out of the sky and smacked him across the face. He'd forgotten about Ginny. She was still at the station. They'd had breakfast together—it seemed like months ago, but was less than ten hours. In those ten hours EarthAction had squared off against Zellers fallers, and he'd found Breckenridge and shinnied up that damn tree. He hadn't thought of her once.

Maybe he wasn't ready for...whatever he'd thought about with her. Maybe he *was* married to his job, the way his ex-wife claimed. Maybe...oh, hell.

"We'd better get her up here, then."

SEVENTEEN

GINNY HAD NOT FORGOTTEN about Frank, but she had plenty of other things to keep her busy. It was noon when she first realized that something had gone wrong. The radio in Bowers's office came alive with traffic as Bruce and Vince Paley rounded up the EarthActioners and confined them to the campground. Even though they had a secure channel they were careful with their words, and she couldn't make out what had happened. Something to do with the protest, she guessed. When she heard the call for the ambulance, she knew that someone was hurt.

By one o'clock the station was alive with rumors. Only one thing was clear—a protester had died. Tony Bricca called a staff meeting. When it was over, the department heads called meetings of their own. Soon everyone knew who had died, and where, and how.

At two-thirty Christina Schnell blew in like a hurricane. The Neskanie's PIO commandeered Bowers's office, sent Ginny out for coffee, and settled down with the phone cradled against her ear. When Ginny came back, Ranger Bricca was there too. Ginny set the coffee on the desk and sat down without interrupting their intense, low-voiced discussion.

She had seen Christina Schnell before, but had never talked to her. The woman was a whirlwind. About forty-five, tall and willowy, she dressed and carried herself like a model. Her smooth black hair was pulled back into a chignon, and she wore a tiny gold cross in each ear. Her voice, deep and husky, had a Spanish lilt.

At that moment she was using it to demand access to the crime scene. Tony Bricca wanted to accommodate her, but he was worried that Frank wouldn't cooperate. His hair, always curly, drooped in damp ringlets over his forehead. The more Christina talked, the unhappier he looked.

"It's your district," Christina pointed out. "And Larry— your boss, the forest supervisor—wants me up there. He wants complete control of the media. Not like last time."

Bricca flushed. It was only two days ago that he had spilled everything he knew about the homicide investigation to that pretty television reporter. His curls drooped even farther. Neither he nor Christina seemed to have noticed Ginny's presence.

"Carver isn't going to listen to me," he complained. "Why can't Larry talk to him?"

"Because he can't reach him. Carver called in about noon, after he'd found the body, but since then he's been as out of touch as a man can get and still keep his job."

Bricca opened his mouth, hemmed, hawed, and floundered so badly that Ginny wondered how he had ever become a district ranger. Perhaps it was Christina's presence that unhinged him. She was formidable.

He was saved, momentarily, by the telephone. Christina took the call. It was evidently from a reporter, and when she hung up a few minutes later she looked even more determined.

"Within an hour we're going to have two television crews here, maybe more. We've got nothing to show them. If they don't get it from us, they'll start poking around on their own. God knows what they'll find."

Bricca nodded glumly. "What do you want?"

"I want to take them up there. The body hasn't been removed?"

"Not yet."

"They'll love it. Plus an interview with Carver."

"Good luck."

Christina chuckled. "He's got buttons that can be pushed, just like everyone else."

The phone beeped again. She picked it up. "Christina Schnell."

A puzzled look spread over her face. "No, he's not here. Just a moment." She looked up. "It's Charlie Zellers's lawyer. He wants Carver."

"What for?" Bricca asked.

She shrugged.

Ginny was already up and at the desk. She lifted the receiver out of Christina's hand. "This is Ginny Trask, Carver's assistant." It wasn't the strict truth, but close enough.

"His assistant?" The lawyer sounded young, unsure of himself. That surprised her. Surely the Zellerses had a company lawyer, someone with years of experience. Admittedly, a corporation lawyer might not take on a murder defense himself, but this sounded like a kid. Now he was talking again. "Didn't Ellen Jacobson speak with you a few hours ago?"

"Yes, she did. Did she get in to see Charlie?"

"I'll say. Ms. Trask, my client has been wrongfully arrested. He has new information—well, it's not exactly new, but he's willing to divulge it at this point in time—that I believe will exonerate him. He wants to make a statement to either Sheriff Holt or Agent Carver. I understand that both of them are at Coffee Creek."

"That's right. Can you tell me what it is?"

"My instructions from my client are to arrange a meeting with either Holt or Carver. I believe he wants to tell them himself."

She had a pretty good idea of what Charlie wanted to say. Ellen Jacobson's comment, the one that had been nagging at the back of her mind for the last hour or so, was starting to make sense.

"We'll have to patch you through. Might take a while." She got the lawyer's phone number and hung up.

"What's going on?" Christina demanded. "What does he want?"

"He wants to talk to Frank."

"Along with everyone else. What about?"

Ginny smiled politely. "I don't know, Ms. Schnell."

"You must have some idea. What do you think it is?"

She patted her pocket. The keys to her rig were still there. "I think I'm going to save my ideas for my boss."

GINNY WAS well on her way when her radio sputtered and the Coffee Creek dispatcher came on, calling her name.

She unhooked the mike. "Trask."

"Relay from Carver. Ten-twenty?"

Location. She glanced out the window, estimating. "Road ten-oh-six, about half a mile above the fish hatchery."

There was a pause, then the radio crackled again. "He wants you to report to the Burnt Meadows campground."

"On my way." She estimated again. "ETA fifteen minutes. Trask clear."

That was a relief. She had been wondering if she should have called Frank rather than taking off without direct instructions. She didn't think, though, that she could have stood much more of Christina and Tony. This was better. She felt like she was on the team again.

Frank was waiting for her. "That was fast," he said, as she got out of the truck.

"I was on my way already. Charlie Zellers wants to talk to you. His lawyer called about half an hour ago."

Frank raised an eyebrow.

"It sounds important. You ought to wear a beeper."

"Then I'd never get anything done." He got into his truck and picked up the mobile phone. A minute later he was back. "It's going to take a while. They'll call in about twenty minutes. Now, Rachel Davis wants to talk to *you*."

"Me?"

"That's right. Bruce is with her. Over there, past the picnic tables."

Why her? If Rachel had something to say, why not tell Bruce or Frank? "Where's everyone else?" she asked.

"We got statements and sent them packing. Meg Nugent and a couple of the others are staying with Gayle Wallace. Rachel says she won't give a statement unless you're here."

Rachel was sitting cross-legged beside a smoldering campfire, hands loose in her lap. She gazed off into the woods, oblivious. Bruce stood watching her from a few feet away. He stepped forward as Frank and Ginny approached.

"Any change?" Frank asked, his voice low.

"Nothing," Bruce said softly. "She looks catatonic. I wonder if we *should* question her."

"You think she's so out of it her statement might not be admissible?"

Bruce nodded.

He might be right. Frank closed his eyes, thinking. He'd questioned dozens of mentally unstable people—suspects, witnesses, victims. Sometimes their testimony held up in court, sometimes it didn't. Right now, though, he expected a confession from Rachel Davis. A confession would give them something to work with, something to substantiate— something that *would* hold up. For the life of him, he didn't see how they could proceed without it.

"Let's go ahead." Motioning Ginny to follow, he walked over to the tree and knelt down beside Rachel.

"Miss Davis? Ginny's here."

Rachel turned toward them, slowly focusing on Ginny with a gaze as hollow as an empty room. After a moment something seemed to flicker behind her eyes.

Ginny knelt down and touched her hand. "You wanted to talk to me?"

Rachel made a croaking noise, cleared her throat, and tried again. "I want to tell you about Alan."

Bruce already had his notebook out. Frank switched his pocket tape recorder on and murmured into it, recording the date, place, and people present. He touched Ginny on the shoulder, cautioning her to wait.

"Miss Davis."

Rachel turned toward him, seeming to see him for the first time. He had the feeling that he was speaking to her over a great distance.

"Rachel," he said gently. "I have to tell you a few things before we start." He advised her of her rights, repeating the formula he had memorized at the beginning of his career. "Do you understand?" he asked.

She nodded.

"Can you tell me out loud?"

"I understand."

"And you want to make a statement?"

"Yes."

"You realize that you can have a lawyer present?"

"I know," she said wearily. "I don't want a lawyer, not right now. I just want to tell her about Alan."

He backed off, leaving the tape recorder in front of Ginny. He didn't think Rachel grasped the significance of hearing her Miranda rights, but he had done the best he could.

Ginny knew what it meant, though. Frank thought he'd found the murderer. She thought he was mistaken.

"What about Alan?" she asked.

Rachel's eyes, dry until now, glistened with tears. "I loved him. I really did love him. And I never told him so."

Ginny touched Rachel's hand. "Do you think he knew?"

"No." She gulped. "That's the worst thing. I don't think he ever knew."

Ginny squeezed her hand and waited.

When Rachel spoke again her voice was low, but quick and flowing. "I'm thirty-eight. I don't have any kids, my family hardly speaks to me. Most of the friends I've ever had hate me. I've never been a nice person. I've always had more important things to think about than being nice."

She stopped, swallowed, and went on again. "I met Alan about six years ago, in Arizona. We were—we were doing something. I'd heard about him before that. The environmental movement's gotten pretty big now, but back then it was more like a family. He'd heard about me, too, but he didn't realize it at first—I'd been using my other name."

She glanced up at Bruce and Frank, standing discreetly back, but not out of earshot. "Red Tail," she said, with a touch of defiance. "That's my other name."

She turned back to Ginny. "Alan really fell for me. I was kind of flattered, at first. It was nice having all that attention. And the stuff we were doing—well, it was pretty exciting." She smiled. "Excitement is a great aphrodisiac.

"I'd bought this house, mostly so we'd have some kind of central place. We had an office there, a telephone. A lot of our members did contract work in the woods—tree-planting, thinning, fire fighting—and they didn't have permanent homes. There always seemed to be half-a-dozen people crashing in the living room. You never knew who would be there for dinner, who might show up at three a.m. Alan fit right in.

"I guess those were the best two years in my life." She sighed, then went on. "Alan talked a lot about Ward. A couple times he went down to California to see him, but I didn't meet him until he moved up to Longmont. Ward and Alan and I stayed up all night, talking. Ward was really interested in what we were doing, and he seemed interested in me, too. I don't think Alan noticed, not right at first. But I did.

"A couple days later Ward called, wanted to get together to talk about some project. We met at a restaurant, out by the freeway. Well—" She shrugged. "We ended up in bed."

From the corner of her eye, Ginny caught a glimpse of Frank heading toward the truck. It was time to call the county jail, time to talk to Charlie Zellers. Somehow, Charlie's story had to fit in with what Rachel was telling them.

Talking about Alan and Ward had brought Rachel back to life. She smiled, laughed, moved her hands around. Ginny could imagine Tomasovic falling for her—she had that same vitality, that same intensity of purpose. They would have come together with a crackle of lightning, like two charged clouds.

Ward managed to keep the affair a secret from his wife, but Rachel was not capable of such discretion. Alan had evidently taken it pretty hard. A few weeks later he left Eugene.

"We didn't hear from him for months, though we did hear about him. He was traveling around the Southwest, Arizona, New Mexico, keeping busy." She smiled. "Alan always kept busy."

As she listened, Ginny pieced Rachel's story together with what she had heard from Teresa, what they already knew about Alan and Ward. It fit. These would have been the two years unaccounted for in Breckenridge's file, the years

Frank figured he had spent blowing up bulldozers and spiking trees.

"Then Teresa got pregnant again. She was always real demanding, wanting to know where Ward was all the time, wanting him home every night. Finally he told her he was in love with someone else. He moved in with me about a month after the baby was born. A few months later she filed for divorce."

That would have been just two years ago. Ginny nodded. She knew what was coming next.

Ward had been looking for another position, something more in line with his environmental activism than teaching. That summer he got his chance. The National Environmental League offered him a job in Washington, D.C., working up scientific support for legislative proposals. It was a desk job, with a lot of travel, and he jumped at it.

Frank was back. He caught her eye and flashed an A-OK. It was all right, then. Charlie had finally told Frank why he had met with Ward. As soon as they had a chance, Frank would tell her, and a piece of the puzzle would fall into place.

Had Charlie told him, too, that Ward was his son? He must have, if Frank was having him released. She smiled to herself, thinking that she had guessed right. It was that comment Ellen Jacobson had made—that once he fell for Debbie, Ward couldn't help himself, "just like his dad." She'd told Teresa Tomasovic the same thing, and it had puzzled Teresa, too—the only time Ellen had ever said anything against her first husband.

Except, of course, that she hadn't meant her first husband at all. She had meant Ward's real father—Charlie Zellers.

Rachel Davis was still talking about Tomasovic's job in Washington. "He said the stuff we were doing wouldn't make much difference in the long run. This job was going to give him a chance to save thousands of acres of wilderness, thousands of miles of streams and rivers.'' She paused. "And he called *us* naive."

He had wanted her to go, but she refused. She wasn't going to play dirty games in Washington. Ginny tried to picture her in the capital, her intensity swallowed by crowds and traffic. She wondered, too, if Washington was just too close to the family Rachel had virtually abandoned. In any case, she hadn't gone.

And after she had refused, Ginny knew, Ward had asked Teresa. He evidently had not cared for the idea of moving across the country by himself. Maybe that was too harsh. According to Rachel, their parting of ways had been loud and public. Maybe Ward had had enough to give him a new appreciation for his wife—former wife, at that point.

Rachel's obsession with him changed from love to disdain, then hardened into a sense of betrayal. She was still passionate—anything she felt, she felt to the hilt. And what she felt now was hatred.

That was how Alan found her when he returned to Eugene a few months later. He moved back in, and for a year the two of them followed Ward's career through newsletters and gossip, jeering at his failures, and even more at his successes. Finally, disillusioned with the legislative process, Ward returned to Oregon.

She still loved him. She went up to Portland to see him. He took her out to lunch, an uneasy meal without much talk. Two days later she was back. They spent the night together, and then nothing for three weeks. Rachel was not accustomed to sitting by the phone, hoping for a call that never came. She charged back up to Portland, to the house where Ward was staying with friends, and demanded an explanation. She got more than she wanted

"He started talking about someone named Debbie, someone he'd known in high school, for Christ's sake. Why would you want to see someone from your high school? She'd seen him on television, and she gave him a call."

At first Rachel couldn't believe what Ward was telling her. He was in love with someone else. He and this Debbie were having an affair, meeting secretly so that her family wouldn't guess. Finally Rachel realized that he had betrayed her again.

"What did Alan think about all this?" Ginny asked.

"He didn't know," Rachel said gruffly.

Ginny didn't believe it. Rachel was not capable of hiding her feelings. Alan must have known, but chose to act as though he didn't, waiting patiently for Rachel to come to her senses.

Or perhaps not so patiently. "Rachel," Ginny asked, "did Alan kill Ward?"

She sat still, staring into the woods again. "I thought so. Until last night, that was what I thought. But now—" She turned, moving her eyes deliberately to include Bruce and Frank, to make sure they were listening.

"Alan told me he met Ward on Friday, at the Burnt Meadows sale. They hadn't seen each other for years, and they had a lot to say. At the end of it, they'd patched things up. Alan was devastated by Ward's death. Yesterday he said there was something he had to do, something he wanted to talk to Carver about." She lifted her chin and looked at Frank. "He followed you last night, after you talked to Meg. He knew something about how Ward died, and when he told you, you killed him."

"Me?" Frank said stupidly. "Lady, if I shoot someone, it's not going to be a hundred feet up a tree. Why would I kill Breckenridge?"

"You tell me," Rachel said.

Frank shook his head. "Rachel, can you tell us exactly what Alan said to you? Word for word?"

Rachel took a deep breath and reached out to take Ginny's hand again. She lifted her head. "Ginny's going to hear everything I say, so don't think you can shoot me, too. Alan said the Freddies were on Ward's tail, that he'd seen them. Freddies with guns." She cast a meaningful look at Frank's holstered revolver. "The only Forest Service employees I've seen with guns are the cops."

Suddenly Frank knew why Alan had chosen those four cryptic letters for his dying message. It wasn't a name at all, but his favorite derogatory term for Forest Service—federal—employees.

He cast a quick, wary glance at Bowers. The Coffee Creek LEO stood solidly, gazing at Rachel with no signs of emotion. He must realize that he was included in the accusation.

According to Rachel, then, Breckenridge had met Ward on Friday, and at that time had seen someone in a Forest Service uniform, carrying a gun, whom he believed to be following Ward. He planned to convey that information to Frank, but had been shot before he had a chance—presumably by the same person, in order to shut him up.

There were only three Forest Service cops Breckenridge could have seen. Frank nodded. Himself, Bowers, and Vince Paley. Paley had not arrived from Sitkum until Friday evening. If Rachel's story meant anything at all, only one possibility was left.

There was also the story he had just heard from Charlie Zellers, the story that still left one big piece missing. Perhaps this was it.

Frank turned to Bowers. "Where were you Friday afternoon?"

The LEO looked at him in amazement. "You're not taking this seriously, are you? The woman's practically crazy."

"Where were you Friday afternoon?"

"On patrol."

"Up here?"

"Sure I was up here. The EarthActioners were already at the campground."

"Did you go down into the sale area?"

"Hell, no! I didn't get out of my rig."

Ginny's mind had started working, too. "We couldn't reach you on the radio," she said. "You were late for the meeting with Ward on Friday, and we couldn't reach you for a good hour."

Bowers shook his head. "I don't believe this."

Frank was having trouble believing it, too, but he couldn't leave it unresolved. "Just answer the questions, Bruce," he said gently. "We'll get it straightened out. Why couldn't Ginny reach you on the radio?"

"I don't know. I didn't hear her. You know what reception's like around here."

It was true, radio reception could be tricky, but something wasn't right. Motive, means, and opportunity. He knew something about the first two already, and now he knew what his next question was going to be. He tried not to look at the gun holstered on Bowers's belt.

"Charlie Zellers sent Tomasovic a note on Friday evening. Four people handled it. Four people could have known where Tomasovic would be at eleven that night."

A wary look came into Bowers's eyes, but he stayed silent.

"Tomasovic is dead, Charlie has finally explained what he was doing there, and the third person is a ten-year-old boy. That leaves you."

"I don't remember a note."

"Eric Sondheim handed it to you. You presumably gave it to Tomasovic—we found it on his body. I've put that note in an envelope, the same kind Charlie used, and held it up to the light. It's pretty legible."

He was still trying not to look at the gun. He'd drawn his own gun in the course of duty more than once, he wasn't a bad shot, but he had no illusions. Bowers was an excellent marksman, and fast.

Bowers was shaking his head. "I don't believe this. Why would I kill Tomasovic?"

"For money, is my guess. Someone paid you. Most likely Bob Blanchard."

"Who the hell is Bob Blanchard?"

"Zellers's company lawyer. The one who drew up the papers transferring ownership of seven hundred acres of old-growth from Charlie Zellers to Ward Tomasovic."

Ginny gave a little gasp. "Because Ward was Charlie's son."

"That's right," Frank said. "Ward didn't know it until just before he died."

That was why Charlie had a new lawyer, Ginny guessed. He didn't trust Blanchard. But a lawyer wouldn't do something like that on his own—he had to have had instructions.

"How much is he supposed to have paid me?" Bowers asked.

"Charlie says there's half a million dollars missing. You could have done it, Bruce. You could have killed both men. You're a good shot, you were out of touch at the relevant times, and money is a big temptation."

Bowers snorted. "Not big enough. You're way out of line, Carver. You'd better start looking for a new LEO."

"There's something else," Ginny said. Bowers spun around to look at her, but Frank, she noticed, kept his eyes on the LEO. "Didn't you tell me you had a brother who died?"

A new look came into Bowers's eyes, wary and watchful. "Yes, I did."

"Where did that happen?"

"Back home, where I grew up."

"Where was that?"

"Eastern Oregon."

Frank kept his eyes on Bowers's right hand, hovering uncomfortably close to his holstered semiautomatic. What was Ginny getting at? He didn't like the new tone in Bowers's voice, or the tension radiating from him like heat from a fire.

"I don't think so," Ginny said quietly. "I think it happened right here, in Coffee Creek. Ward Tomasovic took your brother fishing one day. Your brother drowned, didn't he? Your name was Ney back then, before your mother remarried. Your family used to own that section—the land that Charlie wanted to give to Ward."

Frank glanced at her for just an instant, but it was an instant too long. When he looked back Bowers had drawn his gun. He held it pointed at Frank's chest.

"He killed my brother," Bruce said. His voice was high, tight, but under control. "He just sat there in the boat and let my brother drown."

EIGHTEEN

"MOVE YOUR HAND away from the gun," Bruce said. He needed time to think. He had always been methodical, had always planned for contingencies, and yesterday, when the look of recognition had slowly dawned in Breckenridge's eyes, he had foreseen the possibility of something like this. If only he could have nailed Breckenridge before he had a chance to talk to little Rachel blabbermouth here—but he hadn't.

Instead, Carver had sent him off to Verona, treating him like a snotty kid who wouldn't mind. He'd recognized Ellen Jacobson, all right—Mrs. Tomasovic, from the school cafeteria. He could still remember her slopping extra servings on their plates, him and his brother, and the wrenching mix of humiliation and gratitude they had both felt. He had recognized a lot of people in Coffee Creek, but so far only Ellen and Andy Zellers had guessed who he was.

And then Andy had offered him the chance to get even. He'd wanted to do it for years, but the money made it possible. The money still made it possible, even now.

Carver was going to jump him at the first possible chance. But he was younger, stronger, faster. He had a good plan, and he could think on his feet. He flicked his eyes at Carver's gun.

"Take it out and drop it on the ground."

Carver moved slowly, his eyes never leaving Bowers's face. His hand touched the butt of the pistol and hesitated, just for an instant.

"You try it, Carver, and after I shoot you I'll take out the ladies, too." He meant it, even though he needed Carver for a while yet, and he didn't want to shoot Ginny. You had to mean it, though, to make it real.

Carver's gun dropped to the ground, hitting the packed earth with a little thump.

"Now kick it over here."

Carver gave it a shove with his foot. Bruce moved closer, knelt, picked it up. The two women were motionless beneath the tree, frozen in place.

He pulled a bandanna out of his pocket and tossed it on the ground. "Take this and tie Rachel's hands behind her, around that little tree."

Carver did as he was told, with Bruce watching every move. When Carver leaned his head a bit too close to Rachel's ear, Bruce jerked the gun. "No talking."

While Carver worked, Bruce looked around for another binding. His gaze lighted on Rachel's backpack. When Carver had finished, he ordered him to toss the pack over. Kneeling, he rummaged inside. His hand closed over something hard and smooth. He pulled out a little .22 pistol with a pearl handle. Silly toy. He slipped it into his pocket and kept searching until he found a filmy sash. He wadded it into a ball and tossed it toward Carver. "Tie Ginny to the tree, too."

He didn't need to kill them. He didn't want to—Ginny was sweet, really, and she'd been nice to him—but he went by logic, and logic told him to keep it simple. Their two bodies would be as incriminating as anything they might say, would certainly intensify the hunt Holt was sure to put in motion.

When the two women were secured, he motioned Carver away and checked the bindings. Good enough. They wouldn't get loose before Holt came looking for them. He'd fleshed out the details of his plan, and he was almost ready to go.

He motioned to Carver. "Stick your hand out."

Should he wait? No, he needed Carver, but the man was too dangerous. He took aim and deliberately fired a shot into Carver's right hand.

GINNY WINCED at the shot. Please don't kill him, she prayed. Oh, God, please don't let him die. She could see both of them from where she stood. Frank waited stolidly, his arm hanging at his side, dripping blood. Bowers motioned him toward the parking area. They stopped at Ginny's truck, where Bowers knelt beside the open door, reached in, and yanked two or three times. He pulled out a handful of wires and tossed them into the brush. That took care of the radio.

At Frank's truck they stopped again while Bowers got the first-aid kit out. He watched, still holding the gun, while Frank roughly bandaged his hand. He motioned Frank in behind the wheel. The truck lurched clumsily into movement. Frank steering and Bowers shifting gears. Somehow they got it turned around. They pulled out onto the road, gravel skittering beneath the wheels.

Ginny heard them take the first turn, and then the sound of the truck faded away to nothing. A deep hush settled over the campground. Off in the woods, a thrush repeated a single piping note twice, then once again. Ginny twisted her hands and flexed her fingers, trying to pick at the sash behind her wrists.

"Jesus Christ," Rachel muttered. "Why didn't he kill us?"

"God knows." She couldn't reach the knots in the sash, but she *could* feel Rachel's hands poking her in the back, just above her own.

"He's gonna kill Carver," Rachel said. "Just like he killed Ward and Alan."

Ginny nodded unhappily. She had already figured that out. "See if you can stand beside me. I think I can reach your hands."

They shuffled around the tree, twisting their bodies until Ginny's bound hands were directly below Rachel's. "Now squeeze up next to the tree and push your hands out," Ginny said. "Maybe I can reach the knots."

Ah, that was better. She picked at the bandanna, pulling and tugging whatever she could reach. The fabric was cinched up tight, though, and she couldn't get a grip. Three minutes went by, four, five. She slumped down in frustration. "Damn. I can't get it."

"They'll find us," Rachel said.

"Yeah, but Frank might be dead by then." Ginny looked around the little clearing, so full of people only a few hours ago. They'd had a fire that morning, the one Rachel had been sitting next to when she arrived. The fire circle was only a few feet away.

The air above the charcoal and ashes rippled in the sunlight.

Heat. Something in the fire circle was still burning. Maybe, just maybe... "Sit down, Rachel. I think I can reach the fire." She stretched her foot out, pulled Rachel up close to the tree, and stretched even farther, feeling with her toes. A moment later she nudged a smoldering stick out of the circle.

Patience. Persistence. Nudging the stick closer was not a simple job. It caught on the rough ground, turned at awkward angles. The closer it got, though, the easier it was to move. The tip was still smoldering, the coal shaken back into life by movement. Finally it was close enough that she could bend over and blow. A small flame leaped and flared.

Rachel's hands were closer, but she couldn't see. Ginny gave her directions, until finally the smoldering stick was in position.

"The bandanna's cotton," Ginny said. "What's this sash made out of?"

"Some kind of synthetic."

"Let's see if it melts."

It seemed to take forever. Every minute or two Rachel held the stick out as far as she could and Ginny blew on it, keeping the coal alive. She tried to focus on Rachel's hands, on the pain where the sash bit into her wrists, on the new pain where the melting synthetic burned into her skin, or anything other than what Bruce might be doing to Frank. Finally she felt the sash give. A minute later her hands slipped away from the tree.

She untied Rachel, and the two women stood for a moment, rubbing their wrists.

"It's true, then," Rachel said. "All that stuff about Bowers growing up here, his brother, all that."

"Looks like it," Ginny said grimly. "He must have hated Ward pretty bad."

"He couldn't swim," Rachel said.

"Ward?"

Rachel nodded. "Never even went into a pool."

"So he couldn't have saved the kid."

Rachel shook her head. "When Bowers said Ward just sat there in the boat, I knew." She sighed. "Now what?"

Ginny patted her pocket. The keys to the truck were still there. A moment later, though, when she turned the key in the ignition, she realized that Bruce had disconnected more than the radio. The truck wasn't going anywhere.

"Come on," she said. "Once we get out to the road we'll meet someone. This mountain must be crawling with people."

Rachel nodded and fell in beside her. They crossed the parking area, little puffs of dust rising into the air with each step. The air smelled of dust and warm pitch. Insects hummed in the sunshine, and off in the woods the thrush still called out its single, unvarying note.

Ten minutes to reach the paved road, then another ten before they heard a vehicle. They both flagged desperately. A few minutes later they were riding with a television crew from Portland, heading for a press area Christina Schnell had set up on the landing above the Burnt Meadows sale. By the time they got there, Rachel had spilled the story, in spite of Ginny's efforts to keep her quiet. In the end, she supposed, it didn't make much difference. She kept her own mouth shut until Sheriff Holt arrived.

Events spun forward after that, out of control, dragging her along. Bowers and Frank had been spotted twice along the road, heading east, toward the summit. Nothing had seemed out of the ordinary. That had been Bruce's plan, Ginny realized, when he forced Frank to drive. Kenny McKinney spread maps across a tailgate, and suddenly the landing was crowded with more uniforms, more flashing tin, than Ginny had known existed in Angus County. Possible destinations were put forth, possible plans of action. Radios sputtered and squawked. Rigs left, and more rigs arrived, more people. Dust churned up by all the traffic drifted in lazy veils above the landing.

The crowd kept pushing Ginny out toward the edge, until finally she got tired of fighting and curled up on the front seat of Christina Schnell's car. It was past six, and the sun was hanging just above the treetops. They had, at most, another two hours of decent light. Shadows crept slowly toward the car. Frank might be dead by now—at the very least, he was in pain—and there was nothing she could do. Holt seemed to have forgotten her existence. Hot, gritty tears welled up in her eyes. She dabbed at them with scented tissues from Christina's glove compartment.

This wasn't doing any good. She wadded up the tissues and stuffed them into a trash bag hanging beneath the dash. Like all the cops out there, all pumped with adrenaline, she wanted nothing more than to dash off and *do* something, anything, rather than sit. And like them, she hadn't the first idea of what to do. What she did have, though, was information. She had just spent two days with Bowers. Chances were she knew him as well as anyone in Coffee Creek. She closed her eyes and thought back to their first meeting, letting her mind go blank as she tried to recapture every detail of his appearance and actions.

After a while she pulled her notebook out of her breast pocket and started to write. That was how Deputy Larkin found her half an hour later, when he ambled over and folded his lanky body almost in half to tap on the window. "Ginny?"

She looked up with a start. Three pages of the little book were filled with cryptic notes. "Hi, Bill. Is anything happening yet?"

"Not a hell of a lot. Sheriff asked me to talk to you. Something about Bowers being from around here?"

She slipped the notebook back into her pocket. "Evidently so. Ellen Jacobson thought she recognized him yesterday, when he questioned her about Tomasovic."

"And she thinks he's the Ney boy?"

Ginny nodded. "You should have seen the look on his face when I brought it up—well, that was when he pulled his gun."

Larkin thought for a moment. "I remember the older boy, the one who drowned. Billy, his name was. Tough son of a bitch. Beat up my little brother once."

"You grew up in Coffee Creek?"

He nodded. "I joined the army after high school, then spent ten years with the Portland police. Moved back about five years ago. I'd forgotten all about the Neys until now."

"Did you know Ward?"

"Oh, yeah. Knew who he was, at least. He won a letter for track and field in high school."

"You know what I don't get? How come no one recognized Bowers when *he* moved back here?"

"Well, I've been thinking about that myself. Susan, that would be his mom, she grew up on their old homeplace. I never knew her—just knew who she was. She showed up when I was in high school. No husband, no ring, just two boys with her family name. Billy and Bruce both came into town for school, but we hardly ever saw Susan or her dad. Then, right after Billy died, she was gone. Married some guy from eastern Oregon—God only knows how they met. His name must have been Bowers—maybe he adopted the boy."

"So Bruce's name was different, and no one had seen him since he was a kid."

"Yeah. And of course he must not have said anything. Wouldn't necessarily have any reason to. Old man Ney died years ago. The state took his place over and auctioned it off for back taxes."

"That's how Zellers's company got it?"

Larkin nodded. "They buy up most all the timberland that comes on the market around here."

Ginny was quiet for a moment, thinking. "So Bowers lived at that homestead as a kid?"

Larkin nodded. "Yeah. I think we better go get the sheriff, don't you?"

"IT MAKES SENSE," Holt said. "We just found Carver's rig, driven over the side of a spur road about three miles from here." He showed them on a map. The spot was almost directly above the headwall of Coffee Creek's north fork, the stream that flowed through the old Ney place. "There must be a road going in along the creek."

Larkin nodded. "I doubt anyone's used it for the past ten years."

"Are there any buildings left?"

"Couple. Not habitable."

The sheriff nodded, thinking. "You figure Bruce knows this place pretty well?"

"It's been a long time since he lived there."

"But he's been in the area for over six months," Ginny said. "Bruce is a planner. He's always got Plan A, and Plan B, and then Plan C. He must have known something like this might happen. I'd bet money he was ready for it."

"He's got another rig somewhere," Holt said, making it a statement.

Ginny nodded. "He wouldn't ditch the first one without a backup."

"He's still up there," Larkin added. "We've got road-blocks on the highway and Coffee Creek Road."

The sheriff glanced at the map. "There's no back way out?"

"Not without a four-wheeler." Larkin paused. "I guess he might have a four-wheeler."

Holt sighed. "We need someone who knows this area, knows the old roads, the game trails, the creeks."

Larkin nodded in agreement. "We need Charlie Zellers."

NINETEEN

HIS HAND HURT LIKE HELL. Frank gritted his teeth and pushed through a thicket of huckleberry. Bowers's gun, he knew, was about three feet from the back of his head. A branch whipped loose and smacked him in the face. He winced and slowed down.

"Keep going," Bowers said.

He hadn't realized how much he used his hands going through the brush. He'd worked once with a one-armed man—Bob Cummins. Amazing what the guy could do. He didn't think they'd have to amputate the hand. If he made it to a hospital alive. All those tiny, shattered bones, the nerves curled aimlessly through the pulpy flesh. Christ, he'd better find something else to think about.

He tried guessing again why Bowers had taken him, instead of one of the women. They'd sailed past the checkpoints he and Holt had set up a few hours earlier without a hitch, but Bowers could have done that with Ginny. It was, Frank thought, the humiliation factor. He wasn't likely to forget the sullen look on Bowers's face when he sent him to Verona, after the mix-up with Rachel Davis. It was already obvious that the man held grudges—he'd held one against Tomasovic for over twenty years.

They were out of the huckleberry now. Bowers stopped to check his radio again, running through the frequencies on the little hand-held. Nothing. Frank smiled to himself. Holt knew they'd have a radio and was keeping his people off the air.

While he caught his breath, Frank checked the area out. Just ahead a couple of windfall trees lay across the slope like giant pick-up-sticks. The trunks were too low to go under. It was going to be a hell of a scramble with one hand. Even with two—Bowers couldn't climb over those trees and keep his gun trained on Frank's head at the same time.

He'd have a decent chance, he figured, if he could get just fifty feet away from Bowers. The dense brush was on his side, and the light in the steep little canyon would be fading soon. He risked a glance at his watch. Half an hour since they'd ditched the truck. He'd tried to scramble into the brush then, but Bowers had been too quick, had cut him off before he got away. He'd been looking for another chance every minute since. Perhaps this was it.

He dug his heels into the duff to keep from slipping on the steep slope. They were almost up to the windfall.

"Left," Bowers ordered. "Sidehill."

So much for that opportunity. Frank turned and worked his way along the slope, uphill of the fallen trees. He was certain now that Bowers knew exactly where they were going. He figured he'd guessed at just about everything by now, including the fact that Bowers did not intend to keep him alive much longer.

Holt would have sent someone to check the campground. Thank God Ginny and Rachel were okay—he still didn't know why Bowers had left them alive. He risked a glance back at his captor. Bowers's eyes, blue and very hard, met his. Evidently he could manage the rough ground without watching every step.

"Downhill here, into the creek."

Frank turned and pushed his way through a tangle of salmonberry. The creek, about three feet wide, flowed past with a fluid gurgle. During their hike down the canyon he had tried to mentally superimpose their route on what he remembered from the Burnt Meadows maps. He was pretty sure this creek went through the old homestead at the end of the North Fork Road.

Bowers motioned for him to keep moving downstream. An old trick, and one that wouldn't stop a good tracker. They had to get out of the water somewhere. Still, it would hold a search party up. The creek was slow here, and his boots slipped on the slimy stones. His feet were soaked through within seconds.

They might have found the rig by now. Two people had seen them driving. Once Ginny and Rachel told their story, it shouldn't take them more than half an hour to check the spur roads leading off Prairie Mountain. Bowers had ordered him to drive right over the side, into a ditch about four feet deep. The truck was more or less hidden, but a vehicle that size doesn't go through brush without leaving any signs. If they were looking, they'd find it.

The problem was that the Prairie Mountain road kept going. The track down the back side wasn't paved, but it was passable. If he were in Holt's shoes, he'd fling a roadblock across that back road, a couple more on Coffee Creek and the North Fork, before he started looking for the rig. You couldn't go very far cross-country in these hills, even in a tank. Holt would put a noose of roadblocks around Prairie Mountain, then start pulling it tight.

That was what Bowers expected, and that was why he was keeping Frank alive. Frank was his ticket out of the noose. Once they were out, though, the ticket was as good as dead.

Was Holt making the connection between Bowers and the Ney homestead? If he did, Frank figured he had a chance. If not—he sloshed along the creek, keeping his mind on the scenarios in which he came out alive.

HOLT'S VOICE BOOMED out over the landing as he lined out his forces. Ginny took a mental inventory of who was available: the sheriff and Larkin, with two more county deputies; two state patrol officers; Vince Paley, Kenny McKinney, and a couple others from the Forest Service. About a dozen people altogether, only half of them carrying weapons.

Six of those people had already been dispatched to roadblocks, taking three of the seven rigs equipped with lights and sirens. Right now Holt was intent on getting everyone else up to the Ney homestead as quickly, and quietly, as possible.

She waited, hoping against hope that she'd get an assignment. Two of the district people were on roadblocks, and McKinney was on his way to the Ney place with a county deputy. Within minutes everyone was lined out, and she was standing by herself on the dusty landing.

A great, choking ball of frustration rose in her throat. She clenched her fists, close to tears. Bars of light shot through the trees and lay across the landing like weights, locking her in. She wanted to throw her head back and howl.

"Ginny! Holt wants you on the phone!"

It was Christina Schnell, calling to her from the cluster of greenfleet rigs and news vans parked off to one side. She'd forgotten all about the media people. Now she swallowed, took a deep breath, and walked over to join them.

The half-dozen journalists milled around, talking and adjusting their equipment. One of them was interviewing Ranger Bricca, who looked hot and uninformed but pleased at the attention. Another pair had Christina in a corner, where they peppered her with questions that no one could answer.

"In there," Christina said, gesturing to her car.

Ginny slipped in and picked up the receiver. "Trask here."

"Ginny, good," said Holt. "Charlie Zellers should be showing up at the ranger station in about fifteen minutes. I want you to pick him up and bring him to the Ney place. We've got a roadblock on the Coffee Creek Road. Call me when you get there."

"Ten-four." A pause. "Thanks." She cradled the receiver and gazed out across the landing. The light had turned from yellow to a deep, bloody orange. She had what she wanted and dreaded at the same time. Whatever happened to Frank, she would be there.

Bowers waded to the bank and stepped out of the creek, keeping his gun on Carver. They were a couple hundred yards above the old homestead, in an area he remembered from his childhood. Pushing Carver ahead of him, he skirted through the woods, tense, silent, every sense pitched to its height. As they neared the clearing the sagging barn loomed beyond the trees, a shadow in the gathering dusk.

A twig snapped under Carver's foot.

Bowers shoved the gun against his captive's head. He didn't say anything. Carver would get the message.

They reached the edge of the timber and stopped. A light breeze rustled in the brush. Swallows swooped through the air around the barn, twittering as they pursued their evening meal. Soon they would drift one by one to their nests inside. Already a couple of bats fluttered about in the fading light—the night shift coming on duty.

Bowers stood alert, straining to catch every sound—the creek curling along the far side of the meadow, mice moving through the grass. An owl hooted softly from the timber behind them. No sign of other people.

He poked his gun into Carver's back and the two of them stepped out into the open.

For a moment he could hardly hear over the pounding of his heart. He should have cached the stuff in the woods, like he did with the .22. Then he wouldn't have had to risk exposure like this. That had been a great idea, using a handgun cartridge with a rifle. He'd thrown Carver off the track for at least a couple days.

Holt might already have men in position, ready to open fire as soon as they had a clear shot, but he didn't think so. Too many animal noises. At that moment a pair of does moved into the field between them and the tumbledown buildings. The deer, downwind from a possible ambush, confirmed his belief that they were alone.

Last week, when he finally had the stuff, the old barn had seemed like the best spot. Andy wanted him to go up to Portland to do the job, but he'd refused to move until he had everything he needed. Andy hadn't liked that, but so what? Screw him. Andy Zellers wasn't taking the risks, and neither was that lawyer with the shit-eating grin.

The two men moved into the field. The deer looked up, stared, and fled in great leaping bounds. Carver stopped, startled by the unexpected movement.

"Keep going."

They reached the barn. Bowers paused to let his eyes adjust to the deeper gloom, then motioned Frank toward the back. Halfway across the open space he stopped at what had once been a stall. He could remember coming out here on frosty winter mornings, his grandfather blowing on his hands to warm them up so the cow wouldn't bolt when he touched her teats. October—that's what he'd called her. He'd always named his cows for the month they were born.

"Kneel," he ordered.

Carver bent, grunted, and almost fell over. He stuck his good hand out to steady himself. Finally he was on the ground. Bowers gave him a disgusted look. Well, he wouldn't need Carver much longer. Another hour at the most.

He crouched down and thrust his hand underneath the loose boards by the old stall. There it was. He pulled out a small packet wrapped in dirty canvas and stuck it in his shirt pocket.

"I expected to find a rig stashed in here," Carver said in a conversational tone. It was the first time he'd spoken since leaving the truck.

"Shut up."

"What's that you've got? Money?"

"I said shut up."

"I don't see why. You must be planning to kill me, anyhow. Always the planner, huh? That was one of the reasons we hired you."

The goddamn bastard was trying to make him talk. Use a little psychology, get him to let his guard down, then make a break for it. Well, he'd done a few interrogations himself—he knew the tricks.

"Why'd you come back to Coffee Creek?" Carver asked. "Was it just coincidence that the job you wanted was here, or did you apply *because* it was here? Not talking, huh? I'd guess it was a mixture of both. You'd wanted to get even with Tomasovic for a long time, but you couldn't have known he'd come back to Coffee Creek. I'm guessing you just couldn't pass up the chance to see your old hometown, without anyone knowing you'd come back."

Bowers shoved the gun into Carver's back. "This is the last time I'm telling you to shut up." Suddenly his head snapped up. He heard it now, too. The growl of vehicles coming up the road. Damn Carver.

Headlights slashed across the clearing. They were close, too close. He stood up, keeping the gun pointed at Carver's neck. Three rigs, by the sound of it. Car doors slammed shut. Bowers tensed, his panicked heart thumping so loud he could hardly hear, his stomach and bowels clenched for flight. And then, rising above it all, came a high, keen exhilaration, almost a joy, like a bird soaring upward to the sun.

CHARLIE ZELLERS was waiting in the reception area at the ranger station. He had a rifle. As soon as Ginny pulled up he stepped out to meet her. "Where are they?"

"Holt's got everyone heading for the Ney place."

Charlie nodded. "Bowers might have hidden a truck in the old barn."

He climbed in, standing the rifle up next to the door. He glanced at Ginny. "You got a gun?"

She shook her head.

"Good. Less chance we'll shoot each other."

She pulled back out on the highway and took the turn up Coffee Creek Road. The radio—an older model that picked up only the Forest Service channels—had been silent for the last few minutes. "You know who Bowers is?"

"Jerry Ney's grandson. Should have figured it out a long time ago. Should have figured a lot of stuff out, I guess."

"I know that Ward was your son. I'm sorry, Charlie."

There was an awkward silence. "You know, I've been grieving all this time, but it wasn't until I saw Ellen this afternoon that I could talk about it."

"That must have been hard."

"I should have claimed him years ago, after Nick Tomasovic died. Ellen wouldn't have anything to do with me while her husband was alive, wouldn't take the money I sent, but I should have insisted once he was dead. None of that foolishness with Debbie would have happened—they could have been brother and sister. Ward could have gone to college, come back, worked with the rest of us, been part of the family." Charlie sighed. "But I was too damned stiff-necked. Mary—my wife—was already sick, and I didn't want to add to her burden."

He fell silent again, his fingers drumming lightly on the armrest. "I hardly knew him. I admired what he was doing. I think he was a good man."

Ginny nodded, thinking about the women in Ward's life: his wife Teresa; Debbie Kurtz, his first love and possibly his last; and Rachel Davis, who had sent his marriage up in flames. But this was a man who had paid double child support when he finally had money, who had wanted a second chance with his family. No one, not even Teresa, accused him of willfully hurting another person. His last mission had been to bring together two warring sides, to help them seek a common solution to the old-growth issue. No one's life was beyond reproach. She nodded again. "He was, Charlie. He was a good man."

"Thank you."

"Did he know you were his father?"

"I told him, that one time we talked. He didn't believe me at first, said it would take a little time to get used to the idea. Then I told him I wanted to give him the Ney place." Charlie paused. "You know, that's one of the most beautiful stands of timber in this county. Jerry Ney and his boys logged some, right around the homestead, but most of it's never been touched. There are trees in there worth thousands, just sitting on the stump. Beautiful trees.''

He fell silent. "I've cut a lot of timber in my life, but I just couldn't bring myself to take that stand. About ten years ago, after we bought it, I walked around up there. There's something about that place. I made myself a promise that it would never be cut.''

"And you figured Ward would keep that promise.''

"I was under a lot of pressure from Andy and Joe, especially with this spotted owl business. Everyone's worried we'll run out of timber. When the Forest Service put that new spur in for the Burnt Meadows sale, it opened up access to the Ney place, too. You know, I'm planning to retire in a year or two. Those boys don't want to listen to me anymore, especially Andy. I had to do something.''

"So you had the lawyer draw up papers to transfer the Ney place to Ward?''

"That's right, had Blanchard do it. The little rat.'' Charlie gave a disgusted snort. "Worked for me for years, but he just couldn't keep his mouth shut. Guess he figured Andy was the head honcho now, with me retiring and all. Christ, I can't believe, my own son...'' He cradled his forehead in one hand and fell silent.

Ginny swung the truck around a sharp turn before she spoke again. "Why wouldn't you tell us why you were meeting Ward? Why did you go to jail instead?''

"Because of Ellen. She's had a lot of grief over the years, a fair amount of it from me. I figured this was one decision she had to make.''

They took the North Fork turnoff. She saw headlights up ahead. They were almost at the roadblock. There seemed to be some sort of activity beside the patrol car.

Suddenly her radio sputtered into life. "He's shooting! Get down!" She recognized Kenny McKinney's panicked voice.

Doors slammed, red and blue lights flashed as the patrol car whipped around, spun gravel, and took off up the North Fork Road.

"He's down," Kenny shouted over the radio. "Help! Larkin's been shot!"

TWENTY

THEY WERE IN THE WOODS again, moving fast. Frank's arms were tied behind his back. Bowers had looped a rope around his arms and chest, and now Frank stumbled after him like a dog on a leash. Searchlights shot through the trees. The clearing behind them resounded with shouts, the slam of car doors, revving engines.

He'd tried to get away, once the shooting started, but Bowers had stopped him with a well-placed bullet through the shoulder. Now he could hardly think for the pain and loss of blood. His judgment wasn't worth a nickel. He stumbled, lost his balance, and fell heavily against a tree. Bowers gave the rope a savage jerk. Frank started moving again.

Where the hell were they going? Bowers was in a hurry, but he didn't seem panicked. Through the haze of pain Frank gradually realized that the woods were quiet once more. It was pitch-black, the only light a faint starshine shimmering through the canopy. Branches whipped against his face and legs, unseen roots stretched out to trip him. He followed Bowers blindly, aware only that they were climbing, moving uphill.

WHEN SHE HEARD Kenny McKinney's call for help Ginny hit the gas, ready to dash up the road behind the racing patrol car. Charlie put his hand on her arm.

"Slow up. Let's find out what's going on."

That wasn't easy, with the babble of voices pouring out of the radio. Charlie leaned forward, listening intently.

Kenny appeared to be on foot, keeping in touch with Vince Paley over a hand-held. Deputy Larkin had been shot in the leg—an ambulance was on the way.

"Sounds like he's holed up in the barn," Charlie said. "That's the only place you could hide."

A few minutes later Vince Paley came on. "They're gone," the Sitkum LEO said in a flat voice.

Charlie grabbed the mike and pressed the send button. "Did you find a rig?"

"Who's that?" Vince demanded.

Ginny took the mike. "Vince, it's Ginny. I'm with Charlie Zellers at the roadblock. He wants to know if you found a vehicle in the barn."

"Negative. They're on foot."

They. That meant Frank was still alive.

"He's got to have a rig somewhere," Charlie muttered. "I was sure it would be in the barn." He sat quietly for a moment, chewing on his lower lip. "Could be at Harris Creek."

"Where's that?"

"Next canyon over from the Ney place. There's an old logging road runs almost up to the ridge. Some of the boys drive up there each year to do a little elk hunting. Got to have a four-wheeler."

"We'd better tell the sheriff."

"You tell him. And scoot on over. I'll drive."

THEY WENT BACK down Coffee Creek to town, then east on the highway for five or six miles to Harris Creek. The paved road going up the creek ended in a small gravel pit. They stopped there to put the hubs in, then drove past the silent rock-crusher to a rutted track leading up the ridge. Charlie had been right when he said it wasn't much of a road. Even in the middle of summer, with the ground hard as cement everywhere else, they crawled through seeps with mud up to the rims. Young alders crowded the edges, held back only by the annual passage of elk hunters. They crept along at ten miles an hour.

"Worst thing would be a blowdown across the road," Charlie muttered, peering into the yellow cones cast by the headlights.

They were back to radio silence. Fifteen minutes after leaving the gravel pit, Ginny spotted headlights in the side mirror. "Company."

It was Vince Paley and the sheriff, in Vince's truck. A couple of deputies followed in the only other four-wheel drive available. They all got out for a short conference.

Holt didn't have much to say. Either Bowers was up there or he wasn't. If he was, they'd have to judge the situation when they arrived.

Before they got back in their rigs, Vince asked Ginny if she had any experience with firearms.

She nodded. Her father had taught her to shoot as a teenager. She'd been out of practice until a few months ago, when she decided to apply for the law enforcement job. Since then she'd spent three or four afternoons at the local firing range, getting back in practice.

Vince reached into his truck and pulled out his backup gun, a Colt .45 semiautomatic, with a belt and holster. "You better take this."

She stared, then swallowed and took the proffered weapon. What she was getting into was suddenly much more concrete.

They continued up the road. Though there was little hope of surprising Bowers, they drove with running lights only. Every few minutes Vince flashed his searchlight through the woods, looking for the glint of glass and metal.

Tension hung like fog inside the truck. Charlie concentrated on driving, while Ginny peered into the darkness, not knowing what to expect. "No moon," she commented.

"Won't be up for hours. Just a sliver, anyhow. Full moon's in two weeks."

Deputy Larkin was in an ambulance, on his way to the hospital in Eugene. Holt had called for another ambulance to stand by in Coffee Creek. It was a warm night, but suddenly Ginny found herself shivering.

"What's that?" she called out a few minutes later.

Charlie stopped the truck. "Where?"

"Over there." She pointed up the road. "I saw something gleam."

The other two trucks had stopped behind them. Charlie got out, leaving the door ajar, and crept silently up the road. A couple of minutes later he was back.

"That's it, all right, and no sign of Bowers."

BOWERS STOPPED at the top of the ridge. He stood still, sniffing the air like a wild animal. Frank stumbled and sank to the ground, his eyes bleary with exhaustion. He wasn't going to last much longer. Pretty soon he'd be ready to lie down and let Bowers shoot him. A breeze touched his face, cool against the scrapes and bruises. He had an incredible thirst, and wondered if he might be in shock from loss of blood.

Bowers hunkered down beside him. He'd holstered his gun before they started up the ridge, evidently aware that Frank was in no condition to pose a threat. Now he stared into his face, examining him.

"It's downhill from here, not very far. There's water in the truck."

Frank nodded, grateful to his captor for this small sign of consideration. The more rational part of his mind pointed out that this was a classic hostage reaction, but the rational part of his mind seemed very far away.

Bowers stood up, and they started downhill. The going was a little easier. After a few minutes they hit what seemed to be an old road. The footing was uneven, with ruts and potholes, but there wasn't much brush. When he looked up, Frank caught glimpses of the stars. His shoulder still hurt, but the wound wasn't bleeding as much—his shirt was a mass of sticky, coagulating blood. He caught his breath now that they weren't climbing, and his mind began to clear.

Bowers had to have a rig hidden along this road. They'd find it, Bowers would drive, and sooner or later they'd hit a roadblock. His life would be Bowers's ticket out. He would stay alive just so long as his captor needed that ticket.

His best chance to get away would be at the first roadblock. Once they were in the truck he'd feign unconsciousness—after he got a drink of water. With luck, he might be able to simply roll out when Bowers slowed for the roadblock. He had a feeling they weren't going to stop.

Bowers came to a halt. They stood in the middle of the rough track, listening. The fir boughs above their heads sighed softly as cool air flowed through them down the hillside. Small scurrying sounds came from the duff beneath their feet. Upslope, deer moved quietly through the brush. The woods were hushed, but deeply alive. Despite his exhaustion, his pain, and his very real fear, Frank sensed something of awe. To be in this place at this time was a blessing, perhaps the last he would ever receive.

Bowers gave the rope a tug and started off again, apparently satisfied that they were alone. A few minutes later Frank caught the glimmer of starlight on a windshield. Bowers hurried the pace.

They reached the cab, Bowers in front. Suddenly lights blazed out from nowhere, dazzling their eyes, pinning them against the side of the truck. Before Frank could move, Bowers shoved him in front.

"Shoot, and I'll kill him," he shouted.

"NOW WHAT?" Ginny whispered. She and Charlie were about thirty feet away, hiding in the brush. They had a fairly good view of the pickup truck, visible in the glare of three pairs of headlights. Vince Paley and one of the deputies were in a similar position on the other side.

Charlie shrugged. "Wait here and try to get a decent shot, I guess."

"We're not shooting," Sheriff Holt called out. "We want to negotiate."

Bowers was slowly backing up, taking Frank with him. She could see the gun, stuck into Frank's neck, and the rope around his chest. They reached the back of the truck. Bowers seemed to feel more comfortable with all that metal between himself and the sheriff.

"Okay," he shouted. "So negotiate."

"Put your gun down, let Carver go, and we won't hurt you."

Bowers snorted. "Let me drive out of here with Carver, and I won't hurt *him*."

"Come on, Bruce, you know we can't do that."

Charlie brought his gun up to his shoulder. "This could take all night."

"Have you got a clear shot?"

"No."

"Maybe Vince has a better chance," she suggested.

"If he does, he's not using it."

"What if we move?"

"He'll hear us. You still got that pistol?"

"Yeah."

"Well, get it out. We might need it."

The sheriff and Bowers continued to talk back and forth, both playing for time. Ginny unholstered Vince's gun, knelt back, and braced her arm. This was one of the positions she had practiced at the firing range. Her angle was about the same as Charlie's. If she shot, she'd be just as likely to hit Frank as Bowers. Chances were, though, that she'd miss them both.

"Six inches," Charlie muttered. "That's all I need."

Bowers moved, but not far enough. He seemed to be trying to adjust something, maybe the rope around Frank's chest. Suddenly Frank slumped forward against the tailgate, leaving Bowers exposed.

Charlie fired.

And missed.

Bowers stood back, his gun inches from Frank's head.

Christ, he was going to shoot. Ginny kept her sights on Bowers, closed her eyes, and squeezed the trigger. At the same instant, Charlie fired again.

SUDDENLY EVERYTHING was quiet. Frank's legs gave way and he slithered to the ground. He opened his eyes and looked straight into Bowers's lifeless face.

A moment later he was surrounded by people, all talking at once. Ginny's face hovered among the rest. Someone cut the ropes around his arms and hands, someone else propped him up, someone thrust a canteen between his lips. He took a huge swallow of water, sputtered, and swallowed again. Holt was on the radio, calling for a stretcher. It was all over.

Ginny was gone. He tried to ask for her, but his tongue wouldn't work. Vince Paley was doing something to his shoulder, cutting the shirt away to look at the wound. Assured that he was alive, people started moving away. Suddenly he heard her voice, quite close.

"I shot him. I've killed another human being."

"No, you haven't, honey." That was Charlie Zellers. "Your hand jerked up when you squeezed the trigger. Your shot went high."

"Charlie, I shot him." Ginny's voice was shaky, but sure.

"And now you want to carry that around for the rest of your life? No way. Your shot went high, mine didn't." He sighed. "He killed my son."

Frank managed to gurgle out her name.

"Hey, Ginny," Vince called. "He wants you."

Then she was there, her face creased with concern, her smile the most beautiful he had ever seen. He gurgled again.

"You're going to be okay."

Vince was searching Bowers's clothing. "What's this?" he asked, holding up the little canvas-wrapped package.

Frank lifted his head to see. "Open it," he mumbled.

The words weren't clear, but Vince understood. He unwrapped the canvas and held the contents up where Frank could see. Money first, a lot of it, and then the thing he had expected. A full set of fake IDs—birth certificate, social security card, driver's license, even credit cards. Bowers had been a planner right up to the end. He had always known where he was going.

He lay back down, ready for the EMTs, the stretcher, the tubes, the needles, the drugs—most especially the drugs. He just hoped they would get there soon.

Ginny took his good hand in both of hers. "I love you," she whispered, kissing him on the cheek.

And then mercifully, at last, he let go. He was alive. Unconsciousness rose like a black tide, wiping away the pain. She would be there when he opened his eyes once more.

THE LAZARUS TREE
Robert Richardson
A Gus Maltravers Mystery

First Time in Paperback

A PRETTY PLACE FOR MURDER

In the picture-postcard English village of Medmelton, the air remains thick with enchantment of centuries past. Here, women have strange eyes—one brown, one green—and superstition and magic still rule.

When a famous London poet is murdered beneath the legendary Lazarus Tree, Medmelton is forced into the spotlight. Eventually the curiosity seekers drift away, but the mystery still lingers. And Gus Maltravers, at the request of a friend alarmed by the strange behavior of his stepdaughter, agrees to investigate.

"Richardson returns in top form..."
>   —*Kirkus Reviews*

Available in April at your favorite retail stores.

WORLDWIDE LIBRARY®

CONSIDER THE CROWS
CHARLENE WEIR
A SUSAN WREN MYSTERY

First Time in Paperback

PAST SINS AND PRESENT LIES

The life of a small-town police chief is a far cry from that of a street-smart San Francisco cop, but as Susan Wren knows only too well, murder happens everywhere.

The first victim is Lynnelle Hames, a young woman found dead outside her newly rented house. Lynnelle had a secret—it was the reason she had come to Hampstead. Was it the reason she had died?

When the body of a prominent citizen is found in a well, Susan struggles through a maze of small-town secrets to connect the murders, and find a killer who won't hesitate to litter the trail with more death.

"Highly recommended."   —*Mystery News*

Available in July at your favorite retail stores.

FIRST WIFE, TWICE REMOVED
CLARE CURZON

A THAMES VALLEY MYSTERY

TOXIC LOVE

Two disturbing deaths have Superintendent Mike Yeadings's team spread out from the Thames Valley to Amsterdam, looking for answers.

The first victim, Penny Winter, a divorced mother of two, dies as a result of food poisoning. Someone sent her tainted pâté with intent to kill. The second victim, Anneke Vroom, was a young Dutch national found crammed into an antique mahogany chest. She was shot full of heroin—and pregnant.

As the investigation of the separate incidents develops in sinister parallel, the men and women of the Thames Valley Police Force will confront more untimely deaths before tangled skeins come together to create a diabolical tapestry of murder.

"Clever misdirection." —*Kirkus Reviews*

Available in May at your favorite retail stores.

DEATH by DEGREES
Eric Wright

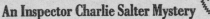

An Inspector Charlie Salter Mystery

LITERALLY—AND FIGURATIVELY—DEAD

The politics and infighting to elect a new dean at Toronto's Bathurst College turns to murder when the winner is discovered dead.

Though the case appears open-and-shut—an interrupted burglary and a suspect neatly arrested—Inspector Charlie Salter believes otherwise when he begins investigating anonymous notes warning that the killer lurks in the groves of academe.

Scandal, blackmail and layers of deception line the corridors at the college...all the way to the dark truth surrounding the killer's identity.

"Excellent series...humor and insight."
—*New York Times Book Review*

Available in June at your favorite retail stores.

To order your copy, please send your name, address, zip or postal code, along with a check or money order (please do not send cash), for $3.99 for each book ordered, plus 75¢ postage and handling, payable to Worldwide Mystery, to:

In the U.S.
Worldwide Mystery
3010 Walden Avenue
P. O. Box 1325
Buffalo, NY 14269-1325

Please specify book title with your order.

DEGREES